Lydia Acquires Adoration

A Pride and Prejudice Variation

Jaime Marie Lang

Book Cover by Jaime Marie Lang

Editing by Bailey and Bloom Ink

Contents

Prologue

The bouquet in Lydia's hand was deceptively simple, yet there was so much meaning tucked among its petals. Holding the assortment of flowers in her hands was oddly surreal. She had spent so many hours fantasizing about her wedding day, envisioning its every detail. Lydia must have been around six when she had watched a bride leave the church on the arm of a tall, well-dressed man. The bride had been so beautiful, her smile so wide and so happy, that it had stuck with Lydia, for all that it had grown hazy with time. Even as young as she had been, Lydia remembered thinking that one day she would be that beautiful and happy.

Gazing down at her bouquet, Lydia fingered a petal of one of the pink roses. It was the most delicate shade of blush, calling to mind the dress she had envisioned for herself all those years ago. She had once dreamed of a light pink dress. It was to be long and flowing, with small, darker pink roses sewn into the sleeves. Though over time, as she—and the latest fashion—had changed, so did her vision. By the time she was twelve, Lydia had learned of floriography, and knew she would one day carry a bouquet of beautiful flowers, all of them full of meaning. It was then that Lydia decided she was going to have a perfect wedding.

It was also the year that Lydia had realized that a wedding implied the need for a husband. With her father as her primary example of a husband, she had not been in a rush to get married, though it did not stop her from dreaming of her wedding. She simply decided that she would find a man better than her father to marry.

Though she had always known she wanted roses and peonies, Lydia had never cared what her groom would look like. Her only wish was to find a man who possessed more kindness than her father. But, of course, her list of requirements in her groom grew and changed as she matured. In her early teens, Lydia had been partial to a man in a red coat, though she quickly learned that men in uniform did not stay in one place very long, nor did they have the funds to support a wife and children in the manner she was accustomed to living. Lydia wanted a lot of children, so men from the militia and the regulars never made it on to her list of potential suitors.

Frankly, she had trouble adding anyone to her list, and if they managed to make the list, they did not stay very long. Shaking her head as she reminisced, Lydia retied the bow at the base of her bouquet, wanting the cream ribbon to fall just so. All she asked for was kindness and a genuine affection for children. Of course, people were so much more difficult to arrange than ribbons. It had been disappointing to realize that society gentlemen eschewed kindness and most of them rarely had any interaction with children, even their own.

She had always thought it was a good thing that she was never in any hurry to marry. Lydia was happy to visit her sisters and mother to play with her much younger brother and little niece and nephews. Or at least she had been.

"Lydia, are you sure?" Elizabeth's gentle voice drew Lydia out of her musings. Focusing on her sister instead of her bouquet, Lydia immediately recognized Elizabeth's deep concern as she said, "You still have time to change your mind."

With a smile, Lydia enveloped Elizabeth in a hug. She would miss all the time they spent together desperately, but she had already made her decision and was not about to change her mind. There was too much riding on what she was about to do and, oddly enough, her soon-to-be husband met her two requirements. Leaning back, Lydia kissed Elizabeth's cheek before saying, "I understand your concerns, but I have made up my mind. I have confidence that it will all be for the best."

Stepping back from her younger sister, Elizabeth nodded her head with a watery smile. "You always were always the bravest of us." Elizabeth reached out and gave her hand a squeeze before wiping at her eyes and slipping from the small anteroom.

The surreal feeling returned or maybe merely intensified. Here she was, on the verge of getting married, her mind filled with anticipation and disbelief at how her life had changed in such a short time. She would no longer be dreaming of that one-day wedding because that day was already here. Even with all of their doubts, her sisters had done what they could to make the hurried affair beautiful, and she would be forever grateful for it.

Someone signaled that everything was ready, and Lydia set her shoulders and lifted her chin. She was ready to walk into the church on her mother's arm. She was confident that despite the rush, the room and flowers would be simple yet beautiful. Lydia's bouquet, filled with her favorite flowers, was everything she had dreamed of. Her new periwinkle dress, though not the pink she had wanted as a child, was stunning in its elegant simplicity. With a smile on her face and every hair perfectly in place, Lydia took a deep breath, knowing that the time had come for her to start a new chapter in her life—marriage.

Chapter One

One Month Earlier

Lydia chased Artie around the tree, delighting in his giggles. She couldn't deny that Gilbert, Elizabeth's new little babe, was absolutely adorable, and Jane's Ellie was a doll. She was sure that Kitty's coming baby was sure to be precious as well. But despite all this, Artie remained Lydia's favorite, not that she would tell any of her sisters that.

She had a very close bond with precocious little Arthur Theodore and Lydia was more than happy to keep him entertained while Elizabeth and the rest of the household adjusted to Gilbert's birth. Swooping down, she grabbed the almost three-year-old boy, tickling his sides.

"You thought you could escape me?" Lydia growled into his ear.

Struggling to speak between peals of laughter, Artie complained, "No, Auntie Lydie, you are supposed to say Fe Fi Fo Fum!"

Laughing at his antics and his deep, little giant voice, she took a moment to catch her breath and kissed him on his nose. She set the boy down and said, "You are correct, my dear. I am sorry. I forgot we were playing Jack and the Giant."

Standing straight, Artie smoothed his clothes as if trying to reclaim his tiny dignity. "We can play it again. This time I will be the Giant."

Lydia kept a straight face despite the incongruous image of her little nephew being the giant. "If you are the Giant, then I guess I will be Jack."

"Yes, you are Jack. You hurry before I get you." Making shooing motions with his hands, Artie urged Lydia to flee.

Taking off, Lydia zigzagged around Pemberley's front lawn, staying slow enough that Artie's little legs could keep pace. Circling another tree that reached high into the sky, Lydia waited for Artie to catch up so that he could say his line and capture her.

When his small weight catapulted against her legs, she steadied herself, laughing as he said in a mock deep voice, "Fi Fie Fo Fum, I smell the blood of an Englishman!"

"Oh no, the Giant has caught me. What will I do?" Lydia laughingly lamented. Little growls from Artie only had her laughing more until she noticed a carriage coming up the drive.

Lydia stilled at the sight as they did not expect any visitors. Apparently, Artie also noticed the unexpected carriage approaching because he announced, "Someone is coming!"

"Yes, it appears so, Artie." Taking up his little hand, she added, "Let us hurry back into the house so we can tell your parents."

With a nod of his head, Artie dashed off, trying to beat his aunt to the front door. He called back, "I will win!"

Hurrying to keep up, Lydia lifted her skirt so she could run after him. She couldn't for the life of her think of who might be coming for a surprise visit. Jane would arrive in a few weeks and Kitty was at Matlock awaiting the birth of her first child. In fact, Lydia was going to be leaving to stay with her soon. Georgianna would be with Mary at Longbourn by now. Mother had been present for Lizzie's confinement, but had just returned to her own estate with her husband and little Mathew.

Lydia glanced back for another look at the approaching visitors as she arrived at the front of the house. She did not recognize the carriage, though it looked vaguely familiar. Nodding to the footman who opened the door for Artie and her, she said, "It looks as if we are to have visitors. I will alert William and the staff." He nodded in return and remained at the door, waiting to assist as needed.

Inside, Lydia could hear the echo of Artie's feet on the marble floor as he raced to his father's study and shook her head at how much energy he always seemed to have.

Lydia walked at a more sedate pace and smiled as Artie called, "Papa, there is a car'age!" Artie still struggled with pronunciation when he was excited. He was such a little gentleman all the time that she loved the moments when he actually acted his age.

Moments later, William was coming out of his study and scooping up his son. "Did you see a carriage on the drive?"

Answering with a vigorous nod of his head, Artie's chestnut curls tumbled into his eyes, obstructing his view as he exclaimed, "Yes!"

"Well then," William started, pausing to smooth the hair out of his son's eyes, "we shall have to go see who has arrived." Lydia couldn't help but smile at the comforting exchange between William and her nephew. She was grateful Artie would grow up with a father vastly different from her own.

She approached a nearby maid and said, "It appears that we are to have guests. I do not know if they will be staying but would you please let Mrs. Reynolds know and have a tea service prepared and sent to the blue parlor. Also, please let Nurse Sarah know she may need to come take Artie up to the nursery." With a curtsy, the maid turned to go, and Lydia hurried to follow William and Artie. She was eager to find out who their surprise guest was.

Sebastian Burgess sighed as he tried to focus on the positive of the situation. Thankfully, Clara, his niece, had stopped looking at him with wary suspicion, though her wide-eyed scrutiny had only faded away when she finally toppled over into Selene's side, unable to fight her exhaustion any longer. Observing Selene as she cradled Clara to her, he realized she looked as worn and heartbroken as he felt. Still, she managed a wan smile when she caught his gaze. He had always been close to his twin sister, and they had only grown closer over the years, especially after they had lost their older sister in childbirth.

He could see the pain in Selene's eyes despite the smile that she managed, and that pain lingered as she looked at Clara asleep at her side. With her jet-black hair and pale complexion, Clara looked very much like her mother, Sophia. He couldn't recall what Sophia looked like when she was young, but as he gazed at Clara, he could picture the resemblance.

He had always been close to his older sister. Not as close as he was to his twin, but he loved her dearly nonetheless. When his father had married Sophia to a wealthy baron, Sebastian had been away at school and could not even attend the ceremony. In her letters, Sophia had said that she was happy enough with her marriage, but he often wondered if that was just her trying to reassure her younger brother. In all reality, there was not much he could have done if she had asked for his help.

He had visited her when on break from Cambridge, and even managed to bring Selene along as well. The estate was beautiful and well managed, even though the master seemed to be absent. Sophia let it be known that her husband seldom visited, and she was content living quietly in the country. When Sebastian had his new brother-in-law investigated, he learned that he mostly kept to London, where he was often seen with his mistress attending the opera or other high society events. He had not been happy to learn that the man was a notorious rake, though it was somewhat of a relief that he did not gamble. There was little risk of his sister falling on hard times despite being stuck with a man who he could not respect.

They frequently exchanged letters, but it wasn't until she neared her confinement that he and Selene received a summons to be by her side. At the time, he remembered thinking that his sister had looked wrong somehow. She had been pale and puffy, her wrists and ankles quite swollen, and, more than that, she was very low in spirit. Apparently, carrying the child had been very difficult and her husband had not visited in four months, leaving her to care for several estate issues on her own while unwell. She did not say it, but he believed she feared for her life.

As fate would have it, her husband, Cornelius Blakesley, had arrived while they were visiting. Finding them there had, for some reason, angered him, or maybe he had already been in a bad mood. Either way, the resulting argument was brought to a halt when Sophia had collapsed in pain, her time coming far too early. By the next day, they had lost their sister but had gained a niece. Remarkably, Clara survived despite her premature birth. She had been tiny, but her indignant screams could be heard from rooms away.

They had been forced to leave the estate the very day of their sister's funeral. Somehow, Blakesley had felt that it was their presence and not his anger that had set off his wife's early labor. He had also been upset that his wife couldn't even do him the courtesy of giving him a son and heir before she passed.

Blakesley had returned to living in London full time, leaving his small daughter behind to be cared for by nurses and staff. Over the next several years, he had only begrudgingly allowed Selene and Sebastian to visit a handful of times to see Clara. Despite wanting a change in his relationship with his niece, Sebastian had been stymied. He did not have the power to do anything. That is, however, until he learned of Blakesley's death in a duel.

Sebastian did not know what Blakesley's will entailed as to the care of his niece, but he would certainly fight for her. He and Selene had fled London that very afternoon in a mad dash for Swarkstone Park. Eager to reach little Clara, they had only stopped when it became too dark to travel safely.

They had arrived to find the estate in chaos. Blakesley, who was more interested in the pomp of high society, had had little to do with his estate, and when his servants learned of his death, they worried about who would take over. Apparently, Blakesley's older half-brother, a one Randell Blakesley better known as Baron Blackthorn, was not a well-liked man. In fact, even the liberal Cornelius Blakesley had disapproved of his dissipation.

Selene and Sebastian did not care a fig for who inherited what, they only wished to care for their niece. Thus, upon their arrival, they went directly to the nursery, and what they had found was not encouraging in the least. They found little Clara, who was only five, in the nursery alone and crying fitfully. While Selene had stayed with her, Sebastian had gone looking for the housekeeper or steward, someone who could put some perspective on all the chaos.

He had found the housekeeper in the kitchen working with a few other staff members, but the rest of the house appeared empty. Upon questioning where the rest of the staff was, the housekeeper simply shrugged. "They left."

Sebastian rubbed at the twitch developing behind his right eyebrow as he tried to cogitate a response. Finding his voice, he asked, "Why would the staff all leave?"

The older woman halted her stirring and locked eyes with him. "Have you ever met Baron Blackthorn?"

"No. You could say that he is not a part of my set."

"Be glad that you have never met the man. Though I suppose you will be forced to deal with him now with this place hanging in the balance. I do not know the contents of the master's will, but I do know his cousin will show himself soon. He will be eager to stake his claim, legal or not." Shaking her head, the housekeeper sighed. "He has visited the manor on several occasions and his behavior has been such that many of the staff have decided that they would be better off leaving before he arrives. The little miss's nurse was one of the first to leave. I do not have the staff to serve you and your sister fancy like, but you are more than welcome to some soup when it is ready." She returned to her task and began chopping something that also ended up in the pot.

"That is very kind of you," he answered almost automatically. Sebastian stood, trying to decide what he should do. What could he do? If this Baron Blackthorn was as bad as he sounded, Sebastian did not want his sister and niece anywhere near the man. They would simply have to follow the lead of the staff and take Clara and flee.

He walked slowly back up to the nursery, trying to come up with a plan. When he reached the nursery, he found Selene in a rickety chair holding Clara, who seemed to have fallen asleep.

He had only just finished telling her what he knew when she blurted, "The Darcys."

Looking at her in confusion, Sebastian questioned, "What?"

"The Darcys live in Derbyshire. They are maybe only fifty miles north of here at Pemberley. You remember them from last season, don't you? We attended the new earl and countess of Matlock's wedding at Pemberley."

Eyebrows drawing together, he asked, "Yes, but how can we be certain that they are even there?"

Running her fingers soothingly along the contours of Clara's elfin face, Selene replied without looking up, "I heard talk that Mrs. Darcy would be entering her confinement this summer and she and her family would be staying at Pemberley to await the birth of their second child." Her fingers stilled as she finally looked up at him. "They are there."

Sebastian did remember them. He had, in fact, been disappointed when he realized that the family was not in London that season.

Rather than comment on his thoughts, he said, "Is this the time to be bothering them? What with a new baby, either there or about to arrive? Wouldn't it be better to take her to our house in London?"

"Look at it logically, Sebastian," Selene sighed. "London is one-hundred and thirty miles from here. That is a several days' journey with a small child that we do not have the proper belongings for and nothing to keep her entertained. Of course, we could attempt to bring her back to our father's estate in Northumberland on the Scottish border, but that is well over two-hundred miles."

Running his hand through his hair in frustration, Sebastian replied, "I would never suggest going to father. Not only would that trip take a week at least, but our stay would be less than welcome."

"I am merely trying to point out your ridiculousness," Selene countered with a scrunch of her nose. "The Darcy's are the closest people we know in this part of the country, and if I know the Darcys at all, they will welcome us with open arms." Then, staring up at him, her expression serious, she continued, "Besides, you know there will be some sort of reading of the will that you shall have to attend. It is best if we remain as close as we comfortably can."

And so they left as soon as they could pack up Clara's meager belongings and partake of the meal the housekeeper offered them. They only made it halfway to Pemberley before they were forced to stop for the night due to a storm. The journey was proving to be difficult as neither of the Burgess siblings had much experience caring for a child, and their interactions with Clara had been limited. They were unsure how to best care for her, especially when the life she knew was no more. The trip left Sebastian feeling as though he was not cut out to look after his niece. Though, to be fair, he certainly had to be better in that regard than the child's own father, who saw her once or twice a year before his death. It was not like Cornelius Blakesley had ever personally seen to her care or comfort. What did that amount to in her five small years? Something less than ten visits? Sebastian had to be doing a better job. Worse was simply not possible at this point.

LYDIA MADE IT TO the front steps just as the carriage was coming to a halt. Standing next to William and little Artie, who was bouncing on his toes with excitement, Lydia tried to hide her curiosity. While it was perfectly acceptable to bounce in enthusiasm at three, it was not fitting at eighteen. Without Elizabeth not yet up to greeting guests and overseeing the house, and Georgianna visiting Mary, the responsibility had shifted to Lydia. She was perfectly capable of seeing to what needed to be done even if she sometimes had to clamp down on her enthusiasm.

It took most of her control to not react to Sebastian Burgess coming down the carriage steps. Having grown close with his sister the last time she was in London for Kitty's season, she recognized him instantly. When he turned back into the carriage and brought out a small, sleep-rumpled girl, Lydia's curiosity spiked. After setting her carefully on her feet, Mr. Burgess handed down Selene. All three of the visitors looked disheveled and out of sorts. There was obviously a story here, but Lydia would wait to hear it.

Moving swiftly down the steps, Lydia rushed to greet her friend. Giving her a hug, she said, "Selene, it is so good to see you and Mr. Burgess. Welcome to Pemberley."

"I know this is rather unexpected, but we have found ourselves in a situation and, well..." Selene stopped speaking and merely shrugged. Lydia studied her friend, concerned at the unusual air of discouragement about her. The familiar playfulness of Selene was absent, leaving behind a changed demeanor. Lydia would simply have to find out what happened and help fix matters.

William arrived with Artie trailing behind him and shook Mr. Burgess's hand. "You are all more than welcome to stay here for as long as you may need. We are friends, after all."

Mr. Burgess nodded in thanks. "Thank you for that. I actually do not know how long we might stay or even what our next steps might be." Lydia looked away from his obvious discomfort and instead watched the young girl with them.

While the adults had been talking, Artie had been investigating the smaller guest as well. The small, unknown girl had been half hiding in Selene's skirts. To Lydia's eye, she seemed to be older than Artie by a year or two, maybe close to five. She had milk-pale skin and a mess of wild black ringlets. Her blue eyes seemed shadowed and afraid in a way that made Lydia's lips press into a hard line. Something was definitely wrong, and Lydia's mothering instincts were screaming at her to fix it.

Approaching the girl, Artie boldly said, "Hello, I am Arthur Theodore Darcy." He offered a little bow, a gesture he had obviously witnessed the male members of his family perform, and continued, "Welcome to Pmbr'ley."

The timid little girl's eyes grew wide as saucers but after a moment of hesitation, she bobbed a credible curtsy and whispered, "Thank you. I am Clara."

Artie's grin grew wide as he asked, "Would you like to play? I have toys."

All the adult eyes seemed to go directly to little Clara, waiting for her response. She bit her lip and then looked up at Mr. Burgess and then Selene. When Selene nodded her head encouragingly, Clara looked back at Artie and nodded her head. With her approval evident, Artie turned to his father and said, "Clara and I are going to play. Please?"

William looked down at his excited son, an indulgent smile upon his face. "Yes, I am sure it will be fine for you to play with Clara." Looking up at Selene and Mr. Burgess, he seemed to gauge something before continuing, "Will you show her the way to the nursery? She will be staying there for the time being."

"I can," Artie nodded before centering his focus on the older girl. "Clara, you can stay in Ellie's bed. She is not here yet." Bouncing on his toes, Artie reached out and grabbed the older girl's hand.

His grin and enthusiasm seemed to be infectious, as he actually had Clara smiling in return. Still she waited and looked up at Selene. "It is fine," Selene assured her. "I will come up with you and help settle you in as long as young master Arthur does not mind."

"Sure. We can share the toys an' play toget'er." With a little tug at Clara's hand, Artie got her to accompany him up the stairs and into the building. Lydia could not help but smile at his welcoming antics. At least some of little Clara's problems, whatever they may be, could be solved with Artie's cheer and kindness.

SELENE FOLLOWED ARTIE AS he showed them the way to the nursery, chatting with Clara all the way. She was not sure why she had thought of the Darcy family in their time of need, but she was grateful that she had. They had welcomed them without a question. In fact, they still had not asked any questions.

Little Artie was, of course, full of questions, but his were innocent enough. He wanted to know if Clara liked to play castle but was very accommodating when she said she had not played it before. He reassured her that he could teach her if she wanted to learn, or she could play with the dolls they kept for when his cousin visited.

Artie, still holding Clara's hand, led them up two flights of stairs before he turned back to Selene and Lydia to say, "This is the last stairs. Do not worry, it not on the roof." Artie beamed at Selene, and she realized he had just tried to joke with her. Selene laughed as was expected, and the little boy's smile widened. He paused for a moment, appearing winded after going up so many stairs with his short little legs.

After their brief break, they made it to the nursery where Artie proceeded to show Clara all his toys before introducing her to his nurse, Sarah. Selene watched as the young maid immediately took in Clara's condition but said nothing. Instead, Sarah knelt down and offered Clara a hug, saying, "Hello, my dear. I am so happy that you have come to stay with us. What would you say to a nice warm bath and getting changed into a nice clean dress? I might even be able to find some bows for your hair."

Eyes wide, Clara nodded. Then licking her lips, she asked, "A new dress and bows? Really?"

The nursemaid smoothed some of Clara's tangled locks back from her face and said, "Of course, my dear! Though it will take some time for them to bring up the warm water. Why don't you play with Artie until your bath is ready?"

Selene's heart ached watching the nursemaid bond with her young nice. Not only did she make it look so easy, but it seemed as though she already had more success with Clara than Selene had. Selene had attempted to remove the tangles from Clara's hair when they stopped for the night at the inn, but Clara's tears and uncooperative behavior had thwarted her efforts. It was obvious that Clara's clothes were patched and made from an inferior fabric. Between that and Clara's hair, what must everyone think? Selene certainly felt like the worst aunt.

The nurse moved away as the children played to a bellpull, probably to request the bathwater and clothing. Lydia, still cheery, turned to Selene and said, "I am sure that little Miss Clara will do fine here in the nursery while you are here. I assume they are sending up her things?"

Nodding, Selene said, "Yes, I am sure that they will bring up her trunk, but I know there is not as much there as should be, even should our stay be of a short duration." Lowering her voice so as to not be overheard by the children, she continued, "Clara is my niece. You may remember me mentioning her before. My older sister died bearing her and sadly, her father, Cornelius Blakesley, died only this week. Mr. Blakesley did not permit me to visit my niece often, but when we learned she had been orphaned, Sebastian and I rushed to his estate. What we found was disheartening, to say the least. Most of the staff had fled fearing Mr. Blakesley's older brother, a baron who has a very bad reputation. There was no one there caring for Clara as her nurse had left days before and maids had only been checking in on her as they could. I do not know if some of her possessions had been taken by fleeing staff or if she was never provided for in the way she should have been." Turning, Selene watched Clara play with Artie for a moment, remembering how the poor child likely never had such toys to play with before. In Artie's presence, Clara's face lit up with an abundance of smiles, surpassing anything Selene had ever seen from her before. With a sigh, she looked back at Lydia and said, "To make things worse, Sebastian and I could only visit her occasionally. She does not know us. She must feel like strangers have taken her." By the end of her small speech, Lydia had fire in her eyes and Selene was grateful it wasn't aimed at her.

Selene noticed Nurse Sarah approaching after speaking with another maid. She wondered how much the woman had overheard but shrugged it off as Sarah appeared kind and had been so very sweet to Clara. Selene could not find it in herself to fear Nurse Sarah's judgment.

Smiling at both Lydia and Selene, the nursemaid said, "We will see to it that the little mite has all she needs. Don't you worry."

Lydia, on the other hand, had moved to envelop Selene in a hug. Squeezing her tight, she murmured, "Nurse Sarah is correct. We will look after her and provide whatever support you might need."

Blinking back tears, Selene allowed herself to relax into her friend's embrace. The whole scenario was just so overwhelming, and she worried that there would be repercussions for their actions. She knew it was not quite the right thing to do to just pack up her niece and flee, but what other choice had they had?

Chapter Two

Sᴇʙᴀsᴛɪᴀɴ ꜰᴏʟʟᴏᴡᴇᴅ Dᴀʀᴄʏ ɪɴᴛᴏ his study without taking much note of anything that he saw. Darcy's home exuded a tasteful and understated opulence that was difficult to ignore, but somehow, he found himself overlooking it. The magnitude of the issues he now faced overwhelmed him. There were so many questions running through his head.

What did Cornelius's will state in regard to Clara? Had he made provisions to see to her care? Would this Baron Blackthorn be a problem? If so, what would it take to claim her? If for some reason the baron was given Clara to raise, could Sebastian bribe him in order to keep her?

Then there were concerns about Clara herself. She had not spoken much at all in the two days they had been together. Compared to little Artie, who he knew was maybe two years younger, she was practically silent. She had mostly only cried or looked around in solemn silence. What had her young life been like up to that point? He had to find a way to protect her.

It took him a moment to realize that Darcy had sat behind his desk and was waiting patiently for him to take a seat. He quickly sat in one of the well-stuffed leather chairs and finally found his voice. "You have my gratitude for offering my family sanctuary."

"So it is sanctuary that you seek. I assumed as much, but I do not want to pry if you do not wish to share. Though I will say that I have learned over time that a trouble shared is a trouble halved. Maybe we can work on the problem together, and if I cannot help you, then certainly one of the Bennet ladies shall."

Even though Sebastian was taken aback by Darcy's ease in accepting and offering help, his comment still managed to make him laugh. "Yes, I can only imagine if they are anything like the Countess of Matlock."

It was actually the now countess that had brought the two families into contact. The then Catherine Bennet had befriended his sister Selene during the previous season. They had both been present when Miss Bennet had been forced to protect herself with her penknife from a rogue gentleman. Not only had she seen to her safety, but she had also seen to the man's care when he had foolishly taken out the knife and started bleeding out. It seemed that the Bennet ladies were a group of women stronger—and possibly craftier—than most.

Sebastian knew it was time to share his story with Darcy. Maybe the older man would have some idea of what he could do or have connections that could help him. Rubbing at the ache that seemed to be building behind his eyebrow, he began to tell his tale. "I learned four days ago that Clara's father, my brother-in-law as was, had been shot in a duel after he was found in the bed of a married lady. After our sister's death at Clara's birth, Blakesley had prevented us from seeing Clara much and I worried what would happen to her in the wake of his death." The rest of the story—finding Clara amidst the chaos, their hurried decisions to flee, and his concerns moving forward—were easier to relate than he had thought it would be. Darcy might be considered solemn and sometimes cold, but the man had been more than welcoming thus far.

When he had finally stopped, Darcy remained silent, his fingers steepled in front of him with a look of deep thought upon his furrowed brow. Eventually, he said, "As the custody of your niece is in question, I would suggest you go on the offensive. It would be best if you could find out who Cornelius Blakesley's solicitor was and be sure you are present for the reading of the will. It should not be too difficult to arrange as you are there to look after your niece's affairs. Do you have a solicitor you trust to represent you in this matter?"

Shaking his head, Sebastian replied, "Though I have a solicitor for when I am visiting London, I would not trust him with something this important. My father's solicitor is quite good, but he lives back in Northumberland near the Scottish border. That is over two-hundred and thirty miles of road, most of it unreliable. It would take a minimum of a week to just travel here, probably longer. Besides, he would never travel this far south to help me. He knows I am out of favor with my father."

"I have a very good fellow that I can suggest. Know him from my Cambridge days. I will send him an express and ask for him to start looking into things. Have you contacted your father?"

Darcy's expression was as understanding as it was serious. Somehow, his penetrating gaze made it easier for Sebastian to say, "I have not contacted my father yet. I know I should have already done so, but the condition at Swarkstone manor was such that I was simply focused on getting my sister and niece away." Running his hand down his face, Sebastian tried to sort out his thoughts when it came to his father before giving voice to his concerns. After gritting his teeth for a moment, he said, "My father has both feet firmly planted in the past. He is fond of older styles and ways of doing things, among which is the idea that his children are to obey him without question. Even having had his children later in life, he is still quite spry for a man of his age. He is of the thought that the new ways of doing things, with agricultural reforms and the like, will be the downfall of the nation. My sister and I spend as little time at our family estate as possible. That being said, I am uncertain how my father will react to the current situation."

"I see." Leaning back in his chair, Darcy continued, "It seems every family has one of his ilk. My aunt, Lady Catherine, is also the sort to eschew modernization, even to the detriment of her tenants and daughter."

It was a relief to hear that Darcy was familiar with the issues he faced with his father. Nodding his head in commiseration, Sebastian said, "I worry what he will think of me stepping in to what he might see as matters that do not concern me over a *mere girl child*." Seeing the way Darcy's face screwed up in anger at the statement, Sebastian grimaced. "Yes, that is the way my father speaks of the females in the family, and it angers me as much as it seems to anger you. My father views girls as little use beyond the ability to use them as pawns in marriage alliances."

LYDIA LEFT THE NURSERY with her mind full of what needed to be done. Selene would stay with her niece for the time being, but Lydia wanted to check in with Mrs. Reynolds about their unexpected guests. She assumed the cook would have been informed that there would be two more for dinner and another in the nursery, but she still wanted to speak with her. The cook always seemed to do better with unexpected changes when someone came by and approved of any adjustments she had made. Lizzie would also need to be informed of the goings-on.

Moving quietly through the hallways and stairways of Pemberley, Lydia soon found herself in the housekeeper's office. She entered the open doorway and greeted Mrs. Reynolds with a smile. "Good afternoon, Mrs. Reynolds."

"And good afternoon to you, Miss Lydia. May I assume you are here to check in on our arrangements for the guests?"

Smile broadening, Lydia replied, "Even had I not had the maid send notice, you would still be aware of our guests. You are aware of everything that goes on in the halls of Pemberley."

Mrs. Reynolds nodded knowingly. Her bearing was mature and responsible, but Lydia could see a sparkle in her eyes when she replied, "Yes, but I am sure you have more information that will be helpful."

"Mr. Sebastian Burgess and his sister Selene have arrived with their young niece, Clara. They brought with them their own valet and lady's maid. I know you probably already have rooms for them in the guest wing and suitable accommodation for their staff."

"I have Polly readying their rooms as we speak, and we can care for their staff when they arrive without issue." Mrs. Reynolds paused, and after studying Lydia for a moment, asked, "Is there something else that you need my assistance with?"

Lydia knew that Mrs. Reynolds was too proper to ask questions, no matter how curious she might be. She would not meddle or seek information for gossip. Mrs. Reynolds was the ideal housekeeper for such a large estate as Pemberley. She knew everything that went on within its walls and saw to it that everything reflected well on the Darcy family.

Lydia said, "I would appreciate it if you could make sure the cook knows that I have every confidence in her, despite the sudden additions. Also, it might be helpful for one of the cheerier maids to be made available to help in the nursery for the time being. Little Clara does not have a nursemaid and could use some extra affection. I will be speaking with my sister about my concerns for little Clara. The poor mite was recently orphaned and has been having a rough time of it."

Mrs. Reynolds tsked in sympathy before replying, "We will make sure the poor lamb is well cared for her while she is here. Don't you worry, Miss Lydia."

Answering only with a smile and a nod, Lydia left the room and made her way to Lizzie's room. Lydia hoped that she would be awake, but with Gilbert's birth only three weeks prior, Lizzie was still taking naps often, and why wouldn't she? Unlike other mothers of their station, Elizabeth insisted on feeding her own babies, so she was waking up throughout the night to feed the little dear.

Happily, Elizabeth answered when she knocked softly at her door. Elizabeth was propped up in bed, surrounded by pillows. She quietly greeted Lydia without ever looking away from Gilbert, who lay sleeping in her lap. Coming closer, Lydia smiled at the maternal image that her sister made.

Sitting carefully on the edge of the bed, Lydia tried not to jostle the two. "And how are you and my little nephew doing this afternoon?"

"We are both well. Little Gil will wake up soon wanting his dinner. He seems to be thriving as far as I can tell." Elizabeth smiled, running a finger along his smooth brow, and Lydia marveled that he did not wake at her touch.

After watching Elizabeth with her new son for a moment, Lydia acknowledged the ache she felt at seeing her sister with her child. Lydia wanted that. She wanted a child, or more accurately, children—lots of children. It was something she craved, like other young ladies desired sweets or Gothic novels. She was determined that someday she would have as many children as God would bless her with. She just had to wait until she found the right man. Biting back a sigh, Lydia commented, "I have come to let you know that we have guests, though you might have already heard."

Looking up, Elizabeth narrowed her eyes at her sister's statement and Lydia could almost see the cogs of her mind turning. After only a slight pause, she said, "I had not heard that we had guests. May I assume our guests were a surprise? You would have said who arrived if it was family."

"Selene and her brother, Mr. Burgess, arrived this afternoon with their niece. They did not say it explicitly, but it seems they need our help."

Sitting up straighter, Elizabeth said, "How so?"

Lydia could not help but smile at Elizabeth's response. Her sister had recently given birth and was still confined to her room, rarely venturing out. However, at the first hint that someone needed assistance, she was quick to respond. Fiddling with a loose thread on the bed's coverlet, Lydia said, "It seems that Selene's niece Clara was recently orphaned and there is some concern about her father's will and the directives made in regard to her care. Apparently, the staff was so worried that Mr. Blakesley's brother would come and take over that they abandoned the estate, including the poor girl's nurse. She had been left all alone." Pausing, Lydia looked at her sister, her eyes sparking. "Her hair is an utter mess of tangled black curls, and she is more withdrawn than I would like. Her appearance makes me wonder if the staff dressed her in castoffs and used the money for her upkeep to line their pockets before they fled."

Fire flashed in Elizabeth's eyes and Lydia knew her sister was with her in her pursuit of protecting the poor girl. The Bennet sisters did not take kindly to people mistreating anyone, especially children. "Anything that she needs, we can provide. I suggest you sort through the clothes we keep on hand as gifts for the tenant children. It will be plain but serviceable until we can make something better. There are plenty of toys in the nursery for her to play with." Stopping, Elizabeth looked at Lydia and grinned bashfully before concluding, "I am sure you have it all well in hand."

"Yes, I do, but that does not mean I do not appreciate your advice. I will keep you informed of the developments as they happen." Lydia leaned in and hugged her older sister. She knew Elizabeth was always frustrated when her physical limitations kept her from being as busy as she wished to be or felt she should be. "On a brighter note, you would have been so proud of little Artie. He actually got the poor thing to give him a smile as he offered to show her his toys. You are raising one fine gentleman."

Sebastian felt consumed by a restless energy. It had been four days, and they hadn't been updated on any developments since then. Although the solicitor had informed them about pursuing the matter concerning Cornelius Blakesley, his will, and the care of his daughter, uncertainty still lingered in everyone's minds. Considering the distance, not even an express rider would have made it there and back in such a short time. The earliest a message would get back to him would be that very day. He had never considered himself a man of action, but the inaction he faced was maddening. Of course, he understood that things took time, but with the fate of his niece in the balance, he wanted to do more than wait for news.

Hearing melodic laughter, Sebastian turned from the groove that he was wearing in the garden path and followed the noise. It did not take him long at all to find the source of the enchanting sound. As he had suspected, Miss Lydia, or rather Miss Bennet, was playing with her nephew and his niece. They appeared to be having a on a large blanket overlooking the beauty that was Pemberley. His sister was there as well, but it was not her laughter that had drawn him. It was Miss Bennet's musical laugh and the carefree abandon that she exhibited in her enjoyment of the moment. Something about it was infectious.

"Are you hungry?" Little Artie's small voice startled him out of his reverie and Sebastian looked down. "We have enough if you want some, too."

Miss Bennet's voice drew his attention back to her as she said, "Yes, please join us." Sitting up straighter, she tucked a stray strand of blonde hair behind her ear and Sebastian swallowed hard. In the months since he had last seen her, it seemed that she had changed in a way that unsettled him. Not that he could pinpoint what it was.

Finding his voice, he said, "Well, if you are going to be so generous, who am I to resist your kind offer?" Lowering himself to a corner of the blanket, Sebastian gaped at the selection and quantities of food.

Seeing his expression, Miss Bennet laughed, saying, "As our cook did not know what treats might tempt Clara or Selene, she prepared what seems to be some of everything they might like. We have been trying each in turn to see if Clara finds anything she likes."

Artie piped up, saying, "Clara does not like the eggs." His scrunched nose and wide eyes were a perfect expression of glee. It seemed that the younger boy was quite fond of their game.

Looking over at Clara, Sebastian was happy to note the changes that had occurred in the last two days. Her hair now fell about her face in neat black ringlets instead of knots, and her dress, while not fancy, did not have patches and fit her well. Hoping to develop a relationship with his niece, he asked, "Did you find anything that you liked?"

Ducking her head, she looked up at him from under her lashes. He waited, hoping that she might actually speak with him. She licked her lips, but then only pointed to what appeared to be some kind of cream puff. Understanding that it would take time did not make the fact that she was not speaking with him hurt any less. Trying to keep the smile on his face unchanged, Sebastian said, "The cream puff?" At her nod, he continued, "I can see how that might be your favorite. I do believe that your mother was fond of them as well."

Clara's blue eyes grew wide at his comment. It was unlikely that she had anyone tell her of her mother, and in that moment, Sebastian made a promise to himself. He would make sure the precious girl his sister had brought into the world would know about her mother and just how much she had loved and wanted her. "Yes, my older sister, Sophia, who was your mother, liked cream puffs so much that she would often steal them from my plate when I was not looking." Blinking back tears that had suddenly appeared in the corner of his eyes, he confessed, "It was a game that we played. I did not like cream puffs, so I let her take mine and I took the gingerbread from her plate."

Selene leaned over and squeezed his hand. Familiar with his pain, she shared the moment with him in silence. Clara watched them intently for a moment, her gaze drifting back and forth between the pair. After a moment's hesitation, she brought out a slice of cake and, putting it on a plate, handed it to him.

Amazed at Clara's action, Sebastian grinned and bringing it to his nose, he sniffed. "This would not happen to be gingerbread, would it?"

Clara giggled, nodding her head in a way that made her curls bounce. She even offered a whispered, "Yes."

Grinning, Artie held up a handful of forks saying, "It is a pic'nic. You do not need a fork, but we have some if you want one."

With his heart warmed by both his niece's kindness and Artie's consideration, Sebastian broke off a bite-size bit of cake with his hand and said, "Thank you for the kind offer, but as it is a 'pic'nic,' I will just use my hands if you do not mind." Then, popping the cake into his mouth, he groaned as the spices hit his tongue. It had been far too long since he had a good piece of gingerbread.

Chapter Three

Eyes widening, Lydia felt her focus shift uncontrollably from cute little Clara and her generous action to Clara's uncle. Had he just groaned? Fighting a blush, Lydia directed her eyes away from the handsome Mr. Burgess and back to Clara's broad smile. It was much safer to look at the little girl's joy than to see just how much Sebastian Burgess was enjoying his gingerbread.

Finding the need to busy her hands with something, Lydia began to clear away some of the remnants of their picnic. She wrapped up the discarded bits and bites of food that the children had rejected in one of the many serviettes that the cook had thoughtfully provided. She was very careful not to look back over at the sterling example of masculinity until she was sure that she could control the expression on her face.

Yes, his actions were extraordinary. It was heartwarming to see the effort he was putting in to bridge the gap between himself and his neglected niece. His efforts to ensure her well-being and fight for her custody were not only commendable but also a testament to the type of man that he was. Few single gentlemen of his age would undertake such a task, and Lydia admired him for his actions.

It was not the time to realize just how attracted to him that she was. Yes, when she had met him during Kitty's season, she had been more than happy whenever they were given the opportunity to spend time in one another's company. It was impossible to deny that his jet-black hair, which stood out against his light complexion and captivating deep blue eyes, made him incredibly attractive. He had been lighthearted and engaging, and Lydia had childishly speculated about the possibility of a future with him. But that was before Clara came into the picture. She was not about to complicate matters by indulging in a girlish crush.

Finding herself under better regulation, Lydia looked up to watch the antics of those around her. Tucking a strand of her escaping hair behind her ear, she could not help but enjoy how well the children got along. Artie's outgoing nature seemed to pull Clara out of her shell little by little, and she was losing some of the haunted look she had when she had first arrived.

Rejoining the conversation, Lydia turned to Selene and said, "I have always loved picnics. There is just something about eating in the fresh air that lends everything a better flavor than eating inside. What do you think of picnics?"

Tilting her head in thought, Selene did not answer right away but after a moment responded, saying, "Though I enjoy them now, I will admit that at first, I found them strange and intimidating. It was only a few years ago, during my first season, that I finally had the opportunity to go on my first picnic. I found it so foreign that I was uneasy. I did not know how to sit or where to put my hands. While I have adjusted to the concept, I still shudder to remember how so very out of place I felt at the time."

Lydia felt her eyes widen at her friend's experience and her inadvertent faux pas and she quickly found herself saying, "Oh, you poor dear. Now I either want to fill your time visiting Pemberley with picnics for you to enjoy so you can catch up on all your missed pleasure or I need to avoid them all together to protect you from feeling uneasy."

Thankfully, Selene laughed, setting Lydia at ease as she said, "While I would not want you to go out of your way to arrange a picnic every day, I am finding that I quite enjoy the way you host a picnic." Then, looking at her brother, who seemed to be quietly savoring his last bite of gingerbread, she grinned, commenting, "And as long as you are sure to provide gingerbread, I think my brother will be happy to join us."

Lydia couldn't bear to watch Mr. Burgess's face after his sister's remark. To distract herself, she turned her attention to the children. They had completely abandoned the adult world and were now immersed in a lively game with two wooden horses. Lydia smiled at them and asked, "Artie, what do you say? Shall we have another picnic while Clara and Mr. and Miss Burgess are still here?"

Sitting up straighter, Artie looked at Clara and, at her nod, exclaimed, "Yes! We should do another picnic." Then, scrunching his nose in a way that Lydia adored, he continued saying, "Next time, bring more gingerbread. Mr. Burgess ate it all, leaving no for you."

Lydia could not help but smile at her nephew and his attempt at humor, despite her slight embarrassment. His scrunched nose always gave him away when he was trying to be silly. He still had not quite gotten the hang of joking, but that did not mean he had given up trying.

Sebastian watched Miss Bennet interact with her nephew and could not help but feel slightly jealous of how easily she got along with the precocious little boy. They had a very close relationship, but then why wouldn't they? She had been part of the lad's life practically since his birth, whereas Cornelius Blakesley's interference had stunted his relationship with Clara.

Pulled out of his rumination, Sebastian realized Artie had just said that he ate all of Miss Bennet's gingerbread. Looking at her in concern, he felt like an utter bore, having ate several slices. When his niece had continued to fill his plate, smiling all the while, he had not given it a thought. The realization hit him that the gingerbread was actually meant for everyone.

Casting a concerned glance at Miss Bennet, he swiftly caught sight of a faint blush spreading across her cheeks. Without wasting a moment, he inquired, "Miss Bennet, is gingerbread perhaps your favorite treat?"

Her blue eyes flicked to him, and then swiftly shifted back away, the blush deepening on her cheeks. Finally, after a slight puff of air filling her cheeks, she locked gazes with him and she said, "It seems that you have found me out. Though I am fond of a number of treats, my nephew is correct. Gingerbread is my favorite."

Sebastian found himself enjoying watching the way emotions played across Miss Bennet's face. Oh, he knew she was slightly embarrassed, but that was not all that he could see. There was humor in her countenance as well, as if she acknowledged the situation she found herself in and embraced it for what it was. There was also something bold about the way she met his eyes, as if she challenged him to think less of her.

He was attempting to come up with a fitting response when Selene said, "Is that a rider approaching Pemberley?"

It was difficult to drag his gaze away from Miss Bennet, but eventually he managed to catch a glimpse of what appeared to be an express rider approaching the mansion. It seemed his respite was at an end. Hopefully, he would at least have news and something to do besides wait.

He looked back to Clara, who was once again playing with one of the wooden horses with Artie. He wanted above all else to give her a proper home and the loving environment that she had been denied thus far. Standing, he gave a bow to the group, saying, "It seems that my time enjoying the lovely picnic is at an end." He only hesitated slightly before looking at Miss Bennet and saying, "If you are so kind to invite me to join another such marvelous event, I promise not to eat all the gingerbread." Turning, he hastened back to the manor house, eager for whatever information was waiting for him.

SELENE BURNED WITH CURIOSITY. Not only was there a rider with news probably about the will they waited so anxiously to have read, but there was something going on between her brother and the delightful Miss Bennet. It was almost difficult to decide which she was more eager to find out more about.

Either way, she would not get more information just sitting on the lawn with the children. Gazing over at a slightly flushed Lydia, she said, "I hope you do not mind if we cut the picnic a little short? I find myself quite interested in the goings-on."

Nodding Lydia, replied, "I can only imagine how concerned you must be. Let us finish packing up what is left of the food. I think the children have eaten all that they were going to eat, regardless."

It did not take long before everything was packed away, and Lydia was asking Artie to go fetch the nearby footman to carry their basket. Clara and Artie ran off together, giggling as they raced to the servant. It had been a good morning and perhaps with the addition of the much wished for news, the Burgess family might get what they needed to continue to care for Clara.

Walking back towards the building, Lydia linked arms with Selene as they followed the children's frolicking path. Keeping her voice low, Lydia asked, "I know you are not used to having a sister to confide in, but I have found it most helpful and would play your confidant." Selene's face, pale and drawn, betrayed her worry through the deep lines between her brows and her compressed lips. It was obvious that the strain was getting to the normally vivacious young lady. Giving her arm a squeeze, she prompted her, saying, "What most worries you?"

"I am afraid that I cannot get what I want. I want Clara to be cared for by my brother and me, because we are the ones who will cherish her the most and attend to her needs without any hesitation. However, I know my wishes do not factor into what the law says. It is not the way of the world to cater to a woman's sensibilities. Men hold the power, and they rarely choose what is best but what is the most profitable to them." She looked at Lydia with a solemn expression and sighed, "Though you of all people comprehend the cruelties that can exist in the world of men."

Lydia wished that the woman she admired and looked to as a friend did not have such a heavy load to bear at the moment. Acknowledging the truth of her statement, she said, "Yes, I have seen such cruelty firsthand. My mother, sisters, and I have all handled it differently, but I do believe that in our own way, we have all found a liberation of sorts in claiming the happy lives we deserve. Even if the news that has come is not to your benefit, you can still fight it, you know."

Shaking her head, Selene replied, "I do not think I have your family's courage. I am terrified that Clara will fall into the hands of an even worse man than her father."

"I think courage comes in many forms. Not all of it looks like an all-out attack. I believe I am most like Lizzie in that we both found ways to cope that allowed us to fight back against our father. My mother, Jane, and Mary were different in their courage, but they still have it." Bumping Selene with her shoulder, Lydia said, "And even Kitty picked it up as well, eventually."

This elicited a laugh from Selene, and she said, "I have heard of your fondness for floriography, and I witnessed firsthand some of Kitty's courage myself when that dastard her mother-in-law paid to hurt her saw the error of his ways. Maybe I just need to stay near you, and it will rub off on me."

Lydia snickered, but said, "You are more than welcome to stick around as long as you need to, though I believe you will find your own courage when it is called for."

Making it to the stairs that lead into the house, Lydia let go of Selene and took up Artie's hand. She understood that Selene and her twin brother were some four years her senior, but twenty-two was not so very old. Though it struck Lydia as odd that she was often giving advice to those older than her. She supposed it must come with growing up so fast.

Making it inside, Artie let go of her hand and turned to face her, his enthusiasm evident in his request. "I want to see Mama and baby Gil, Auntie Lydie. Can we go now?"

THE FOLDED PIECE OF paper on the table before him was in no way threatening, but that did not stop the tremor that ran through his hand as Sebastian moved to pick it up off the table. So much hung on the information in the folds of crisp black and white words. Looking over at Darcy, who sat across from him, Sebastian swallowed and then broke open the seal.

MR. BURGESS,

I apologize for the time it took me to find the information you seek, but I was finally able to confront your Mr. Blakesley's solicitor and the reading of the will is to be held at Swarkstone Park on May

twenty-fifth. I am uncertain, but I suspect the other interested parties
may have wanted you to be absent from the reading, for I can find no
legal reason you would have been excluded from this information. I
am at this time making my way to Swarkstone and hope to meet you
there with all haste.

In my investigation on the other parties, namely Randell Blakesley,
Baron Blackthorn, I have found enough evidence that would suggest we
could take the matter to court over your niece's custody should the need
arise. I will provide additional information when we meet in person

Yours,

H. Herrington,

412 Whitley Square

London

SEBASTIAN TOOK IN THE information before handing over the letter
to Darcy. He respected him and knew that any advice he might give
would be valuable. Tapping a finger against his leg as Darcy read, he
tried not to wonder just how bad Randell Blakesley must be. That
the solicitor had stated that they had recourse should the will be
unfavorable, hinted at something more than merely disreputable.

"What are you thinking?" Darcy's question pulled him out of his
thoughts, and Sebastian looked into the man's serious gaze.

In a moment of self-awareness, Sebastian glanced at his hands and saw that they had involuntarily clenched into fists due to his mounting agitation. He made a conscious effort to relax his hands by stretching out his fingers. "I am glad that we finally have a time and place for the reading of the will. However, it worries me that Mr. Herrington has already suggested that we might fight the will should it be necessary."

"Yes, I noticed that as well." Darcy seemed to hesitate a moment before continuing, "I know we are not exceptionally close, Burgess, but you have been supported my family in the past. I want you to know that you have the Darcys' support in your quest to care for your niece, and I do not believe I am out of line by saying that you have my cousin's support as well, should you need it."

"I do not know what exactly I will be facing, but I appreciate the support, nonetheless. I believe that I should leave for Swarkstone Park at first light. If I do, I should be able to get there by nightfall and will forgo the need to stay at an inn along the way." Memories of the horrendous night at the inn on the way to Pemberley with Selene and Clara briefly invaded his thoughts before he returned to the situation at hand. "I do not feel comfortable bringing Selene and Clara with me to Swarkstone. Would you—"

Waving off Sebastian's almost request, Darcy interrupted, saying, "You do not even need to ask it. They are more than welcome to stay here under our protection while you see to matters. In fact, I was wondering if you would mind if I sent one of my footmen with you.

A show of strength is never amiss when dealing with men as suspect as this Randell Blakesley."

Sebastian nodded, rising to his feet. Casting a hard gaze at Darcy, his eyes revealed a firm resolve, he stated, "Normally I would not feel the need, but when it concerns my lost sister's only child, I will not hesitate to do whatever it takes. Thank you, I will accept your offer. If you will excuse me, I will leave you now and see to my preparations for my departure."

Chapter Four

It took Selene all of her training that had come with being a debutante for her to resist pacing the room. Instead, she calmly sat on the chair provided and took small sips of her tea, trying to hide her frantic concern for her brother's trip to Swarkstone Park. Despite her desire to pace, she found herself unexpectedly seated and sharing a cup of tea with Mrs. Darcy.

Selene was taken aback when Mrs. Darcy, who had recently given birth, welcomed her into her sitting room for a soothing cup of tea. Then again, the Bennet ladies all seemed to be rather singular. Who was she to say that a woman had to stay in bed for weeks after having a child? Maybe it would be something she would know herself one day. She had thought she might have such an outcome, but then Cedric had died, and her hopes were crushed before they even had the chance to take root.

Smiling at Selene over the rim of her teacup, Mrs. Darcy said, "I know that it is half scandalous that I am already up and about within my own rooms, but I have always been an active sort. Even when I broke my arm, I had trouble staying in bed."

"If half the stories I have heard from Kitty are true, I am not surprised," replied Selene. She would always be grateful for having met Kitty the previous season. They had become great friends and often exchanged letters. Kitty was very close to her older sister and often would share anecdotes that would have them laughing until they cried. Studying the other woman, Selene was happy to note that she appeared just as hale and hearty as the last time she had seen her, despite her recent ordeal. Selene said, "It is good to know that you are well on your way to recovery, Mrs. Darcy."

Waving her hand dismissively, she insisted, "None of this 'Mrs. Darcy.' Please call me Elizabeth. I know you are close with both Kitty and Lydia and use both of their names. I wish for the same."

Meeting Elizabeth's emerald eyes, Selene's own eyes lit up with a smile. "I am more than happy to comply, Elizabeth," she said, her voice brimming with warmth. "But only if you return the favor and call me Selene."

"Selene, I would be interested in talking about the situation you find yourself in." Elizabeth's comment had Selene's eyebrows rising.

Tilting her head, Selene said, "I am uncertain what information has been passed to you, but my brother has gone to Swarkstone to be there for the reading of the will of Cornelius Blakesley, my niece's father. We hope that there will be no issue with us taking on her care." Looking into Elizabeth's steady gaze, Selene found herself biting her lip before saying, "I know it is useless to worry, but I cannot help it. So much depends on the outcome of the will reading."

Nodding her head in commiseration, Elizabeth explained, "I would be just as worried if I were in your shoes. I love all my sisters dearly and if something happened to one of them, I would fight tooth and claw to take care of any child they left behind. We are very alike in that way."

Selene was slightly surprised by Elizabeth's fierce reaction to the situation. The woman had only met Clara once, but she seemed very protective. Maybe it was her recent dealings with motherhood coming through? It was said that a mother was the most ferocious of predators, her maternal instincts making her a force to be reckoned with.

Interrupting Selene's thought, Elizabeth continued, "I may have just had a baby, but my mind is still as sharp as ever and I want to help. If you are willing, tell me everything you know about your niece's situation and her father and that way, when your brother returns, I will be ready to delve into strategy and tactics with everyone."

Why did it feel as if Elizabeth was talking about preparing for war? Putting down her teacup in its saucer, she said, "One would think that it was you who had spent time in the regulars and not your brother-in-law, with your talk of strategies and tactics."

"I will admit to picking up the phrase from Theodore. While my life now revolves around activities that don't require strategy, there was a time when it played a crucial role in my everyday decisions," explained Elizabeth. "But less of me. Tell me more of your niece."

"You may recall that I told you I lost my sister in childbirth. Frankly, everyone seemed to be shocked that Clara survived. She was so very tiny." As Selene spoke with Elizabeth that morning, their conversation shifting from Sophia to Clara and oddly enough, chess, she came to appreciate Elizabeth much better.

They spent most of the afternoon in each other's company. Selene even held baby Gilbert when he was awake. All in all, it was time well spent, though she wondered just how things were proceeding with her brother.

SEBASTIAN HAD ARRIVED AT Swarkstone relatively swiftly, with "relative" being the key word. With only three people inside the carriage and little baggage, they were able to keep a swift pace. They actually made good time, even with having to stop a number of times to rest the horses at coaching inns. Still, with fifty odd miles to cover, they had not arrived at Swarkstone for a good eight hours. Sebastian had been more than ready to escape from the swaying of the carriage by then.

He had not been ready to come face to face with Clara's other uncle the moment he entered the front hall. Randell Blakesley, Baron of Blackthorn, was not what Sebastian thought he would be. Though he was uncertain what he had pictured, whatever it was, it was not this. The man was not imposing, at least not in a physical sense. He was shorter than Sebastian by a good four or five inches, and not even padding could have helped to hide his lack of physical physique. While his clothes were fine, they lacked the distinctiveness of a dandy, fop, or rake, making his style difficult to categorize. Wherever his tastes ran, they were expensive.

If Sebastian had passed him on the street, he would not have thought twice about him. Yet locking gazes with the man made Sebastian want to shudder. His pale blue eyes lacked the emotion one would normally expect. No, there was no emotion in those depths, only cold calculation.

When the man smiled and held out a hand for him to shake, Sebastian reacted without hesitation to return the gesture, though his first thought afterwards was that he would need to wash his hands. There was just something about the baron that was off-putting. Sebastian did not know what it was, but something in the back of his mind told him to be wary.

"It is good to meet you, Burgess. I hope your journey to Swarkstone was not too difficult."

Fixing a bland smile firmly upon his face, Sebastian responded the only way he knew how. "The journey was pleasant enough. Thank you." What else could he say? It would not do to tip his hand too soon by telling the man he thought him an oily tick. That would get him nowhere.

Holding on to his lapels, Blackthorn seemed to chuckle to himself. "Good, good. It is nice of you to come to the reading of my brother's will. I did not know you were at all close to him. Really, your sister died what? Five years ago? I would not have thought you would have kept up the relationship."

Tilting his head, Sebastian fought to maintain his smile, saying, "I had a rather vested interest to do so."

Sebastian's careful observation helped him to take note of the slight tightening of the man's lips and a narrowing of the eyes, but Randell Blakesley only responded by saying, "Oh?"

"Yes," Sebastian began, "He was the father and guardian of my beloved niece."

Nodding vigorously, the older man exclaimed, "Ah, yes, little Laura, our niece."

Sebastian could feel the tick behind his right eyebrow starting up again. Had the man just called their niece Laura? He might have been forced to say something ill-advised if not for the hand on his shoulder distracting him.

The man who had come up to him helped further by saying, "Baron Blackthorn, you must excuse me for interrupting, but I really must speak with Burgess here for a moment. You understand—business matters to attend to."

The man did not even wait for a response before pulling Sebastian away and drawing him into a room off the hallway and shutting the door firmly behind them both. "I apologize for the sudden interruption and getting the introduction backwards, but you looked like you could use a bit of a rescue." The gentleman offered a card before introducing himself. "Herold Herrington at your service."

Sebastian studied the card. Not only did it tell him that the man before him was the man he had been meeting at Swarkstone, but it was made from high-quality paper and spoke of wealth. The card was quite impressive, but Herrington himself was equally so. If he had to guess, Sebastian would guess Herrington to be maybe Darcy's age. His attire may have been simple and subdued, but the fine tailoring and choice of fabric hinted at a higher price point, even in its muted hues. Then, too, there was something about the way the man looked at him over the rim of his glasses that spoke of discernment.

Relaxing into a more natural smile, Sebastian said, "It is good to meet you. Darcy spoke of you highly. I would shake your hand, but I feel as if I should really be washing mine after shaking hands with Baron Blackthorn."

Chuckling under his breath, Herrington said, "I can well understand the feeling. There is something about that man that is off."

Rubbing at his still twitching eyebrow, Sebastian responded, saying, "Would you believe that he just referred to our shared niece as Laura? And this is the man who I fear may become the guardian of my niece."

Clasping him on the shoulder, Herrington said, "As I said in my letter, I have every confidence of being able to fight such an occurrence, and we do not need to worry about that yet. Take on only those problems that you are sure you have to face, Mr. Burgess. Do not borrow trouble that does not yet exist."

It sounded like fine logic to Sebastian. If only he could completely control his anxiety. "Though I am quite happy to hear we will have a case if it comes to it, I am left wondering just what kind of man we are dealing with here?"

Looking Sebastian in the eye, Herrington asked, "How much do you know about the Blackthorn family?"

"I THOUGHT I TOLD you it would be best for that Burgess fellow to get the incorrect information about the reading of my fool brother's will," snarled Baron Blackthorn. The man stalked around the room as he berated Chester Eliot. It was a tableau that Chester had endured many times before.

"Yes, sir, and I bribed the clerks at the firm quite well. It appears that this Herrington fellow, tired of being given the runaround, took matters into his own hands and personally confronted your brother's solicitor. As I have told you before, Niles Coulson is not a man who can be bribed into compliance. It is why your brother chose him to be his solicitor."

Slamming a fist against a column, the baron shouted, "Then you should have used threats! It's as if you want me to throw you into debtors' prison and force your mother and sister from the cottage they live in. You know your father handed the deed over to me before his death."

Chester humbly bowed his head and whispered, "I am fully aware of that, sir. Rest assured, I will work harder to do better."

The baron sneered at him for a moment before returning to his previous rant. "I will not be opposed in this. There is too much at stake."

"Yes, sir." Chester knew from experience that keeping his responses to a minimum would serve him best. Letting the baron rant for a time always made it easier for him to handle later. Dealing with the man was a necessary evil for which Chester cursed his father for every day.

They had once been a respectable family, but his father's desire to see them become more than they were led to gambling and angry money lenders. If his father had not amassed huge piles of debt and went to Blackthorn for a loan before his death, Chester would never have anything to do with the man. Now he worked for baron Blackthorn, and the once luxurious lifestyle of his mother and sisters had been replaced by long days toiling away for a seamstress.

His gaze slid around the room as the baron stormed about, only half listening to his tired complaints of misuse. It was all the same complaint at this point in his rant. The baron complained ceaselessly, "Father never should have allowed such a settlement. His wife's money should have gone to him and then me not be handed down to her child! I was his firstborn. I deserve it all."

It was a common enough problem. You could see it's like all the way back in bible times. The old baron had two wives, and each wife had a son. The first wife passed away shortly after giving birth to the heir, the present Baron Blackthorn. Not content as a widower, the old baron had married again, and his second wife also birthed a son. The fact that he had a half-brother did not bother the current baron. It was the fact that his father's second wife had an airtight settlement that left all the monies and the estate she brought into the marriage to her son, Cornelius.

When the current baron had swiftly run through his inheritance with his fast lifestyle, the grumbling had begun. Left with a derelict estate that he could not parcel off due to an entailment, he began saying his father should have seen to the upkeep with his second wife's funds. Eventually, his complaints had shifted and now he believed that, as the firstborn, he should have received everything. In his mind, Cornelius should not have received anything, as he was only a second son. The baron believed that his younger brother should have had to shift for himself.

"Do you understand?" The baron questioned, and Chester was pulled back from his thoughts.

It did not matter what had gone before the question; he knew what was expected of him. Nodding his head, he replied, "Yes, sir." Chester couldn't understand the baron's reasoning behind trying to twist his younger brother's will in his own favor, but he was in the man's service, come what may.

Keeping his eyes averted in a show of respect and his head tilted down, Chester hid his smile. Even though he was compelled to carry out the man's plans, he couldn't help but derive a perverse joy from imagining their failure. He was only human, after all.

Sebastian sat, fighting the nervous anticipation that ran through him, knowing that the reading of Cornelius Blakesley's will would be read in a few hours. Waiting had never been something he was good at, and Sebastian found himself wishing that he was back in London, where he could blow off some steam at *Gentleman Jack's*. Going a few rounds with someone and working up a sweat had always been one of his preferred methods of killing time. It was not, however, an indulgence he could anticipate here in the country.

Running into Baron Blackthorn so soon after his arrival had been bad luck, but at least he had not had to spend too much time with the man. He had avoided sharing a meal with the baron the evening before by claiming exhaustion and asking for a tray to be brought to his room. The food that had been brought was meager and the tea lukewarm. Despite that, Sebastian did not regret his choice.

Sighing, Sebastian let his head fall back against the back of his chair. It was easy to see evidence of the lack of staff in the care that was being provided. Apparently, even getting warm water for him to wash up with was a chore without the needed staff below stairs. Davies, his normally unflinching valet, seemed to be frustrated with the conditions and had gone down to fetch the water himself. Though with as long as it was taking, he wondered if Davies was having to boil it himself. The lack of efficiency was becoming increasingly frustrating, though he didn't hold the remaining staff responsible. Sebastian could not truly be angry at the people who had fled their positions in fear.

If Herrington's claims about Baron Blackthorn were even partially true, he wouldn't blame anyone for wanting to escape the estate and avoid such a contemptible man. Herrington had described him as a spendthrift who did not think twice of abusing staff or people he saw as somehow less than him. It was said that the baron considered those with a lower rank as unworthy of respect, showing no mercy to anyone, regardless of their gender. Hearing that made Sebastian glad that his sister and niece were safe at Pemberley.

Herrington told him that all that was left of the man's inheritance from his father was a crumbling manor and an estate full of terrified tenants. It seemed that Blackthorn was notorious for his underhanded practices and fits of violence and was said to be sustaining himself through the profits of his blackmail schemes. It would make sense that the baron saw Swarkstone and his brother's holdings as a needed infusion of funds. If Cornelius Blakesley had left his wealth to the baron, Sebastian would wish him well. His only concern was Clara and her wellbeing. He was ready to find out what he could of the will and be gone from such a poorly run place.

Chapter Five

"NOW REMEMBER WHAT WE said about leaving the baby plants where they are. We are only taking out the weeds. The plants that look like this." Lydia held up an example for her young nephew again. He was a very enthusiastic helper but sometimes his enthusiasm could be become a danger to her seedlings.

Looking over, she noticed that Clara was watching her carefully and then finding a weed, she pulled it and held it aloft. Her gaze questioning. It concerned Lydia that the little girl chose not to talk for the most part. Nodding, Lydia encouraged, "Yes, perfect, Miss Clara. That is exactly the kind of plant we are looking to pull." Leaning over, she hugged the girl to her side. Careful to keep her dirty hands away from Clara's dress, she kissed her on the forehead. Smothering Clara with the affection she suspected she had never received came naturally to Lydia. She believed everyone deserved love in their life, especially children. It was a tragedy that not all children would get the love they deserved.

Lydia did not know how long she would have with little Clara, but she was going to show her as much love as possible in that time. She could only imagine how stark the child's life must have been for her to be so timid now. Taking a moment to watch Clara as she worked in the dirt, Lydia marveled at her delicate features. Even with her black curls contained with a bow that morning, a few strands were still escaping to frame her elfin face. She was so precious, and she deserved to be treated as such. Hopefully, she would come out of her shell a little and begin to share some of herself sooner rather than later.

The reading of the will was scheduled to begin within a matter of hours. Then they would have to wait until Mr. Burgess made his way back to Pemberley to learn anything vital. It was the perfect morning to vent her frustration on weeds. Gazing beyond Clara, she caught Selene's eye. Her normally talkative friend was becoming just as quiet as her niece, Clara. Selene tried in vain to smile, but it never made it to her eyes. Lydia could see that Selene was just as anxious, if not more so.

Pulling on her arm with a grubby hand, Artie got her attention, saying, "Auntie Lydie, I think we did all the bad plants."

Realizing that he was correct, Lydia smiled. "You are right! I suppose we are done for the day in the garden, and it is time for you both to go back up to the nursery."

"No, Auntie Lydie. There are other bad plants over there. We can get them next."

Lydia shook her head, trying to suppress a laugh at his playful antics, fully aware that giving in would only spur him on. She was firm when she said, "No, those weeds are for another day. It is time for you to go back to the nursery with Clara."

Clara nodded obediently and stood calmly while Artie pretended to pout and stick out his little lower lip. Lydia knew better than to be swayed. Wiping her dirty hands on the large cloth she had brought, Lydia stood and shook out her skirts, then wiped Artie's hands as well. Clara and Selene were occupied in a similar manner, albeit with less humor. Pursing her lips, Lydia tried to come up with a way to lighten the mood for the two.

One of the gardeners came over to gather the tools and whatnot and Lydia smiled at him in thanks. It had been an odd adjustment to have so many staff present when she came to Pemberley for the first time. She knew that the family could get by with less but learned that William often employed people who found themselves in need. It was one of the reasons Pemberley's staff were so known for being hardworking and loyal.

Then, each holding a child's hand, they moved with them into the house. Projecting a bit of levity in her tone, Lydia said, "You know, I think I heard Nurse Sarah say that she was getting a special treat from Cook this morning."

This instantly had Artie's attention and looking back he cried, "Clara, did you hear we can get a special treat!"

Clara grinned and nodded, setting her curls bobbing around her head. Though Clara did not say anything, Selene responded, "Won't that be lovely?"

Nurse Sarah, who joined the excitement, asked, "Did you have fun gardening?"

Nodding, Artie said, "Yes, we got more bad plants. Auntie Lydie said we can have a special treat."

Not missing a beat, the kind nurse said, "Oh, of course, but you will have to get cleaned up first. We can't have you ruining your treat with dirty hands and clothes."

Lydia watched Nurse Sarah shepherd them off towards the nursery. They would be washed up in no time, she was sure. Sarah was very good at her job and, even with the addition of Clara, she kept their routine running smoothly. It was time that they had a treat and a story, and most likely a nap.

She did not press Selene for conversation as they both walked to their rooms. Lydia could understand her need for contemplation at such a time. Lydia poured water from her ewer into the basin so that she could wash her face and hands. She would change and then go spend some time with Elizabeth and baby Gilbert while the children napped. Maybe she could convince Selene to join them. She wanted to keep Selene distracted while she waited for her brother's return. Though Lydia was starting to run out of ideas.

SEBASTIAN WATCHED THE MAN across from him arrange the papers before him into a neat stack before speaking. Herrington had implied that the man, one Niles Coulson, was, if not on his side, honest to a fault. If problems were to arise, at least it would not be from any underhanded actions on his part.

Clearing his throat, Mr. Coulson began, "As all relevant parties are present, I will begin by reading Cornelius Blakeley's will. Once I have read it through, we can begin discussions on the matters that are most relevant to the current parties. Please do not interrupt with questions until such time when I give you leave to do so."

And so began a long-winded recitation full of legalese and jargon. Oddly enough, Sebastian was reminded of one of the lectures he attended back in Cambridge given by an older don. He felt like he only comprehended every third sentence, and he was certain he would fail the upcoming test.

From what he could interpret, there were certain bequests to servants for their loyal service. A town house was left to a lady of his acquaintance, presumably a mistress of long standing. Though two other women also received lump sums. Sebastian thought Clara was being referred to as the minor female child in most of the document, if he wasn't mistaken. He noticed that her name had been listed only once at the beginning when naming her his heir. Care of the minor child was being left to the relative best suitable, with instructions and provisions in the accompanying codicil with oversight to be handled by the solicitor on retainer Niles Coulson.

Did that mean that the person in charge of Clara's care was not listed in the will itself? What were the instructions and provisions? Glancing over at Herrington, Sebastian saw he did not appear at all concerned. Hopefully, that meant the information thus far wasn't concerning.

Following instructions and not wanting to appear ignorant, Sebastian waited for the man to finish speaking. Blackthorn, however, did not appear to be of the same mind, as he interrupted in a huff of frustration. "Enough of all this, blather! Just tell me of…" The glare delivered by Mr. Coulson might not have been enough to stop Blackthorn mid sentience, but the rather burly assistant coming around to rest a hand on the man's shoulder seemed to do the job.

Sebastian bit his lip to keep from smiling at the baron's inappropriate behavior. He knew it was not the time to be caught smiling. He wondered if there were often people at will readings needing to be kept in line. If so, having formidable assistants was a wise precaution. Mr. Coulson once again began reading the will. It did not take him long to finish the document once silence had been enforced.

Looking at all the men in the room, Coulson said, "Now, are there any questions?"

Finally, given leave to vent his spleen, Blackthorn shouted, "Are you telling me that my brother left all of his property and money to his sniveling brat?!" The man would have stood if not for the large hand that was once again at his shoulder.

"Baron Blackthorn, this is your only warning. These proceedings will be held with dignity and decorum. If you are unable to uphold these strictures, you will vacate the premises."

Glaring daggers at the solicitor, Blackthorn griped, "You cannot kick me out of my brother's home. It should by all rights be mine." Despite speaking in a controlled manner, his tone conveyed a cutting and peevish attitude.

Unswayed, Mr. Coulson countered with cool civility. "As per your brother's will, Swarkstone Park is now under the ownership of Clara Sophia Blakesley."

"But she is female and a minor! She cannot manage a property," he scoffed.

Nodding, Mr. Coulson replied, "In light of her minor status, the individual chosen to oversee her care will also be responsible for managing her properties and investments."

With his eyes widening as if he had stumbled upon a stroke of luck, Blackthorn absentmindedly brushed off a bit of lint from his trousers and remarked, "Then I will take care of the brat. She is my niece. I suppose family being what it is, I shall take her in."

Leaning back in his chair behind the desk, Mr. Coulson steepled his fingers. "That is not how this works. Your brother listed who he wanted to care for his child in the accompanying codicil. Only when all other options for guardianship have been exhausted are you listed as a possibility."

Standing and slapping his hands down on the desk between them, Blackthorn shouted, "Then what did he leave me? I never once heard my name listed while you were muttering on in legal jargon."

"No, you wouldn't have. Your brother left you nothing. He was, in fact, very specific about leaving you nothing." Then, making eye contact with the large assistant, he nodded. "It is time for you to take your leave. As I said, I will not have you disrupting the proceedings. Bankes will see you out. Please vacate the premises within the hour." What followed involved a lot of screaming and more cursing than Sebastian had heard since leaving school, but eventually, the small man and his servant were out of the room.

Then it was just the three men sitting around the desk, Herrington and Sebastian on the one side and Mr. Coulson on the other. Without the stifling presence of Blackthorn, Sebastian felt some of his tension bleed away. At least the baron had not been the one named Clara's guardian.

NILES COULSON LOOKED AT the young man across from him and wondered how he might take the information in the clause. He did not appear to be a greedy man, but he would soon find out one way or the other. Shifting his gaze, Coulson nodded to Herrington. He had never met the man in person but they dwelt in similar circles and he had only heard good things about the other solicitor.

Pulling out a sheet from a folder on the desk, he addressed the younger man, saying, "Mr. Burgess, I believe you are here regarding your concern for your niece, Clara. You will most likely be very relieved that you and your sister are both listed as possible guardians of your young niece. However, there are provisions that must be met."

Sitting forward in his chair, Mr. Burgess asked, "Provisions?"

"Yes, the codicil is essentially a list of provisions. Though unusual, they are in effect and legal." Coulson read the curiosity on Herrington's face, which was to be expected. Being someone who worked with wills, he understood that finding novel approaches often felt like unraveling a challenging puzzle. Mr. Burgess, however, simply looked confused. Taking pity on him, Coulson explained, "A year or so ago, Cornelius Blakesley was ill and feverish; from what I understand it was a rather harrowing experience. For a time, he drew closer to his daughter, becoming more interested in her welfare. It was at that time that he created the codicil."

Though it looked as if Burgess might comment, he hesitated and then asked, "What are the conditions to guardianship?"

Looking down at the sheet before him, Coulson considered the situation before glancing back up and saying, "First off, you must prove that you have the child's best interests at heart.

Unsurprisingly, Baron Blackthorn has already proven himself unsuitable. Conversely, you have demonstrated your worthiness to care for the child."

Herrington questioned, "While I am not about to make things more difficult for my client, I wonder what action of his has shown that he has her best interests at heart?"

"Why, quickly removing her from an unhealthy situation. I have spoken with the staff here. Mr. Burgess and his sister arrived swiftly after my client's death and, on finding Clara without adequate care, removed her." Coulson watched both men as they took in his statement before continuing by asking, "Where is Miss Clara? Though as a father, I applaud your actions. As her solicitor, I will need to know."

Tilting his head, Mr. Burgess's eyes narrowed only briefly before saying, "My sister and I are friends with the Darcys of Pemberley. Not only are they close enough to make the journey possible, but we knew that they would be at home and welcoming. Their son is quite taken with his guest to the nursery."

The Darcys were a very fine family, indeed. It was evident that Mr. Burgess had a greater level of connections than was widely acknowledged. Nodding, Coulson merely said, "It was a wise choice to take her to a place where she could be cared for with a staffed and well provided nursery. I am aware of the staff at Swarkstone Park having fled in fear of the baron."

When neither man commented nor questioned his statement, Coulson continued, "The second provision is that the person who gains guardianship must live at Swarkstone at least a portion of every year in order to oversee its upkeep and care for the tenants. This was put in place so that when Miss Clara comes of age, she will be assured of a solvent estate to serve as her dowry. The estate must remain profitable in order for the guardianship to not fall into jeopardy." From the look on both Herrington and Burgess's faces, they were aware of the irony in that provision. Cornelius Blackthorn rarely visited his daughter or estate and only the care of a good steward had kept the estate solvent.

"The third, and probably the most problematic provision, is that he requires that whoever claims guardianship be married. He states he does not care if it is you or your sister who claims guardianship, but that you must be married. He allows for a thirty-day grace period from the reading of the will should neither of you be married at the time of his death. This is the one provision which could stymie your guardianship, as I believe neither you nor your twin are married."

Pinching the bridge of his nose, Mr. Burgess questioned, "So one of us must marry in order to care for Clara?"

"Yes. At the time, I believe my client felt his failings as a father stemmed from not having a mother to offer his daughter. For a time, he had planned on remarrying but became...distracted by other pursuits." It was not for Coulson to say that the temptations of London captivated Cornelius Blakesley, leaving little room for thoughts of his daughter or the responsibilities of his estate. Pushing forward with the last provision, he continued, "The final provision grants me the authority to oversee Miss Clara's guardian. I am tasked with ensuring that Miss Clara's guardian carries out their responsibilities in accordance with my judgment. As for the money that Clara will inherit, you shall only have control of the interest after I see proof of your marriage and officially name you and your wife as guardians. You are granted the authority to utilize the interest for the purpose of caring for Clara and her estate, however, I will need a detailed record of the funds' allocation."

Married? He or Selene had to be married in order to care for Clara. There was really no question about it. One of them would have to marry, but how to go about it? Mr. Coulson continued talking, but Sebastian found himself lost to anything besides the issue he had been presented with the word marriage. He could not force his sister into an unattainable situation. Marriage was not a simple thing, especially where there was no love in the union, but at least as a man, he would not be so wholly under someone else's power as his sister would be. It would have to be him who married. He would not allow Selene to make the sacrifice that he knew she would be so willing to commit to. Nor would he risk Clara falling into the hands of Baron Blackthorn.

A loud clearing of the throat had startled Sebastian. Opposite him, Mr. Coulson's voice carried a firm tone as he addressed him. "Mr. Burgess."

Sebastian forced his gaze to focus on Mr. Coulson, who, it seemed, had been trying to get his attention. Embarrassed that his inattention had been so easily noticed, Sebastian apologized, saying, "I am sorry, please go on and I will endeavor to pay closer attention."

Offering a kind smile, Mr. Coulson nodded, stating, "Mr. Burgess, I may not know you that well, but I feel safe in assuming that you are even at this moment planning for a wedding in the near future. I wish I could say that it was unnecessary, but I cannot. If you do not comply with the provisions in the codicil, Randell Blakesley, the Baron of Blackthorn, will be allowed to take up the attempt, as per my client's wishes."

With a firm shake of his head, Sebastian adamantly replied, "No. I will not risk my niece falling into that man's clutches. I will be married by the deadline given." With only a thirty-day deadline, he had no clue who he would find to marry. Nevertheless, he remained committed to make it happen, no matter the challenges.

Mr. Coulson began stacking up the papers about the borrowed desk, only pausing to say, "I will need to meet your wife and see the wedding license. I will plan to meet you here. The day after you arrive with your new bride. Kindly provide me with the details of your scheduled wedding date and your expected arrival at Swarkstone Park."

Sebastian found himself nodding and moving to stand while saying, "Yes, that is acceptable. I will be sure to keep you informed." What else could Sebastian say? He was in no position to object, and everyone in the room knew it.

Putting the last of his papers away in a satchel, Mr. Coulson came from around the desk and clasped Sebastian on the shoulder briefly before saying, "Good, good, I will also expect to meet with Miss Clara as well to ensure the girl is properly cared for. It would be wise to hire nursery staff and prepare for an extended stay at Swarkstone. It will require some effort to turn the property and what remains of the staff around after such extended neglect, but I have faith that you will prove capable of doing so."

Despite being grateful for the acknowledgment, Sebastian could not think of a response besides the tight nod that he offered and walking with the man to the door. His mind was overflowing with responsibilities and lists of things that must be done that he felt completely unequal to.

"I will see myself and my staff out after I leave word with the housekeeper and the butler that they are to take instruction from you. I know you have things to be about, but I hope to hear from you soon." After shaking hands with both Sebastian and Herrington, Mr. Coulson was off down the hallway, his large assistant speaking with him as they went. Sebastian wondered if the man had had any difficulty seeing the baron off. He did not seem harmed, so at least that was something.

Chapter Six

Chester was glad to offer his master the flask of brandy as they were unceremoniously escorted to their carriage by the solicitor's man. The spirits offered would not only shorten the baron's rant, but also induce a deep sleep thanks to the swaying motion of the carriage. While he had expected no other outcome, it was apparent that the baron was beyond furious over his exclusion and expulsion.

He rarely paid much attention to his master's rants. There was not much point really and paying attention simply gave him a headache to go along with his stomach ulcer. Between swigs of the brandy, the baron continued to rant even as they made their way through the little village near Swarkstone. Exclaiming loudly enough to be heard by all and sundry, "...have the gall to ignore me in his will. If he was not already dead, I would have him killed! And the solicitor, he was something else entirely! How dare he not give way to my demands? He is nothing compared to me. I am of a higher class of men. I am a baron!" The exclamation would have been more impressive if it was not immediately followed by a hiccup.

Drinking heavily on an empty stomach left the baron snoring soon enough, and Chester could not fight the sigh that escaped him on realizing the man was finally asleep. It was a long trip back to London, and he did not look forward to dealing with the baron's anger along the way.

He was certain that he would be back at the law firm soon enough, once again bribing clerks to get a chance to see the clause regarding the child's care. It seemed that all possibility of the baron having access to his brother's funds revolved around the little girl. So far, his dealings with Baron Blackthorn had revolved around greasing palms and threatening people of a certain sort. The baron lived at the periphery of society where he could impress and sway those below him. As far as he was aware, he had never attempted to *influence* someone with real power or backbone. Or, for that matter, interfere with the life and wellbeing of a child. The scum of the earth and men with things to hide were more his area of influence.

However, the men in the meeting that morning had all seemed like good and honest men. Was it possible that the baron had finally come up against a force that he was incapable of overcoming with blackmail and underhanded tactics? It would be a welcome possibility, but Chester knew better than to celebrate prematurely. Things were sure to get worse before they got better. If they got better.

SETTLING BACK INTO THE cushion of his carriage, Sebastian let his mind wander. As late as it was, he knew that there was no hope of sleep for him. On the other side of the carriage, Herrington had drifted into a doze, but Sebastian would not be that lucky.

He had chosen to drive straight to Pemberley without a stop at an inn for the night. The journey was only eight hours long and they could manage it without stopping. Summer had granted them extra hours on the road, and with the full moon illuminating the night sky, their journey felt secure. Sebastian had just wished to be done with travel, so he had told his groom that they would only stop and change horses before continuing on. He anticipated arriving at Pemberley only a few hours past sunset.

He had been glad that Herrington had been willing to come back to Pemberley with him. Sebastian was sure to have many legal questions arise in the coming days, and it would be most convenient to have the man at hand. He was sure that Herrington would not be able to stay through his taking over Swarkstone Park, but one step at a time.

There were so many things to consider at the juncture before him. The most straightforward choice to consider was taking over management at Swarkstone. He would like to think that he would enjoy feeling actually useful. One of the reasons Sebastian spent so much time away from home was his father's inability to let go of the reins back at his home of Trowbridge Hall.

Not one for any modernization or modern ideas of any sort, his father, Augustus Burgess, Viscount Trowbridge, felt that Sebastian could have a say in things once he died. The man insisted that his son's radical ideas would spell doom for their estate, and he would be happy to be dead when that happened. Modernization and leaving the old ways would in fact be the downfall of the nation, or so his father believed. Of course, there were other reasons he never returned to visit Trowbridge hall, but it was all tied to his father's need to maintain ultimate control. That and his low opinion of women.

Sebastian had no desire to follow his father's advice of using this time to sow his wild oats and enjoy his youth while uninhibited. That was not the kind of man that he was, though lately he had been increasingly bored with the endless rounds of calls and entertainments to be had in London. So it would be nice to bring meaning to his life by being able to pick up the reins, so to speak, even if it was for the protection of his niece's holdings.

He could not even begin to contemplate how he would face the most difficult of the provisions. Marriage. Such an important step in one's life was not to be undertaken lightly, but with a deadline, things shifted. He worried about making the right choice. How did you make the correct choice when you had less than thirty days to find a bride?

Lᴇᴅɪᴀ sᴛᴏᴏᴅ ᴡɪᴛʜ Sᴇʟᴇɴᴇ at the window as William went out to greet the men descending from the carriage. They had received word that Sebastian and his solicitor, a friend of William's, would arrive late that evening. She could feel the tension in her friend's body as she stood next to her.

"He looks as if he has the weight of the world on his shoulders," whispered Selene. They could see her brother's outline in the light of the flickering torches that had been left out for their arrival. She continued, "I fear whatever he learned was not good."

Lydia was not about to say that she agreed with her friend. It was not the time to be pessimistic and so giving Selene's arm a squeeze, Lydia said, "You do not know that. He has had a long day full of news and travel. Of course he is weary. Do not think the worst, not yet."

With a nod, Selene sighed. "I suppose you are right."

Drawing her friend from the window, Lydia encouraged her, "Let us greet them and make sure they get a bit of something to eat. You know they will not have taken a proper meal."

Walking together to greet Mr. Burgess and Mr. Herrington, Lydia was not surprised when her friend rushed the last few steps and enfolded her brother in a hug. In fact, she had already greeted Mr. Herrington and asked him if he would care for tea or if he preferred to retire to his room before the siblings broke apart.

"It has been a long day and if you do not think it rude, I would appreciate retiring for the evening."

"You are not rude at all, Mr. Herrington," Lydia assured him. "Your room has already been prepared. Gregson will see you to your room and see to anything that you may need." The footman she gestured to, who stood quietly nearby, nodded, ready to assist.

Coming over, William clapped Mr. Herrington on the back. "It is good to see you, Herrington. We will have to play a game or two of chess before you return to London."

Mr. Herrington seemed to perk up at the mention of a game. "Oh, have you kept your game up all the way out here in the wilds of Derbyshire? Who do you play?"

"My sister, Mrs. Darcy, has been known to topple his king on a regular basis. Though sometimes she will let him win." Lydia laughed, eager to interject some levity in to the somber and tense atmosphere.

"Then I will just have to play her as well," replied Mr. Herrington. Lydia was glad to see that he seemed pleased to play a skilled opponent rather than be put off by the fact that a woman was winning. He continued, "Well, if you do not mind, I will say good night now and see you all in the morning."

At this, Mr. Burgess spoke up from where he stood, his sister still pulled into his side. "I cannot thank you enough for all the help that you have provided. Sleep well."

Herrington smiled, and with a nod to them all, headed to the stairs. William shared a look with Lydia. She suspected he was in favor of postponing conversation until the morning but did not know how to approach the subject. She surmised that whatever Mr. Burgess had learned would not be handled in even a few hours, and that it would be better for all to get a fresh start in the morning.

They stood and watched Mr. Herrington go, escorted by Gregson up the stairs. Lydia looked around at their small group and, seeing their various looks of concern, she nodded her head and addressed everyone. "It is rather late and not the time to have a conversation about the reading of the will. We are all tired and worn, Mr. Burgess especially. We can discuss matters after breakfast when all of us are present and we have gotten some sleep."

It seemed for a moment Selene might argue with her statement, but then she looked up at her brother standing beside her and sighed. Mr. Burgess might still appear strong, but Lydia could detect how his shoulders drooped, and his eyes seemed shadowed in the candlelight. It was clear that he was in no condition to start a lengthy conversation about the emotional and concerning topic at hand.

Patting her brother's hand, Selene said, "Lydia is correct. We will learn all in the morning."

Chapter Seven

Sebastian held still as his valet shaved his face, giving into
his need to move about at that point in his morning's ablutions
would have consequences. Despite being granted a reprieve of sorts,
Sebastian had found little sleep and no answers in the intervening
night. When he had deemed a decent hour to ring for Davies, he had
already been up for hours pacing his room.

Thanks to Davies's thoughtful gesture of bringing him coffee, he
now felt less sleep deprived. He was, however, also more eager to
roam. A need to expend nervous energy pulled at him. Waiting until
the razor was away from his face, Sebastian asked, "If you were given
thirty days to find a bride and wed, what would you do?"

Davies looked at his master momentarily before he wiped the
lather from the blade in his hand with a towel. It almost seemed
as if he would not answer, but Sebastian knew he was a man of
deep thoughts. Davies had never steered him wrong in the past when

he had asked him for advice on a subject. Davies was not the most loquacious of men, but he was exceedingly steady. Finally he said, "I would look to a woman I already knew. As the heir of a viscount, many women would marry you with no courting at all. Any woman you met and attempted to court and marry in thirty days' time would most likely look at it from a standpoint of security and materialistic concerns, which is fine for many people. However, if you do not mind my saying so, I do not believe you would be happy in that sort of arrangement, sir. Yes, I believe you would be better off looking at women you already know to an extent, where there is already a certain amount of amiability or even affection."

What Davies said contained much sense, though Sebastian did not feel as if he had been magically granted any answers. Nodding, he held still once more so that Davies could finish, and he could go pace somewhere else. He needed to think, and he did that best while moving.

Soon enough, he was outside of Pemberley, winding his way through one of the many gardens where Sebastian had begun to think. Davies had said that he should look to one of the women he knew already. It made sense; to a certain extent, he would know something about their disposition and preferences. The question that he was left with, however, was if he had liked a woman he had met enough to want to marry her, wouldn't he already be married? Or at least engaged?

Spending much of his time in town, he had met any number of debutantes and rarely found himself impressed. Or at least impressed enough to want to do something about it. There was also the fact that many of those who spent their time in town did it because they chose to. They enjoyed it there. He did not, or at least he did not like it as much as he once had. He had to think that picking one of the women he had met in London would not go well if he was set to spend the majority of his time going forward in the country overseeing Swarkstone.

Regardless of the way his marriage was starting, he hoped that he could at least develop a closeness, a friendship of sorts. Love may be off the table, but he did not want the contractual cold thing he saw so often in town. Maybe he would do well if he decided what he wanted in a bride? It would help him narrow down his list of potential brides, so to speak. Not that any names had come to mind.

He wanted a woman who would be willing to spend time with him and his niece. If he had to choose something to put at the top of the list, it would have to be that she treat his niece and sister with love and kindness. He would not permit any cattiness or meanness of spirit to hurt either of them. It was something he too often saw among those of the ton.

Being a gentleman, he was not privy to the world of women, but he had overheard enough backhanded compliments and seen the tears in the eyes of debutantes at balls to know nastiness when he saw it. Then too, his sister shared much of what transpired when she went round making calls. They were close, and he did not want to lose that by marrying the wrong woman.

Beauty was something he could put on his list, or at least attraction. He wanted children of his own, and being attracted to his wife would certainly help matters. It might be best if she also wanted children. While sharing a child could potentially foster a strong connection, he knew that thought was for a much later time.

So kindness and love for his niece and his sister, mutual attraction, and a desire for children. What else? Did he really want nothing else besides being a good and loving person? Stopping to ponder the question, he examined the bright pink blooms on the plant in front of him. He had no idea what it was, but it was beautiful. Looking around, he realized that the flower garden he had been ignoring in his distraction was really quite beautifully done.

Reaching out, he fingered the edge of a bloom just beginning to bud and was startled when he heard, "Those are gladiolus."

LYDIA HAD WATCHED MR. Burgess wander through the garden before she spoke, saying "Those are gladiolus."

It was obvious that he had seen neither her nor the gardener that had been moving about the flower garden that morning. Startling at her voice, he turned away from the plant that she had been carefully cultivating since moving to Pemberley and looked at her. Though he was well dressed and presumably freshly shaved, he still seemed to be subdued. It was clear to Lydia that he had gotten little to no sleep.

Was the news truly so very bad? There had been talk of fighting the other relatives in court in order to see to Clara's care. Was that no longer the case? Regardless of the questions whirling through her mind, Lydia knew it was not the time to attack him with her own concerns when he so obviously was struggling with his own. Accepting her shears from the gardener, she stepped around him to trim a few sprigs for the flower arrangements she had risen early to work on.

After a moment, Mr. Burgess said, "I do not believe I have seen their like, but then again, I am not one to study flowers often."

Turning to him, she gestured to the basket over her arm full of blooms. "I love flowers. Not only are they beautiful, but they are often useful. There is even a language of flowers which I have always delighted in."

Tilting his head, Mr. Burgess smiled. "Oh? What can you say with flowers?"

Lydia decided he looked much better with a smile brightening his previously worried features. Looking into her basket, Lydia pulled out an aster with its star-like bloom and purple hue. "Asters represent love and wisdom. While the gladiolus you were looking at, with its sword-like shape, is said to represent strength." Shifting a few of the blooms, Lydia carefully drew out an iris and continued, "Irises represent hope. So if I were to present you with an arrangement of flowers of all three, I would be saying I hope for love, wisdom, and strength to prevail."

Carefully watching Mr. Burgess as she spoke, Lydia saw the moment of understanding flash through his eyes. He was quick to ask, "And has that been your task this morning? Gathering blooms to help us along?"

"Having a pretty room to have a hard discussion in cannot hurt matters. I have never known flowers to make things worse and if I help the group make wise decisions with my own form of encouragement, all the better." Lydia flashed him a warm smile, hoping he would feel encouraged by her expression and words.

She was concerned with how downtrodden he had seemed when he first came into the garden. She had always known him to be a kind and happy gentleman, and it was a pity that he seemed to have turned a hard corner in life. Both he and his sister Selene only wanted what was best for precious little Clara. That poor girl who seemed nearly afraid of her own shadow deserved only the best love and care. Lydia had decided the moment she met the little sprite that she would do all in her power to help the Burgess siblings protect and care for her.

Lydia hoped she wasn't imagining things as she saw a hint of burden lift from Mr. Burgess's shoulders when he smiled back at her. Maybe that was relief in his eyes when he said, "Thank you, Miss Bennet. Your support at this time means a lot to me and my family."

"I could imagine doing nothing else." Gathering flowers for a few arrangements to show her support was not much, but it was one of the best ways she knew how. She always loved speaking with flowers. "I will leave you to your contemplations for now, though do not lose yourself so much that you forget to come in and partake of some breakfast. Otherwise I might have to send one of the footmen out searching for you to bring you as I would Artie."

Giving Mr. Burgess a small curtsy, she moved on. The gardener followed closely behind her as she checked over her buds and blooms, and she couldn't resist gathering a few more flowers that she spotted along the way. Lydia had things she wanted to accomplish before she broke her own fast.

EVERYONE HAD GATHERED TOGETHER in a rather homey sitting room, and despite how comfortable it was, Sebastian still did not feel at ease. He knew he had eaten. His sister pestered him about his empty plate, but he could not for the life of him remember what he had consumed. Food was there and then it wasn't, and he could not say what it had been at all. Now they were all gathered with tea or coffee in hand, waiting for him to speak.

His time was up. They were all looking at him, waiting for an explanation of what he had learned at the will reading. Even Mrs. Darcy, so recently out of childbed, had come downstairs and was staring at him with a penetrating gaze.

Finding the need to clear his throat, he took a sip of his coffee and said, "Though there were a lot of legal words I did not completely follow, in essence, the will stated that Clara was her father's primary heir. Except for a few bequests to the staff, Clara is the main beneficiary of the estate. Baron Blackthorn was not well pleased to learn that his brother had left him nothing but was, after a few expressions of anger, escorted from the property."

Herrington, present in a chair near Darcy, added, "I do not believe that is the last we will see or hear from Baron Blackthorn. He has a reputation in some of the seedier parts of London for being swift to mete out retribution to anyone who dares to slight him. He is evidently in need of an infusion of funds that his brother's estate would provide. At present, his main source of income is derived from engaging in blackmail." Sebastian could see the distaste that Herrington had for Blackthorn in the way his face scrunched up when he said the word blackmail. It certainly did not speak well for the man to use blackmail as a sort of income rather than his own hard work and effort. Then again, he had known the man was disreputable soon after he had found out about him.

Mrs. Darcy spoke up at that point, addressing Herrington, saying, "It is always easier to deal with men like him when you have enough knowledge going into matters. Thank you for letting us know Baron Blackthorn may be an issue. Our family has dealt with underhanded gentlemen before and has come out on top. We will know how to protect ourselves and those we care for." She might have smiled at Herrington as she spoke, but there was iron in her words.

Sebastian had met all the Bennet sisters at one time or another, and they all shared at least two traits. The first thing he had seen was kindness in their treatment of others and those they loved. Every action they took and every person they encountered were touched by their overwhelming kindness. The other side of that coin, however, was a core of steel. They allowed no harm to come to anyone if it was in their power to protect them. If you threatened one of them or theirs, the knives came out, sometimes literally.

Looking at the woman who had welcomed them into her own, Sebastian said, "I would like to thank you for being so willing to include my sister, Clara, and me in that group."

Herrington put down his teacup and sat forward in his chair, saying, "As the rest is more on the legal side of things, I will explain matters. There was a clause that Cornelius Blakesley added to his will, detailing the parameters for her care. The first being that the guardian must prove that you have the child's best interests at heart. Niles Coulson, the solicitor handling the matter, explained that he believed that both Mr. and Miss Burgess had demonstrated that in bringing Clara away from such a dysfunctional household and taking her to a place that she could be safe and well cared for."

"Of course we have her best interests at heart!" cried Selene. "She is our niece, after all."

Rubbing at the twitching behind his eyebrow, Sebastian replied, "Yes, she is our niece, and we care for her dearly. However, she is also Blackthorn's niece, and he referred to her as both Laura and the brat." The look on the faces of everyone in the room seemed to match the feelings that Sebastian had developed towards the man.

Continuing where he had left off, Herrington said, "The second provision is that the person who gains guardianship must live at Swarkstone Park at least a portion of every year in order to oversee its upkeep and care for the tenants. In actuality, this is a very wise parameter. That way, when Miss Clara comes of age, she will be assured of a solvent estate. Also, the estate must remain profitable in order for the guardianship to not fall into jeopardy."

Sebastian knew what was coming and still he cringed when Herrington once more began to speak. "The third provision is going to be the most problematic for you. Because it is where Cornelius Blakesley stated that whoever claims guardianship must be married. Now he lists both Burgess siblings as possible guardians, but whoever claims guardianship must be married. He allows for a thirty-day grace period from the reading of the will."

There was absolute silence in the room for a full minute before Selene asked, her voice trembling, "And if neither of us are married within the thirty-day deadline, what happens with Clara?"

Clearing his throat, Herrington responded, "The will states that her care falls to Blackthorn if neither of you choose to meet the provisions set forth. I do not believe becoming married would be an impediment of any sort to him, though I would pity any woman bound to him in such a way."

"Then there is no choice." Swallowing convulsively, Selene said, "I have had a number of offers I could—"

Sebastian stood and shook his head vehemently as he moved to his sister. "No, I will not let you sacrifice yourself in that way. Think, Selene. We would just be giving Clara's care to another man with questionable intentions. You refused those men for valid reasons. I will not hand you and Clara over to someone I cannot trust."

Selene took Sebastian's hand and, squeezing it, whispered, "But what other option is there? It is not as though you have been courting anyone. Whoever would you marry?"

"Me. He will marry me." In an instant, the room went from quietly tense to filled with breathless astonishment as Lydia's statement hung in the air.

Chapter Eight

LYDIA WAS AWARE THAT her announcement would create a stir, but she knew she had to speak. If she did not, so much could be lost. Opening her mouth, she boldly said, "Me. He will marry me."

While she had not done anything dramatic, hadn't screamed or broken a vase, she still had all eyes on her with those five small words. Squaring her shoulders, Lydia prepared to face the questions that she knew would come as soon as everyone fully processed what she had said. She would convince everyone of the soundness of her decision and her level of conviction. Lydia would worry about speaking to her mother and other sisters later. One battle at a time.

She knew in her heart that somehow this was the correct thing to do. How could it not be? There was a small child who she was growing to love whose wellbeing hung in the balance.

Across the room, she met Mr. Herrington's gaze. The solicitor did not wear a mask of shock like some of the others. His head was tilted slightly, and his gaze narrowed. The first to speak, he calmly said, "That would solve the issue rather handsomely. That is, if all parties can be brought into accord." Looking briefly over at William, where he sat with Elizabeth, Lydia could see where she thought the first obstacle might arise from.

Elizabeth and William sat silently, hands clasped tightly and, for the moment, ignoring the room. As was often the case, they were looking to each other for strength and support. It hurt Lydia to see her sister's lips pressed together so tightly as she gazed into her husband's eyes. Lydia knew that her simple statement had brought her pain. Elizabeth would be worried for her, Lydia knew it, but she hoped that Elizabeth would not attempt to stop her. Lydia dreaded the possibility that Elizabeth would be disappointed in her choice.

Realizing that Elizabeth and William would not say anything at the moment, Lydia turned instead to Selene and Mr. Burgess. Choosing to face her friend, Lydia rested her gaze on Selene. The black-haired beauty sat with her mouth slightly agape, but when their two blue gazes met, her mouth closed, and she sat up straighter. Opening her mouth again, she seemed to struggle for a moment before saying, "I would be honored to have you as a sister." Then, swallowing mightily, she continued, "However, do not feel you must do this. My brother and I can find a way to manage without such a sacrifice on your part."

Shaking her head, Lydia responded, "You do your brother a disservice by claiming that it would be a sacrifice for me to marry him. One day, he will hold the title of viscount. Who is to say I am not doing this because I crave a title of my own one day?" Lydia attempted to inject some levity into her tone, adding, "Besides, he looks well enough. I wouldn't want to undermine his confidence by implying that I didn't think he was handsome." This elicited a small smile from Selene as she looked up at her brother, who stood next to her. Lydia had been hoping she could make her laugh, but she would take a smile.

Bolstering her courage, Lydia decided it was time to face the man that she had basically just proposed to. Fighting the desire to bite her lip or look away, she met Mr. Burgess's gaze. It was not the time to be bashful; it was the time to be bold. He was a few steps away from her, standing next to Selene. His forehead furrowed slightly as his eyes met hers, evidence, she supposed, of the astonishment she had caused.

"You would be willing to marry me?" Sebastian's question came in halting tones that gave voice to his confusion more than the words spoken.

With a small nod of her head, Lydia replied, "I would be more than willing. I am convinced that it is the correct thing to do."

Scratching at his eyebrow, Mr. Burgess asked, "But why? Why would you choose to sacrifice a love match and opt for a marriage of convenience with me instead?"

"There is that word sacrifice again. After today, I would prefer not to have it brought up again." Striding across the room, she stood in front of him, chin raised and said, "Let us make things clear. If I marry you, would you respect me and my decisions?"

Mr. Burgess's brows drew together in a flash as he exclaimed, "Of course! I would never treat someone as important as my wife without respect. Why?"

Shaking her head to silence him, Lydia continued asking, "Would you see to my comfort and care and that of any children that result from our union?"

Perhaps seeing where she was heading, Mr. Burgess merely said, "Yes."

Tilting her head, she softened her voice and asked, "Would you ever belittle or demean me or any of our children, Clara included?"

Eyes widening, Mr. Burgess was quick to respond, crying vehemently, "No, I would never, *could* never, treat you or any children in such a way." Taking a step closer to her, Mr. Burgess peered down into her eyes, questioning, "How could you believe I could behave in such a way?"

As she gazed into Mr. Burgess's deep blue eyes, Lydia made a mental note to stay focused. It was not the time to be distracted. She had convincing to do. Leaning forward slightly, she smiled before saying, "I do not believe you would ever be that kind of man or husband. I have every confidence that if we marry, you will take care of me and our children to the best of your ability. You are a good man, Mr. Burgess, and you are willing to go to great length to ensure your niece's care and security. I am only trying to point out that I am willing to do the same, and I do not believe that it will ever be a sacrifice on my part. You would not let it be."

Sebastian found himself captivated by the woman who so boldly faced him. Her blue eyes flashed with challenge, and he wanted to answer it in the most basic way, but he would not. Not when he had just expressed her faith in him so eloquently. Still, he had a hard time looking away from the invitation her parted lips so unknowingly offered.

She had just offered to solve all his immediate problems, but in accepting her kind proposal, he worried that he might harm her. Could he be that selfish? Could his need to care for Clara move him to do anything but be selfish and accept the lifeline that Miss Bennet offered?

Despite her assurances that she was not sacrificing anything by marrying him, he worried she would be disheartened to lose out on a love match. All of her sisters and even her mother had eventually obtained a love match. Would she be satisfied with him when she could have waited to find the love of her life?

She met all the qualifications he had thought of that morning. He could not think of a better woman for the care and companion she would show to his niece. She was overflowing with love and motherly tendencies already. She was also friends with his sister. Miss

Bennet passed the last requirement he had come up with high marks. Sebastian had always found himself drawn to blue-eyed blondes, and it was safe to say that he found her highly attractive.

In fact, he had long been aware of her in a physical sense, but he had decided it was not something he would, or could, act on yet. Sebastian had thought that when he was ready to settle down in a few years, she might also be in a similar mindset, and if their goals aligned, he would be pleased. Was it possible that events outside his control might be encouraging him to cross a boundary he had erected for himself? Was there a chance that the timeline he had anticipated was being advanced?

He was only twenty-two years old. Young for marriage, but really, if he was to take care of his niece, he had no choice. On the other hand, Lydia was eighteen, but at least that was the typical age women started to marry. Girls had certainly married younger.

There would definitely be friendship and affection between them, whether or not what they had developed into anything more. And if he wanted more and nothing developed, surely he was mature enough to move past it. They had every chance of happiness in a marriage together, even without love. Right?

If it was just for him, he would proceed without hesitation. After all, all the benefit was on his side. His concerns about the consequences for her weighed heavily on his mind, but who was he to second guess her decisions? He had told her he would respect her and her decisions as his wife.

Reaching out, he took up her hand, feeling how small it felt in comparison to his own. Squeezing it, he asked, "Are you sure?"

With a firm nod of her head, Miss Bennet replied, "I am." That was it, no dithering or indecision. If she had no hesitation, how could he? Sebastian understood that in order to respect her, he needed to begin by respecting her choice to marry him. Understanding the importance of a strong start, he made a conscious decision to begin with determination and establish the desired tone for their relationship.

Drawing her hand up to his face, he placed a feather-light kiss on her knuckles. "Then, Miss Lydia Bennet, it would be a privilege to marry you. You have my word that I will do everything within my power to see to it that you never come to regret your decision."

Lydia was still recovering from the flash of heat that radiated up her arm when Mr. Burgess's lips had grazed her knuckles when Elizabeth spoke up. "Now that you have both had your say, I do believe it is time for other conversations. Mr. Burgess, I rather think you should speak with William."

Lydia peeked up into Mr. Burgess's face. Was it possible to see hope written in someone else's eyes? Whatever it was that she saw in his eyes caused a shiver to run down her spine. While she suspected she had given him hope for the first time since the reading of the will, she also wondered if he had the same hope she had for a congenial marriage, more than congenial, if the butterflies in her stomach were anything to go by.

He still had her hand clasped in his own, hovering in the air between them. Now would come the hard part, convincing the people who loved her so dearly that this was the right thing to do. Giving her hand a squeeze, he bowed over it before releasing her fingers. She tried to smile encouragingly even as she heard her sister say, "I would like to speak with Lydia alone."

Turning to her sister, Lydia saw the rising panic in Elizabeth's eyes. Yes, a conversation was in order. Approaching Elizabeth, she offered, "Why don't I help you back up to your room, Elizabeth? We can talk while you rest."

When Elizabeth began to get the mulish look in her eye that Lydia recognized, she worried she had miscalculated, but it seemed William had also seen the careful way her sister was sitting. Leaning in, he kissed his wife's forehead, saying, "Listen to Lydia, dear. You have already been below stairs far sooner than the midwife would like. Do it for me, Lizziebet."

Looking at her husband, she rolled her eyes and scrunching responded, "I am not made entirely of glass, you know. I am made of stronger stuff than that."

William nodded in agreement. Then, helping her to her feet, he said, "I know you have a core of steel, but I do like it when you allow me to pamper you. Speak to your sister and get some rest while you can. I will speak with Mr. Burgess."

Soon enough, Lydia was helping Elizabeth to change into a nightdress and lie down. Though Lydia wondered what sort of conversation was going on in William's study, she chose not to fret over it. Elizabeth had first checked on baby Gil and his nursemaid in the room adjoining hers. It had been a simple matter to set up a small nursery for first Artie then, Gil in what had once been the mistress chambers. That way Elizabeth and William were close enough to see to them as they desired, and Elizabeth could continue to feed the babies as needed. Artie had only moved to the Pemberley nursery once he slept through the night.

Elizabeth settled into bed with a sigh and Lydia was glad that she had managed to get her sister to lie down. Lydia had only just climbed on to the bed next to her when Elizabeth said, "Tell me what you are thinking, sister mine, because I do not understand. How could you contemplate marrying without love?"

Resting her head on the soft pillow, Lydia positioned herself on her side, her gaze fixed on her sister's worried face, as she started explaining. "Oh, but there will be Elizabeth. I would never marry without love."

Eyebrows drawn together, Elizabeth screwed up her face, asking, "Then do you have an affection for Mr. Burgess that I have never suspected?"

Lydia frowned. She had walked right into that one. She was not about to explain her girlish imaginings she had indulged in when she had first met the handsome gentleman. No, there had to be a safer route. Backtracking a little, she said, "Not in the way you are implying, no. Though I have always thought there might be something there one day. He is horribly handsome, after all, and I enjoy spending time in his company."

Gripping Lydia's hand tightly, Elizabeth asked, "Then what do you mean?"

Lydia worried she would never be able to fully convey the connection she felt to Clara, but she was going to try. She had to explain her reasoning, and she started by saying, "I know I will love that little girl more than all, but perhaps her own mother had she survived. You have not spent much time in her company, but Elizabeth, she is such a lost little sprite. She reminds me much of what we must have been as little girls. I cannot explain it, but I fairly burn to mother her. She soaks up love and affection with a sort of astonished hope that it is nearly painful to see. In marrying Mr. Burgess, I will be able to provide all the love in the world to that child. So yes, my marriage to Mr. Burgess will abound in love."

Half sitting up, Elizabeth argued, "We girls always promised mama that we would never enter into matrimony without a foundation of respect, affection, and love. I just find it hard to see you give that up, no matter how noble your decision is."

"That man downstairs has nothing but respect for me, Elizabeth." Shaking her head against the pillow, she fought her frustration with how much Elizabeth did not see what she saw. Mr. Burgess was going to be her husband if she had anything to say about it and he would be family. As family, she was going to protect him, even if it meant going against her older sister. But how to get her to understand? She continued, "You saw his hesitation. That was not for himself, it was for me. There I was, the literal answer to his prayers to keep his niece safe, and still he hesitated. I bet you anything that he was considering the issues I might face. He respects me enough to believe me when I say this is what I want to do."

Laying back down, Elizabeth said, "Fair."

Well, at least Elizabeth had acknowledged Lydia's point. That was something, right? Continuing her argument, Lydia said, "As for affection, I do not believe that is something that I will lack." Lydia blushed just remembering the way he had made her feel, kissing her hand and bowing over it. If he could keep that up once they married, she would be very happy indeed. Clearing her throat, she added, "We have been on friendly terms for a while now and I can only see our relationship improving."

Raising her eyebrows at her sister's blush, Elizabeth gave Lydia a considering look but said nothing about it. Instead, staring Lydia straight in the eye, Elizabeth demanded, "But what about love, Lydia? And I am not talking about the love you will have for Clara. I am talking about passionate love. You would give that up?"

Sighing, Lydia rolled over on her back and looked up at the canopy above her sister's bed. Elizabeth's romance was the stuff of legends. Of course, she would want her youngest sister to experience the same level of happiness and wedded bliss. How could she make her understand? Lydia explained, "No, I am not giving up on that kind of love, Elizabeth. I have just decided that I am willing to start my marriage without it. I am betting that with enough work and cultivation, Mr. Burgess and I will find our own path to the sort of love you speak of."

After that, they lay in silence and Lydia hoped that she would prove to be as good at cultivating her relationship with Mr. Burgess as she was with flowers. She had always wished for the kind of love Elizabeth spoke of. What girl didn't? She was just willing to work at it.

Sebastian looked across the desk at Darcy, strangely happy that he was having the conversation with him and not his cousin and brother-in-law, the former colonel. He had a feeling there would be a lot more intimidation going on had the situation been different. It was enough to have to face Darcy.

Not that Sebastian begrudged the hard look he was receiving from Darcy. He was attempting to marry his sister by marriage. Had someone asked for Selene's hand in such a manner, he was uncertain what he might be compelled to do. Even knowing that it would weaken his position, Sebastian broke the silence by saying, "Would you be the person I should apply to for Miss Bennet's hand? Or do I need to be contacting someone else?"

Darcy leaned back in his chair, tilting away from Sebastian, his jaw set. Sebastian waited while he felt the scrutiny of Darcy's stare. He knew Darcy would speak eventually. Fighting the need to squirm, Sebastian was grateful when Darcy finally said, "While she is staying with me, I have permission to approve of the match."

Sitting forward, Sebastian began, "Mr. Darcy," his voice filled with resolution, "may I have your blessing to marry your sister by marriage, Miss Lydia Bennet?"

Tapping his fingers on the desk between them, Darcy smiled grimly at Sebastian before saying, "You put me in an uncomfortable situation, Burgess." He hesitated just long enough to make Sebastian worry he would be denied, before continuing, "I have long liked you, Burgess. I was impressed by you when we first met last year. The fact that you are working so hard to care for your niece only makes me like you more, and I can't help but want to offer my assistance. And yet, the assistance that you are requesting directly impacts my sister-in-law and thus my wife."

It was not hard for Sebastian to understand what Darcy was referring to. Mrs. Darcy had always seemed the protective sort and if her response was anything to go by, she would not be happy. Fighting the desire to tug at his cravat, Sebastian acknowledged the issue, saying, "Yes, I understand that, and if there was another way, I would take it."

Darcy gave a brief nod, responding, "If I believed that you were anything less noble in your intentions, I would deny you, no matter Lydia's thoughts on the matter."

Was that a good thing? It sounded as if Darcy was approving of his match with Miss Bennet. "I can assure you that I have nothing but the best of intentions where Miss Bennet is concerned."

At that, Darcy smiled widely and leaned forward in his chair, asking, "Are you familiar with the phrase *the path to hell is paved with good intentions?*"

Feeling uncomfortable with the change of subject, Sebastian felt his brows draw together in confusion. Still, he answered, "Yes, I have heard it used a time or two. In fact, I had a professor who said that it meant that good intentions are worthless unless followed up with action."

"While that is one interpretation, let me give you another, if I may." Darcy paused and Sebastian found himself nodding despite the rising unease that he felt. Darcy continued saying, "Regardless of your intentions, if you make Lydia unhappy at any point, you will find yourself in hell."

Though the words were overtly threatening, Darcy's tone had never changed, and the casual calmness of his statement made it all the more foreboding. Feeling the need to protect himself, Sebastian began, "You have to know that I would never hurt Miss Bennet."

Waving him off, Darcy said, "That is the only reason I am allowing the marriage to take place. However, you have to know something as well. I know you know, on some level, Lydia is the youngest of five sisters. What you may not understand is that means she now has four brothers who are all quite capable of seeing you regret anything you should do to make her unhappy. Though only one of us has a title, the rest of us are not without our resources." Darcy finished the speech with a smile the likes of which Sebastian had never seen before, and he decided it was an excellent thing that he was a good man. He would not want to be in the unfortunate shoes of someone who had the gall to hurt one of the Bennet sisters.

For a moment, Sebastian sat there unsure if he should attempt to put Darcy at ease or if he would be better off just looking as intimidated as he felt. He vaguely wondered how the conversation was going between Miss Bennet and her sister. He hoped it was going better. It had to be.

Leaning back in his chair, Darcy continued, "Do not suppose you are getting away totally free of intimidation and threats. I have no doubt that Theodore will want to have a conversation with you at some point. For that matter, I am sure that Gabriel and Bingley will as well."

Sebastian tried to swallow, though his dry mouth did not make it easy. Was Darcy implying that the last ten minutes had not counted as intimidation? Swallowing again, Sebastian said, "I will look forward to having conversations with each of them."

Rubbing his hands together, Darcy said, "Now that we have that out of the way, let us talk settlements."

Chapter Nine

It felt odd to Lydia to be searching out the man that she was engaged to. She wanted to have the chance to speak with him and possibly plan both for their wedding and what would need to be arranged for returning to Swarkstone Manner. Only she did not know where he was. Could he possibly still be with William?

Lydia wondered if William had been hard on him. She hoped not, but she knew he was very protective of those he loved, and Lydia counted herself lucky to be in that group. It was an odd situation, and none of it was Mr. Burgess's fault; he had been just as surprised by her proposal as her family had been. The whole engagement and marriage would be a huge adjustment, not just to her, but to everyone.

Looking into the library, she found no one. Just where was the man? She was going to have to find a way to track Mr. Burgess down with more expediency. Lydia also supposed she should find out what he wished for her to call him. She could not very well call her own husband or fiancé, Mr. Burgess, all the time. She knew his Christian name was Sebastian, but would he allow her to use it instead of Mr. Burgess?

Noticing one of the footman Lydia took the opportunity to ask, "Evans, have you seen Mr. Burgess about? There were a few matters I was hoping to discuss with him."

Pausing, the tall man gave a respectful bow of his head before saying, "I do believe that Mr. Burgess and Mr. Herrington are both in the master's study with the master."

Hiding a grimace, Lydia worried that William had been taking advantage of the situation to put the fear of God into the poor man. They had been at matters entirely too long, in her opinion. Still she smiled at the footman, saying, "That would explain why I have been unable to find him elsewhere. Thank you, Evans"

In no time at all, she was knocking at the door to William's study and impatiently waiting for permission to enter. If it had been another time, she might have barged in, but she was, after all, trying to make people think she was a mature woman capable of getting married and running a household. It would not look good to act like an impatient child at the moment.

The muffled "Enter," had her turning the handle in a flash. Taking in the occupants of the room, she noticed the three men huddled over some paperwork on the desk. Narrowing in on Mr. Burgess, she noted that he did not seem harassed or worn, which she hoped was a good thing. Mr. Burgess was quick to rise from his chair and approach her with a smile, which she returned. "You have all been secreted away for so long that one would think you are not intending to come out." Seeing a few guilty glances at the clock on the mantel, Lydia realized that they may have simply lost track of the time. Looking at William, she declared, "William, please tell me you granted us permission to marry long ago, and you are not still raking him over the coals."

Laughing at her statement, William said, "No, Lydia dear. I granted my permission a while ago. We are only going over everything necessary for your settlement."

A flash of a smile from Mr. Burgess had Lydia shifting her attention to him as he said, "I am sorry if you have felt neglected by our inattention, Miss Bennet. I had no notion how long we had all been sequestered."

Feeling oddly generous despite herself, Lydia smiled broadly at Mr. Burgess before catching herself blushing. Looking at the others in the room for a moment before glancing back at him, she said, "I suppose I cannot get angery at you if you were working on my behalf, but it is nearly time for tea. Will you be able to break in say, half an hour? Or should I have tea sent for you?"

Mr. Herrington looked down at the sheets on the desk before him and began to arrange them in some semblance of order. Looking back up at Lydia, he said, "I think that we are mostly done with our negotiations for now. I will just need to write up a final draft for them to sign."

Meeting Mr. Burgess's gaze, Lydia wondered what the negotiations had entailed, but supposed she would ask him when they had a moment alone. Not looking away this time, she spoke to Mr. Burgess, saying, "Well, then I suppose I will expect you gentlemen in the blue parlor for tea in half an hour." She supposed that she would have to be patient and wait for Mr. Burgess to be available to discuss matters such as the condition of Swarkstone and finding a nanny or governess for Clara.

Bobbing them all a little curtsy, Lydia turned to leave them all to their discussions, only to have Mr. Burgess grasp her hand as she moved past him. After a slight hesitation where he was looking down at their clasped hands, he said, "Thank you for coming to check on us. I look forward to discussing matters with you over tea." She fought her rising blush when he smiled at her and gave her hand a little squeeze. If he was going to be sweet like that, she could surely be patient.

SELENE WATCHED AS LYDIA moved around the parlor, rearranging pillows and adjusting trinkets as she waited for the gentleman to show. It was obvious to Selene that her younger friend was becoming anxious.

"Are you becoming worried about the decision you made to marry my brother?" questioned Selene. She would hate to learn that her friend regretted such a momentous step. As much as her doing so would help them, Selene would not want her brother and friend to be stuck with an unhappy union.

Lydia immediately rushed to Selene's side and, sitting next to her, grasped both her hands. "Oh, no! I am sorry if I ever made you think that." Offering a smile, she continued, "I regret nothing. I suppose you could say that I am becoming impatient. It is only that now that my mind is made up that I have realized just how much needs to be done. There is so much to do and decide, and I want to get about deciding on it. Only I do not want to do it on my own. I want to include your brother in the decisions, which I cannot do until he shows up." Lydia punctuated her statement by once again glancing at the doorway she expected Sebastian to come through.

Laughing, Selene allowed relief to course through her veins at her friend's reassurances. Lydia had always been impatient and energetic, so it would make sense that she would be eager to conquer the next challenge before her, even if that challenge was to get married and set up a household in the next thirty days. And of course there was really a lot to decide on, the mind boggled at all that would need to be done in a very short period of time.

Setting her sights on the girl who would be her sister, Selene grinned. Squeezing both of Lydia's hands strongly, she said, "Is there anything I can help you with?"

Releasing her hands, Lydia moved to embrace Selene in an excited hug, exclaiming, "Thank you for being willing to help! I know Elizabeth will give her all to help with things, but I worry she will push herself too hard and overexert herself." Selene saw the flash of concern in Lydia's eyes as she sat back from her, and Selene wondered how the conversation with Elizabeth had gone. It did not seem that Elizabeth was sanguine with the concept of her baby sister getting married. It was true that Elizabeth had just had a child, and Selene silently prayed that this would be the only obstacle preventing her from assisting her sister with the wedding. Lydia continued saying, "I know planning a wedding in short order is possible, but it will take staying focused. That is why I so want to speak with your brother who has been holed up with William, going over matters all afternoon."

Growing reflective, Selene put her mind to the list of things that would need to be accomplished if they only had thirty days to present Sebastian and Lydia to the solicitor at Swarkstone as a married couple. Pondering aloud, Selene said, "The first question that comes to my mind is, are you going to wait for the banns? There is just enough time if we tell the curate tomorrow, though simply getting a common license would be more convenient."

Shaking her head, Lydia flopped back across the settee, saying, "And now you see why I feel the need to discuss matters with your brother. We must first agree on the manner of our marriage before we can begin planning for anything else though the gentlemen have not seemed to come to that conclusion yet. They have been concerned with other matters."

Wrinkling her nose, Selene huffed, "Men seem to look at the matter of getting married differently than women. I suppose they have been discussing things like dowries and settlements which I will not say is unimportant. Your brother would do well to see that you have a good jointure. You will be a viscountess after all, and you deserve to be provided for should the worst happen. But I can truly understand your frustration." Shaking her head, she added, "My brother could have at least taken a break to check in with you."

The masculine voice coming from the doorway saying, "I could have done what?" had Lydia sitting up and smoothing her skirts with a muffled yelp. Selene was forced to smother a snicker at her friend's antics.

It was nice to see that Lydia was still Lydia, regardless of her recent decisions. There had always been something enjoyable about the way that Lydia flirted with the line of propriety when it came to some of the more restrictive norms. After all, why did a lady have to always sit upright in her chair with a perfectly straight spine when in her own home? Selene did not mind that her friend made herself comfortable when it was just the two of them and it was hilarious to watch her try to right herself when the men entered.

SEBASTIAN ENTERED THE BLUE parlor to the sound of his sister talking and caught only half of what she said, but knowing it was about him, he asked, "I could have done what?"

It was apparent that he had surprised the girls because Miss Bennet jerked upright. He found that he quite liked the little sound she had made as she tried to smooth her skirts and act unaffected. He enjoyed how natural she was, unlike so many of the ladies of the ton Miss Bennet had never put on excessive airs. Sebastian found he quite liked the way Miss Bennet's blush highlighted the blue of her eyes.

Selene covered a snicker with a cough and said, "I know that you had settlements to agree on and other manly endeavors locked away with Mr. Darcy, but you could at least have checked in on dear Lydia at some point. Had you even told her that Mr. Darcy had approved of the match?"

Tugging at his cravat under the strength of his twin's stare, Sebastian fought his own blush. That had been rather badly done. "Yes, well..."

Rolling her eyes at Sebastian, Selene stood and moving away from where Lydia sat chided him, saying, "Come sit next to your fiancée, there is much to speak of and decide on."

Happy to obey, Sebastian sat down next to Miss Bennet while Herrington took up a seat across from the couple. Darcy, however, hovered by the door, eventually saying, "I would love to join you all, but I will take the moment to go check in on Elizabeth and the children."

No one was offended when he hurried away. In fact, Sebastian had great respect for the love the man showed to his family and especially the wife that he held so dear. Even if that love had prompted to try to put the fear of God in him. It was for a good reason; he supposed.

Acting as hostess, Lydia served everyone tea and various little bites of food. For a while they were occupied by the food and drink, but once Miss Bennet sat back down, Sebastian asked, "What had you wanted to speak about and decide on Miss Bennet? I am at your disposal."

Gazing at him over the rim of her teacup, Miss Bennet said, "While there are many things we must decide, almost all of it revolves around how we choose to marry, by banns or a common license. If we alert the curate today, he can read the bans the day after tomorrow and we could be married in a small ceremony the day after the last banns are read. That is, if you can also alert your parish as well. It would put us within the thirty-day requirement, but we would have to act today. Or if we choose to forgo having banns read, we could simply arrange for a common license. It would give us more control over our timetable."

"It would not be an issue for me to send an express to where I attend service in London. I must admit that I have little care one way or the other, as long as we are able to meet the timetable set forth." He hoped he did not offend his prospective bride, but he really did not care one way or another about details of the wedding ceremony.

Rubbing at the back of his neck, Sebastian continued, "Do you have a preference?"

Tilting her head in thought, Miss Bennet said, "Having the banns read will add a level of respectability to our nuptials. With as rushed as things are, it still might be best to proceed as normally as possible."

Sebastian could understand her point: there were too many people in the world who were happy to point the finger at the appearance of impropriety. Why give them something to crow about? Catching Miss Bennet's gaze, Sebastian said, "Then, with your permission, I will leave to speak with the curate after we have finished with tea. What else must be decided on? I must admit when it comes to planning a wedding ceremony, I really am at a loss."

He was relieved when Miss Bennet smiled, saying, "Now that I have the date of the wedding and the fact that we will have the banns read, I can plan nearly everything with the aid of my sister and Selene at least regarding the ceremony; there are however other things to take into consideration."

Eyebrows narrowing, Sebastian asked, "Such as?"

Ticking off her questions on her fingers one at a time, Miss Bennet began, "When are we leaving to take up residence at Swarkstone Park? Will there be enough staff to have things run smoothly, or should we begin the process of hiring additional staff?"

He had to admit that it was somewhat reassuring that Miss Bennet seemed to have an understanding of what they must do. However, her list of questions made him realize just how much they had to decide. "Frankly, when it comes to moving into Swarkstone, I am uncertain how we should proceed. I did not come away feeling that the staff there were of the caliber you or I are accustomed to. Yes, they were short-staffed, but everyone seemed almost lackadaisical when it came to their work and responsibilities."

Sebastian was beginning to feel overwhelmed, contemplating all that they faced. They might very well need to replace most of the staff beyond helping to bring around the neglected estate. He had lost himself in his thoughts until Miss Bennet reached out and took his hand. "We could always visit the place before the wedding and begin looking into matters." Then, blushing bright red, she seemed to have realized what her statement might have sounded like, and she quickly amended it with, "Well chaperoned, of course."

Herrington added his opinion, saying, "Miss Bennet certainly has the right of it. Much of what you will have to do besides the wedding can only be determined by inspecting Swarkstone Park and looking into matters there."

The rest of the tea passed swiftly as they all began discussing not only Swarkstone Park but also what they each believed to be important to a well-run household and estate. The more time that Sebastian spent in Miss Bennet's company discussing matters, the more he realized how much he was glad that he was not approaching the problem alone. It was rather nice to have someone to work with, like Miss Bennet.

NIGHT WAS FALLING, AND Lydia was weary. She was not surprised by her desperate yearning for her bed after a day packed with decisions and ever-changing circumstances. Still, she was not headed for bed. Lydia was on the way up to the nursery. She had children she wanted to see. That it would do her heart well to see, and so she continued up another flight of stairs instead of heading to her room.

Artie and Clara would most likely be asleep already, but after such a busy day, Lydia wanted to be sure they were both well. She had long enjoyed spending time with children, and she always looked forward to any moment she spent with them. There was something refreshing about spending time with children that lightened her heart. The way they saw the world was unlike adults, appreciating the wonders that often went unnoticed. Not only had she missed spending time with them, but she worried about how Clara was adjusting to her new environment. Clara's life until this point had been bleak, to say the least. There was no telling how she would handle falling asleep in a new place.

It seemed that her choice to visit the nursery had been fortuitous, as she could hear faint crying as she approached. There were a few candles lit, but for the most part, the room was cast in shadows. Following the sound, Lydia came upon Nurse Sarah murmuring to little Clara as she cried in her small bed in the corner.

Concern filling her, Lydia knelt next to the pair. "Whatever is wrong?"

"Tis not much, Miss, only Miss Clara seems to be unsettled this evening. Little master Artie fell right to sleep after their story, but Miss Clara cannot seem to settle."

Lydia's heart went out to the poor sprite in an unfamiliar place with unfamiliar people. She must feel so alone. Whispering to Nurse Sarah, she said, "Why don't you take a break and get yourself some tea and a bit of a bite to eat? I will see to Miss Clara for a time."

Looking at Lydia with wide eyes set in a tired face, Sarah asked, "Are you sure, Miss?"

Smiling at the kind woman, Lydia nodded. "Yes, of course, you have willingly taken up the extra responsibility of Clara without complaint. You deserve a bit of a break. Meanwhile, I will spend some time with Miss Clara. It is what I came up to do, anyway."

The look of relief on Nurse Sarah's face was more than enough. In no time at all, Sarah was sweetly kissing Clara on the forehead and leaving the room. Watching her go, Lydia was grateful that Elizabeth and William had found a very good nursemaid in Sarah. She would have to ask them how they had gone about finding her, as she would certainly need someone of a comparable caliber and disposition to help with Clara.

Lydia looked down into the tear-stained face below her and felt her heart turn over. The little girl was watching her, almost uncertain. Was the poor thing afraid of the dark? Or just plain scared? With a sigh, Lydia said, "Oh, Clara, I wish I could make things better for you. I promise I am trying, though. Would you like to try rocking in the rocking chair with me?"

Her slight nod had Lydia lifting the girl up into her arms, and they moved over to the rocking chair by the window. Clara's hands tightened themselves in the fabric of Lydia's dress and for a time Lydia just held her as she rocked. Letting the child feel the warmth of another person in the night, letting her come to accept that she was not alone.

"You know Clara, when I was a little girl, I was often afraid too." whispered Lydia. Looking down into the wide blue eyes, it was easy to spot their wonder at such a statement. She continued, saying, "Someone eventually made sure that I wasn't afraid anymore. Would you mind If I tried helping you not to be afraid? Would it be all right for me to help make sure that you feel safe and protected?"

Lydia waited while Clara seemed to think, but then biting her little lip, she nodded her head, sending her black curls trembling. Smiling at Clara, Lydia said, "Good, then I will start tonight, making sure you are safe and able to fall asleep without fear." Eventually Clara seemed to snuggle in closer to Lydia, tucking her face into Lydia's shoulder, and Lydia began to hum an old lullaby.

Clara's weight on Lydia shifted, going from clinging to loose and heavy, and Lydia knew that she had finally slipped into slumber. Still, she continued rocking and humming slightly under her breath. Little Clara had been so long without warmth and affection, and under

Lydia's care, that was going to end. Before the month was complete, Clara was going to be her daughter.

DARCY WATCHED HIS WIFE stare at the flickering candle beside their bed. He knew that the day had not been an easy one for her. With Lydia's sudden declaration that she would marry Mr. Burgess, their calm life had been somewhat upended. While Elizabeth wasn't particularly disturbed by her sister getting married, Darcy thought that she was upset by the absence of any romantic connection between the couple.

Darcy let out a sigh as he wrapped his arms around his wife, pressing himself against her back. Resting his chin on her shoulder, he whispered, "Talk to me, my love."

After only a moment's hesitation, Elizabeth whispered, "How can she risk never knowing the sort of love you and I have?"

Smiling, Darcy said, "Few are blessed with the sort of love we enjoy, Lizziebet."

Elizabeth huffed, crying, "But why isn't my sister willing to hold out until she can find something like it for herself?"

"It is not a bad match, you know." Darcy endeavored to help Elizabeth see the brighter side of the situation. It was not like Lydia would change her mind. She was too like Elizabeth to back down now.

"I know that technically, the match is amazing. My little sister will be a viscountess after all." Darcy could not see her face, but he could easily picture her rolling her eyes to match her tone.

Tightening his embrace slightly, Darcy kissed Elizabeth's cheek. He loved how feisty his wife could be. Still, he said, "More than that, Mr. Burgess is a good man. He is kind and will be a conscientious master of Swarkstone Park and eventually his father's properties. Sebastian Burgess is nothing like your father or even that fool that Kitty had to deal with before she married Theodore. He is committed to caring for Lydia and any children they may bring into the world. I believe he will prioritize their happiness and safety. Or do you doubt his motives?"

Sighing, she responded, "No, I believe he is honestly a good person. He will not mistreat Lydia."

"So, your chief concern is that they are marrying without having a passionate love for each other?" asked Darcy.

Darcy could feel Elizabeth's firm nod even as she said, "Yes. She deserves to be adored, Will."

Chuckling, he asked, "Have you seen the way he looks at her when he does not think she is looking, my love?"

Turning in his arms, Elizabeth looked at Darcy. "Are you implying that there is something between them?"

Smiling into Elizabeth's eyes, Darcy brushed his nose against hers lovingly before saying, "I think they both like one another already. It will only take time before they fall as madly in love with each other as we are."

Scrunching up her nose, Elizabeth complained, "But you cannot know for sure."

"No, I can't," he said, his words trailing off, "but that is the essence of hope." After a long day, he was ready to fall asleep next to his lovely wife. Pulling her close, Darcy enjoyed the fact that the bump of baby Gill was no longer separating the two of them, and together the two of them drifted off.

Chapter Ten

"Roses are always lovely, and I am sure that we can make something rather elegant without much effort," enthused Selene. Sebastian watched as his sister and Miss Bennet talked animatedly about flowers over their breakfast. Though he had not found much to contribute to their conversation, Sebastian found himself happy that Selene got on so well with Miss Bennet. It had to bode well for their future felicity.

As much as he was glad that the ladies were enjoying themselves, Sebastian still felt the need to talk to the only other gentleman in the room. Turning to Herrington, he said, "Thank you again for helping with the settlement papers. I know that Darcy and I have given you a lot of unexpected work."

"Think nothing of it." Buttering his toast as he spoke, Herrington continued, saying, "I enjoy being able to see Darcy again. Besides, I chose this profession for a reason. I enjoy it. There is something so satisfying to me about wills and legal documents like settlements."

Sebastian considered his words for a moment and could see a certain amount of sense to what he said. "I suppose documents are certainly easier to control than people. I am glad you have found enjoyment in what you do."

Taking a bite of his eggs, Herrington chewed and swallowed before saying, "As am I. As a second son, my father encouraged me towards the regulars, but when I opted for the law instead, he helped me to establish myself. I will be glad to get back to my practice and my home in London."

Sebastian knew that Herrington would be leaving for London sometime that morning, though he would coordinate with Mr. Coulson to see that the proper paperwork was filled in London. He was very grateful for the older gentleman's willingness to help him, though, to be fair, he was paying for his services.

A footman entered the room with a message on a tray offering it to Miss Bennet. She accepted it and thanked him. He did not wait for a reply, so Sebastian assumed that there was not an express rider waiting for a response. Pausing with his coffee cup halfway to his mouth, Sebastian looked at her with worry. He hoped nothing was amiss. Putting his cup back down on its saucer, he asked, "Is there something wrong, Miss Bennet?"

Fingering the correspondence in her lap, Miss Bennet gazed at him fleetingly, saying, "It is from my mother. I wrote to her and my other relatives yesterday about our engagement. I am fairly certain I will have shocked her by my announcement." She laughed, but Sebastian noticed the light had left her expressive blue eyes. Putting her serviette down, Miss Bennet pushed back from the table, saying, "If you will excuse me."

Sebastian watched her go with rising worry, uncertain of what he should do. It was obvious that Miss Bennet was distressed, but she had not asked for any support. Picking his coffee cup up, he took a sip as he considered how to proceed. Would it be presumptuous to follow her? He wanted to follow her, but would that be too forward? What exactly would be the proper thing to do? They were engaged, after all, and that should give them a little more leeway. Should he give her enough time to read the message in private?

"Well?" Selene asked, her voice filled with exasperation.

Looking at his sister, Sebastian nearly choked on his coffee under the force of her glare. It was obvious that in his hesitation, he had, in her opinion, chosen to do the wrong thing. Setting his cup down, Sebastian pushed back from the table and hurried out of the room. If Selene felt it was right for him to follow Miss Bennet, then he would no longer hesitate.

Finding Miss Bennet did not take long after a helpful footman pointed him in the direction of the gardens. All too soon, he spotted her sitting on a stone bench surrounded by blooms. It seemed she had read the missive on her lap, or had at least opened it. Trying not to startle her, he cleared his throat as he approached.

Sebastian caught the sight of tears on her lashes, but she blinked them away before saying, "Mr. Burgess., I must confess I had not expected you would follow me."

Stepping closer, he said, "I would hope that does not mean that I am unwelcome."

Shaking her head, Miss Bennet responded, "Not at all. I have always enjoyed your company. I do not foresee that changing now."

Sebastian found that despite his concern over her wellbeing, Miss Bennet's confession of enjoying his company made him smile. Sebastian noted a second bench positioned next to her own and sat down. "Then I will remain." Watching closely, he saw Miss Bennet's smile grow when he sat down. He found he liked being able to make her smile grow. Looking at the letter in her lap, he was compelled to ask, "If I asked about the content of your message, would you consider me impolite?"

Miss Bennet's gaze drifted down to the letter wincing as she explained, "My mother informs me that she will discuss our supposed engagement when she arrives later today."

Sebastian knew that parental love was a complicated thing. His memories of his own mother were hazy at best. He rarely got on with his father. Though he had sent word to his father to keep him informed, he knew his father would not react well. That was one express he did not anticipate with joy.

Miss Bennet had a strong bond with her mother from what he recalled. He could easily see how she worried. Those who we were held closest had the most power to inflict pain. Sebastian reasoned, "I do not know your mother well, but my impression of her was good. I cannot imagine that she would be critical of your decision."

Letting out a heavy sigh, Miss Bennet dropped her shoulders. "No, Mother was by no means critical, but neither was she positive or supportive in any way. I worry about the confrontation when she gets here."

Sebastian did not like seeing Miss Bennet, who was normally so full of enthusiasm, so lost. She was all strength and kind fire, and he wanted to make sure she stayed that way. Looking her in the eyes, he declared, "While there is a chance that it may not escalate into a confrontation, I want you to know that I will be by your side if it does."

LYDIA BLINKED RAPIDLY, NOW wanting to cry for an entirely different reason. The cold missive from her mother had hurt. She had known that convincing her mother of the soundness of her choice would be difficult. The brief letter stating that she would not belabor the point via correspondence and to expect her arrival as soon as she could manage it was not entirely a surprise. But the reality of her mother's hesitation hurt more than she thought it would.

Lydia hoped her family would be supportive of her marriage, but there was a chance they wouldn't be. She would not be surprised if she was about to face not only her mother but all of her sisters, all come to scold her for her foolishness. Oh, she would handle them all without too much strife, and she had every confidence that she could convince them of the soundness of her decision eventually. But the fact that she knew for a time that none of her family would be happy for her and her choices stung.

Yet here was Mr. Burgess, saying that she would not be alone when facing her mother and her disapproval. Looking him in the eye, Lydia was quick to share her pleasure, saying, "You have no idea how heartening that is, Mr. Burgess. While I think that I have convinced Elizabeth of the wisdom of my choice, that will not in all reality be enough. My mother and three other sisters will most likely descend on me with various levels of disapproval. I was just starting to feel overwhelmed, and yet here you are, willing to face them with me."

Turning on the bench so that he was facing her more fully, Mr. Burgess hesitated for a moment, his brows drawing together as his lips pressed in a line before he said, "Miss Bennet, you have agreed to join your life to mine in marriage. That is no simple matter to me. At the very least, I hope we will be friends working together to see one another happy and secure. As my wife, I want you to feel happy and protected, treasured even." Pausing, his blue gaze seemed to pierce Lydia's heart, and he continued, "That does not start after we say our vows. In my opinion, it starts now and moves forward with every choice I make, hoping to do right by you. So, of course, I will stand by you when you face your mother and all five of your sisters defending your right to choose me."

With a speech as poignant as that, Lydia really did cry. Holding her handkerchief to her face, Lydia attempted to hide her tears. How had she ended up engaged to such a wonderful man? Her mother and sisters may be unhappy she was not marrying with romantic love in mind, but at the rate he was going, love was not going to be that far of a journey.

Here was a man who wanted to support her and see her treasured, to help her face her problems. She would certainly not be in the marriage alone. It would be a wonderful partnership. A partnership that had apparently already begun.

Lydia was startled when he sat next to her on her bench and, pulling her hands gently from her face, pleaded, "Please tell me I said nothing wrong."

Shaking her head, Lydia smiled through the tears. "No, these are nothing more than happy tears—tears of relief. You do not know how much I love the idea of working together with you."

Mr. Burgess's slumping posture and slow smile were so arresting that Lydia giggled. He only nodded, saying, "That is fine, then. Just as long as I have not mortified you, Miss Bennet."

Biting her lip, Lydia hesitated before asking, "Would it be forward of me to ask that you call me Lydia?"

Sitting up straighter, he said, "Not at all. I would be more than happy to call you Lydia. Of course, I will ask you to call me Sebastian in return."

"Sebastian it is then." Lydia nodded happily, adding, "I like it so much better than the formality of Mr. Burgess."

Turning so that they sat shoulder to shoulder, Sebastian looked out over the garden. "Frankly, I do, too. I am not much for the formality that is often found in high society, though eventually we will have to get used to being addressed by our titles on occasion. After all, you are marrying the heir to a viscount."

Wrinkling her nose, Lydia sighed. "I suppose we will just have to wish your father a long and happy life, putting it off as long as we may."

This caused Sebastian to burst out laughing. "Do you know how many women out there hoped to marry me with the sole goal of becoming a viscountess? It wouldn't shock me if a few of them had already plotted to remove my father and hasten the proceedings."

"Well, it is a good thing that you are not marrying any of them. I doubt they would make you a good wife. Planning patricide is never an inducement to marriage." They both laughed at her observation, enjoying their time together in the garden. That is until the next two letters were brought out to her.

Sᴇʙᴀsᴛɪᴀɴ ᴡᴀs ᴍᴏʀᴇ ᴛʜᴀɴ happy to stand next to Lydia at the top of the stairs, waiting for her mother to descend from her carriage. In the course of a few hours after breakfast, she had received multiple replies to her announcement of their engagement. The first had come from her mother to be followed up by her sisters, Mrs. Bingley and Lady Matlock. She assured him she would also get something from her middle sister, Mrs. Mary Bennet, but that the distance between them would delay her response.

Even as they stood side by side, Sebastian could detect a fine tremor in her form. Reaching out, Sebastian took her hand in his own and gave it a gentle squeeze. He was there to support her, though hopefully it would all be well. "Do not worry, your mother loves you and, besides, we are in this together."

He did not hear what she might have said in response because the door to the carriage was open, and Lydia was hurrying down the steps. Following her at a more sedate pace, Sebastian watched as Lydia caught her younger brother as he launched himself out of the carriage into her arms. If it was not already obvious that she was a favorite of all the children, it would soon be with the way the little boy giggled.

"Lydie, I bac!" cried the small, laughing voice.

Grinning broadly at her much younger brother Lydia, said, "Yes, Mathew, you are back. It feels as if you only just left. Are you excited to see Artie?"

His head nodded up and down with enough vigor to set his hair falling wildly in his eyes. Sebastian could not help but smile at the enthusiasm, but hurried to the carriage where his future mother-in-law was descending the steps. Bowing, he said, "Mrs. Hawkins, it is a pleasure to see you again."

Though he smiled at the older woman, her responding glower made him feel as if he were being studied like an odd specimen of insect. Narrowing her eyes, she murmured, "Mr. Burgess." No greeting, only displeasure.

"Mama." Lydia interrupted his uncomfortable moment with her mother. "Please do not take your displeasure out on Sebastian. I have arranged for us to have tea together after you have settled into your room. Unless you would like to head to the blue parlor now?" Lydia stood next to him, still holding little Mathew gently in her arms, but her eyes had grown hard.

Sighing, Mrs. Hawkins cupped her daughter's cheek. Lydia did not look away from her mother, and it seemed to Sebastian that the two of them were having a conversation that he was not privy to. After a moment, Lydia's mother nodded and said, "I will meet you in the blue parlor once I take a moment to get Mathew settled."

Holding her arms out for her son, the little boy moved to his mother with enthusiasm, if not grace. Then, together with the nursemaid and lady's maid that followed from the carriage, they all moved up the stairs and into the house. At the top of the stairs, Mathew was set on his feet, and he took off running in circles about them.

Sebastian could sympathize with the child cooped up from a long carriage ride so recently himself. Though Mrs. Hawkins was only a few hours away, it must have felt like forever to a small boy.

When they reached the hall that led to the stairs, Lydia asked, "Mathew, will you do something for your big sister?"

Swiveling to view his older sister exuberantly, he cried, "Yes!" and catapulted himself at her legs.

"In the nursery there is a new little girl named Clara. Can you be nice to her for me?" Fluffing his hair fondly, she said, "She could use a good friend like you."

Leaning over, Mrs. Hawkins scooped up her rambunctious son. "Won't that be nice? Meeting a new little friend."

Lydia and Sebastian stood there watch her mother go up the stairs with her son and the quiet nursemaid. Offering her his arm, they walked together into the blue parlor, being sure to leave the door open for proprieties' sake. The maid was just bringing in the tea tray and Lydia thanked her, and moving to the tray asked, "Would you like some tea while we wait?"

Sitting down on the nearby settee, he answered, "That would be lovely." He studied Lydia as she prepared him a cup of tea. Contemplating the interaction with her mother, he said, "I know I said I was here to support you when you speak with your mother, but it seemed as if you were defending me on the drive."

Handing him his teacup, Lydia set about pouring her own cup, saying, "It is always easier for me to protect someone else than to stand up for myself. While I started out anxious about how my mother was going to react to my choice, when I realized she was more upset with you, everything changed." Taking a seat next to him on the settee, she took a sip of tea and sighed. "I am sorry if she says anything hurtful to you."

With a slight tilt of his head, Sebastian tried to meet Lydia's gaze, his words laced with confidence. "Lydia, I am well able to weather a few unkind words."

"Yes, I suppose you are." Lydia smiled at him. Then, wrinkling her nose, she added, "I only wish it were unnecessary for you to weather them. I was the one who proposed the solution to your issue, after all." Lydia's smile grew cheeky as she finished speaking, a mischievous glint in her eyes. Sebastian found himself quite entranced.

Putting down his teacup on the little side table, Sebastian turned to Lydia. He wanted to make sure that she understood. Looking into her beautiful blue eyes, he explained, "Lydia, she is your mother and from what I can tell, she loves you dearly. Any upset results from her concern for your happiness. As someone long without a mother, I do not mind her wanting to protect you at all. It is a good thing. Once she realizes I am just as eager for your happiness as she is, then things will proceed much more smoothly."

"That was remarkably well said, Mr. Burgess. This might go better than I hoped," said Mrs. Hawkins from where she stood in the doorway.

LYDIA KNEW SHE SHOULD not have been startled when her mother came in, but she was, nonetheless. Smiling at her mother, she stood. "Hello, Mother. Would you like some tea?"

"That would be lovely. It is not exactly hot out today, but the carriage ride felt very close after a while." Settling down in a chair next to Lydia, her mother's gaze followed Lydia's every move as she prepared her cup of tea. Only once Lydia had finished and taken her seat did her mother speak up, demanding answers. "I have heard Mr. Burgess's words. I want you to explain to me why you are trying to marry, without paying notice to all I taught you."

Setting her shoulders, Lydia faced her mother. She did not enjoy going against her mother to whom she owed so much, but that did not mean she would back down. Not when she knew she was in the right. "Mama, you taught us girls that we must be cognizant of finding respect in any match we make. I won't pretend ignorance of why respect is so important, not when I saw the lack of it every day in my young life. Just because the arrangement I have agreed upon with Sebastian differs from what you expected me to choose does not mean I acted unthinkingly. I would say that Sebastian has the utmost respect for me."

Her mother looked at Sebastian and then back at Lydia before saying, "No offense to Mr. Burgess, but sometimes it is hard to tell if someone really respects you until it is too late. Do not make the same mistakes I made. I beg you."

"Mama! You are letting your past cloud your judgment on the matter. Just because I am going about this matter quickly does not mean I have not thought it through. It most certainly does not mean that I do not know Sebastian's character. Think, Mama. Would my father have ever stood by you to speak with your mother?" asked Lydia.

"No, your father never would have supported me in such a way," she acknowledged. Then, leaning forward, she gripped Lydia's knee. "But darling, you do not have to be the one to make this sacrifice. Protecting his niece is all well and good, but it does not have to be you that he marries. I am sure between your sisters and myself, we could find Mr. Burgess a perfectly suitable wife in the time he has. Why are you taking this on yourself?"

Lydia tried not to growl; she really did. Why did everyone have to use the word sacrifice? When Sebastian made a noise, she looked over at him and realized that he had noticed the sound she had made and was attempting not to laugh. When he shrugged helplessly, she wondered if he was also thinking about the day before when he and his sister had used the word sacrifice and Lydia had reacted so badly to the word. Feeling a smile twitch at the corners of her lips, Lydia rolled her eyes at Sebastian before turning back to her mother. "Because, Mother, I *want* to. I will say this only once. Marrying Sebastian will not be a sacrifice on my part, and I will not have anyone saying it is."

Grabbing her mother's hand, Lydia said, "Did you meet Clara when you settled Mathew into the nursery?"

As her mother's brow furrowed, Lydia could practically see the woman's maternal instincts come to the fore. Lydia knew that her mother would never leave a child in distress; in that they were both alike. So, it was not a surprise when her mother said, "Yes, the poor mite was much quieter than any of you girls were at that age."

Nodding, Lydia took a sip of her tea before responding, saying, "I knew you would be able to see it. That girl is in need of love and affection, and I mean to be the one to give it to her. I want to be the mother figure Clara deserves."

Lydia saw when her mother began to accept what was going to happen, her shoulders drooping ever so slightly. She murmured, "But to marry without love, darling? Now that I have known love with my Bertram, I cannot imagine you not having it." As she took a fortifying sip from her own cup of tea, her mother let out a sigh, her wariness evident.

Lydia wished her mother were not so upset about her match, not when she was so happy about it and had such hope. She knew she could not force her mother to come around. She would simply have to prove herself happy as time rolled by and the marriage progressed. Patting her mother's hand, Lydia said, "You are going to have to trust that I can judge for myself, even if it is not the choice that you would make. I know in my heart that I will be happily married to Sebastian.

No one knows what the future holds, but I have decided to hope for the best."

Shaking her head, her mother said, "I will not try to stop you, Lydia, but I find that I am not happy for you either, not yet. I am sorry, dear." Taking a deep breath, she looked at Lydia and Sebastian and continued, "You said that you are planning on having the banns read and that your wedding will be on the seventeenth of June. Bertram was unable to come until closer to the ceremony date due to some obligations on his estate, but Mathew and I will stay for the duration. How may I help"

Lydia beamed at her mother. She knew it would be hard for her to accept her choice, but it meant so much that she was still willing to help her, regardless. Looking at Sebastian, Lydia saw his encouraging smile, so turning back to her mother, she said, "Actually, Sebastian and I were planning on a very simple affair with a few flowers at the church and a small breakfast for only family afterwards. So there is not much help needed with the wedding. There is, however, the issue of inspecting Swarkstone Park. We have to take up its management immediately after we marry. What do you say to going with us to inspect the staff and grounds? I have a feeling both will need a lot of attention."

Chapter Eleven

It had taken little time to arrange for the excursion for the three of them to evaluate her daughter's future home. They would only be there for two days before having to turn back around and endure another long carriage ride. They had discussed stopping and breaking up the trip with a stay at an inn but decided against it. With only two full weeks before the wedding left, there was too much to do to waste time stopping at an inn.

Eight hours of riding in a carriage is enough time to give anyone enough time to think about pressing matters. For Fanny, the carriage ride to Swarkstone, though tiresome, was enlightening. For a time, all Fanny thought about was how much her baby girl was giving up by committing to the man on the other side of the carriage. Eventually, she looked at the issue more deeply. Was it really so important to start off a marriage passionately in love?

Yes, her second marriage had proceeded so much better than her first, in part because of how much she loved Bertram, but that was not all that made the difference. She and Bertram both put the other first and were respectful and conscientious of each other's feelings and needs. If Lydia and her intended did the same, who was to say they would not have a happy marriage?

She also considered the fact that she loved Bertram more today than the day she married him. Lydia's arguments had been sound. Just because they were not starting out in love did not preclude building to that, eventually. It occurred to Fanny that she could be unnecessarily fixated on her daughter not being in love. If Mr. Burgess did, in fact, respect and care for her daughter, even if he did not love her deeply, then everything might turn out all right.

It had only taken as far as their first stop to see to the horses for Fanny to decide that she would observe the young couple together, looking to either prove or disprove the man's respect and affection for her daughter. She knew you could learn a lot simply by observing how two people interacted when uncomfortable or tired, and an extremely long carriage ride would provide both circumstances.

While at first Lydia had seemed too drowsy for conversation, now she was chatting happily, saying, "I spoke with Elizabeth and William yesterday about how they found such a wonderful nursemaid."

Nodding, Mr. Burgess responded, "She does seem to be all that is good, especially with someone as energetic as your nephew. Did they have any advice on obtaining someone for Clara?"

Sighing, Lydia shook her head, clarifying, "Sadly, they came upon Sarah quite by accident. She was the daughter of one of the tenants and the oldest child of seven when her mother mentioned that she was to begin looking for work to help with the family's finances. Elizabeth offered her a position as a maid. That was shortly before Artie was born. Things naturally developed from there. As for finding someone for Clara, she said that there are agencies we could contact if there was no one suitable from Swarkstone."

Fanny watched as Mr. Burgess paid attention to her daughter, as she spoke, as if he was truly interested in what she had to say. He was doing all the right things so far. Mr. Burgess, eyebrows raised as he said, "I can certainly see how she would have plenty of experience with children having six younger siblings. I cannot imagine trying to support that many children as a tenant."

Fanny thought he was wise to be concerned. That many children was a lot to feed on a tenant's income. Then, too, one had to take into consideration how they would get along in life and provide them with training to support themselves. Though there was not much you could do to stop children from coming.

Tilting her head, Lydia said, "I have always wanted a large family myself but until just now, I had never considered the expense of having many children. Though I suppose the matter is somewhat different as an estate owner."

"I know that people's opinions of a large family differ. My father would have stopped at one child if my older sister had been born a boy and probably thought three children made for a large family." Leaning forward in his seat towards Lydia, he asked, "What do you consider to be a large family?"

Wrinkling her nose, Lydia replied, "Would you think me crazy if I said I have always wanted at least six children? And would actually be happy with more?"

Hearing her daughter's desire for so many children set Fanny laughing. Only a girl who had never suffered through morning sickness and labor would ever be so easy with the idea of having more than the required heir and spare. When she felt both of their gazes settle on her, Fanny explained, "You say that now, Lydia, but just wait until after you have had your first. You may change your mind."

Lydia only huffed in response, but Mr. Burgess frowned. "I think it is a splendid thing to want a large family. Despite my deep love for my twin, I constantly wished for more siblings to create a larger, lively family dynamic. I will be delighted with as many children as Lydia and God are willing to provide me." Fanny watched the grin spread across her daughter's face and admitted that, at least in their desire for children, they were a good match.

When the carriage went over a rut, Lydia was suddenly thrown forward and practically into Mr. Burgess's lap. Watching as he caught her daughter and carefully helped set her to rights was reassuring. His solicitous attention to her daughter's wellbeing allowed the knot in Fanny's stomach to loosen a little, though Fanny had to bite her lip to keep from giggling at the way they both blushed at the accidental contact. Maybe it was a good thing that she had agreed to come and help the pair view their future home and not for the reasons that she had originally thought.

HER PRETTY FACE SCREWED up in confusion, Lydia looked at Sebastian and asked, "You did tell them we were coming, right?"

Sebastian looked down at Lydia and nodded. "Yes, I sent a letter, and the rider assured me that he put them in the hands of the housekeeper."

Mrs. Hawkins shook her head. "I know that you said that the estate was badly run when you were here last, but you would think they would at least be capable of greeting the new master."

His spirits sagged with every impact of his fist on the hardwood. Sebastian banged on the door again. What kind of estate did not have at least one footman available to answer the door to callers?

Sebastian looked down at Lydia as she murmured, "I wonder," and reached out to turn the doorknob. The door creaked as it swung slowly open on complaining hinges.

They left the door open for all and sundry to enter. Shaking his head, he held the door open for Lydia and her mother to enter before him. All three stood gazing about the entry hall in confusion for a time before Sebastian said, "I was hoping we could speak with the housekeeper and steward while we were here, but I never thought we would have to go searching them out once we arrived."

The staff who had followed them in a second carriage had, by that time, followed their master and mistresses into the building. The two ladies' maids looked at each other with wide eyes while Davies turned to Sebastian, saying, "Sir, as I am somewhat familiar with the layout of the house, I propose you stay here while I search out at the very least the housekeeper to come meet with you and take you to your rooms." With those words, he exited the room and embarked on his stated mission.

Tomkins, the very large footman from Pemberley that had also come, said, "The grooms and I will bring in the luggage and see to the horses. I will find you once we are done."

It took fifteen minutes for Davies to return with the housekeeper. Entering the hall, Davies announced the housekeeper, saying, "Mrs. Netter, the Housekeeper, Sir." It was only the years of knowing Davies that enabled Sebastian to read his annoyance both with the situation and possibly the woman herself in his tone of voice.

Resisting the urge to glare at the woman, Sebastian managed to keep his voice even when he said, "Mrs. Netter, did you not receive my letter letting you know we would be arriving this afternoon?"

Seemingly unfazed, the woman, who appeared to be of middle age and stocky build, shook her head. "No, I received the notice of your arrival, but with as short as we have been on staff, I did not feel my time was best used waiting around for you to show."

Sebastian could once again feel his eyebrow twitching. Bringing his hand to his head, he massaged it as he said, "I would never expect you to waste your time, however most estates I have visited have a footman on staff to see to the front door. I have never once in all my years been to an estate where the front door was just left open and unattended."

Shrugging, Mrs. Netter gestured with her chin to the now closed door. "We had two footmen, but they left." With a put-upon sigh, she added, "I had one of the stable boys doin' chores up around the front of the house so's he could let you in and fetch me, but he must have been called back to the stables for some reason or another. I set up three rooms as you asked, and dinner will be ready in an hour or so. I suppose you would like me to show you to your rooms."

Sebastian stared at the woman, dumbfounded at her attitude and the situation. He was grateful when Lydia's mother inserted herself by saying, "Yes, that would be lovely. It has been a long day full of travel. I would love the chance to wash up and change."

With a nod, the woman started up the stairs and gestured for them to follow. "I don't have the staff to fetch and carry as you might be used to, but your maids can make themselves useful and get you some water."

With the woman gone and Davies occupied with fetching water, the three travelers congregated in the sitting room, connected to the ladies' rooms. Shaking his head, Sebastian collapsed back into the chair that he occupied with a little more force than he had intended.

Lydia sighed from where she sat next to him, saying, "This is going to be a very interesting two days."

Looking over at Lydia, he grimaced. She was worried about the next two days; he was worried about the next year or so trying to bring everything and everyone into line. Not that he was going to bring her spirits even lower by saying so.

Mrs. Hawkins interrupted his morose thoughts by saying, "Now do not go making a mountain out of a molehill, you two. We will eat and rest tonight. Tomorrow we will meet the staff and inspect the house. If what you find is not to your liking, and frankly, I do not know how it will be, well, this wouldn't be the first estate to have a total turnover of staff." Giving her daughter a hug, she continued, "You know as well as I do that good staff can be found. It is not an impossible job."

THERE WAS NO GETTING around the fact that the welcome they received on their arrival had been horrible. Lydia had hoped that in the morning things would not be as bad as they seemed. She was wrong. And every room she entered on her tour with Mrs. Netter brought home the point a little harder. Even Longbourn, as badly staffed and oppressed as it was, was better run. It was a struggle to keep the distaste off her face as she walked through the rooms, continuously finding them not up to her standards.

The housekeeper's nasal voice interrupted Lydia as she inspected the dust-coated mantel, saying, "Swarkstone Park does not boast the same grandeur as estates like Chatsworth and Pemberley. There are no magnificent pieces of art or family heirlooms, but I am sure that you will find it sufficient."

Maybe she hadn't hidden her distaste well enough after all. Lydia had not wanted a confrontation yet, but she felt she could not let the comment slide. "Mrs. Netter, I would never condemn a house for its lack of pretension. I did not always live at Pemberley. In truth I am a simple gentlewoman and I am not above the simple elegance that I think Swarkstone Park is capable of. What I am above is the lack of cleanliness and attention to detail that is so evident in every room I have inspected." Reaching out, she ran her handkerchief along the edge of the mantel, and it came away visibly coated in grime and dust. Handing the handkerchief to the housekeeper, she stated, "Help me understand how, as the housekeeper of Swarkstone Park, you find this sufficient."

The woman colored and nearly glared at Lydia before responding, "We haven't enough staff to see to everything. You knew that already. If you want things different, I suggest hiring enough people to get all the work done as you would like it. Or, if you are so displeased, you could put on an apron and set about cleaning yourself, if your standards are so high and mighty."

This just was not going to work. It was no wonder things were so slipshod if this woman was in charge. Lydia had hoped that she would not have to be replaced, but she could already see working with her would be imposable. Not with that attitude. "I thank you for your opinion, Mrs. Netter. If you are so understaffed, then you must be sorely needed elsewhere. I will not waste any more of your time. Please go about your duties as normal. I will come speak with you about this later in the day."

Giving a slight bob of her head, the woman left without saying another thing. Lydia watched her go, debating whether she should continue checking the rooms or if she should give up for the moment and search out either her mother or Sebastian. Shrugging, Lydia left the room. She had already confirmed what she had come to expect. The entire house needed a thorough cleaning and much better management.

She would find her mother and see what she had discovered in her own investigations for the day. Hopefully, it would not all be bad news. Leaving the sad little parlor behind, she went in search of her mother somewhere above stairs. Lydia was glad to have Tomkins following her as she went about the place. At least he was a friendly face. Everyone she met was so gloomy and sullen.

She did not trust her ability to find her way around yet, but at least she had not gotten lost. Making her way up the stairs and into the servants' quarters, she found her mother with her lady's maid. If the strike of her step on the floorboards was any indication, her mother was not the least bit happy. Peeking her head into the room, she asked, "What has you in a tizzy, Mama?"

Hands on her hips, her mother shook her head, exclaiming, "Most of the rooms are not fit for habitation. It is no wonder there are no staff. I would not put a dog in here." Gesturing to the sad excuse for a window, she continued, "The window leaks and there is mold running along the pane. I cannot imagine that anyone could keep warm in here come winter."

"No, staying warm is always a struggle." Hearing the voice, Lydia swiveled to face a young servant girl who looked to be about thirteen who stood in the hallway. Her dress, though neat and clean, was worn and patched. Blushing, she said, "I am sorry for speaking out of turn. I just came up to fetch an extra pin."

Lydia noticed that the girl's ample hair was falling out of its pins. Shaking her head, Lydia said, "Do not worry about it. I am glad for your input. My name is Lydia Bennet, I am engaged to Mr. Burgess, who will be taking over managing the estate for his niece, Clara. This is my mother, Mrs. Hawkins. What is your name?"

Bobbing a curtsy, she said, "May, Miss."

Her mother smiled at the girl, asking, "Are all the staff rooms this bad?"

Shrugging, May answered, "For the junior staff like me, it is." Then, looking away, she added, "The senior staff, well, it would not be my place to say."

Lydia met her mother's gaze, and she saw the hard look settle into her eyes. Neither of them was happy about such findings. "Thank you for taking the time to speak with us, May. Please know that Mr.

Burgess and I will endeavor to improve matters for you and everyone else."

"Of the twelve tenant families connected to Swarkstone, two of their homes are in need of repair. Frankly, it has been difficult to help them as I should have. While Mr. Blakesley would approve of repairs and the like eventually, his responses to my requests were never prompt. In fact, it always took quite a bit of time to get the approval and needed funds associated with repairs and necessary improvements. Keeping the estate running well was never his focus." Concluded Mr. Burton.

Sebastian studied the man who sat across the desk from him, finding that he did not dislike the man as he suspected he would. With as badly run as the household was, he had had little hope when it came to meeting the steward. He was finding, however, that this Mr. Burton was to all appearances earnest and hardworking. It would take time to confirm his observation, but as things stood, he would not mind working with the man.

Remembering the reason the man had not been present at the time of their arrival, Sebastian asked, "What of the fire you spoke of? Have you been able to catalog the damages?"

Mr. Burton nodded, and Sebastian noticed a smudge of soot on his forehead that had been hidden under his hair. It was obvious that he had tried to wash up before coming to meet him, but the man still smelled of smoke and there were remnants of a hard morning's work about his person. He answered, "The fire on the Adams farm only affected the barn, not the house. It will need repairs, or possibly to be completely rebuilt. I tried to inspect it this morning, but parts of the wreckage were still smoldering and too hot to know for sure."

"How is the family coping?" asked Sebastian.

"Well enough, I suppose. Their neighbors have come together to help them. Mrs. Adams and their youngest boy have been taken to a neighboring farm. The smoke and soot in the air were making her cough excessively, and the apothecary felt it would be best to remove her until the air clears."

"I am glad that the neighbors were so willing to help." Leaning back in his chair, Sebastian taped his finger against the desk for a moment, thinking of his next steps.

He had never been the one in control of an estate. His father did not even allow him to express his opinion about their estate in Northumberland. This made Sebastian hesitate, but only slightly before he continued, saying, "I have no intention of being the same type of estate manager. I want to be more involved and certainly more responsive. However, per my conversation with Mr. Coulson, I will not have access to the funds needed to make repairs until after my marriage. Is there anything that must be handled before the eighteenth of the month that you need funds for? I may be able to provide some of my own funds to get by until then."

"No, there are no repairs that are that urgent."

"What about the apothecary for Mrs. Adams? Has he been paid?" asked Sebastian.

"I...well... I took care of that." Stammered Mr. Burton, as he blushed.

The more that Sebastian knew about Mr. Burton, the more he liked. Paying for the tenant woman's care out of his own pocket should not have been necessary, but that he had been willing to do it because it needed to be done was commendable. Sebastian said, "Before I leave, I will give you a small amount of funds, both to reimburse you for the cost of the apothecary and to hold in case of an emergency. You should not have to pay for things out of your own savings."

Eyes widening, Mr. Burton leaned forward, saying, "Thank you. That will certainly make things easier."

Sebastian was about to ask about something else when he heard a commotion in the hall. Shaking his head, Sebastian fought back a groan of frustration, it seemed that there was no end of problems with the household. Looking at Mr. Burton, he said, "Excuse me for a moment while I address that." Standing, he quickly moved to investigate whatever was amiss.

As he opened the door and looked into the hall, his forward motion came to a sudden halt. Mrs. Netter, her face a mask of disgust, was shouting at Lydia, saying, "And you would think to criticize me? I have worked as the housekeeper at Swarkstone for years. Not once did I hear a word of complaint from the master! I know what I am about, but you? You know nothing! You are barely more than a child fresh from the schoolroom. That you would think to better know how to run a household is laughable." Her cold bark of laughter only stopped her diatribe for a moment before she started up again. "Girls like you are raised to be pretty, not useful, and certainly not capable of anything of note. Or rather, you are not capable of anything besides embroidery, snide gossip and bearing heirs. Look at you! You know I am right, or you would have said something by now. You are nothing but an empty-headed chit who, after marrying the new master, will be left behind while he goes back to his entertainments in London. If you think you can remove me from my post, think again. You have no power, and I will not allow you to try to take mine." The woman finally came to a stop. Most likely to breathe. As she took several shuddering breaths, her eyes flashing fire and hate.

Sebastian almost said something, but then he saw the look in Lydia's eyes. She was not cowed in the least. He could not name the look on her face, but the last time he had seen it was when his sister's governess had caught him trying to sneak a frog into his sister's bed. If her look was anything to go by, Mrs. Netter would not stand a chance.

Lydia simply tilted her head, asking, "Are you finished with your tantrum?"

Mrs. Netter's only response was to make a strangled squeaking sound. Sebastian half wondered if the woman was getting enough air. She was turning an odd purple color that was certainly not good for her health.

Chapter Twelve

Lydia could not believe a grown woman, in service no less, would have the temerity to behave in such a manner. How Mrs. Netter thought she would retain her position after such a show of impropriety Lydia would never know. At this rate, the woman was practically fit for bedlam.

Taking a deep breath to control her anger, Lydia began in a calm voice saying, "Mrs. Netter, I do not particularly care what Mr. Blakesley thought of your work here at Swarkstone Park. His thoughts are irrelevant, as are, quite frankly, your opinions about me. Opening your mouth to spew such filth only shows evidence of your ignorance. What *is* relevant is that I am not satisfied with your work here. Not only is the work being done slipshod, but you are not seeing to the staff that are present as you should. You are petty, small-minded and cruel to the staff who serve under you. I am surprised anyone has remained working here under your tenure as housekeeper. I will not have that in my home. Before you started your rant, I was going to see you were let go with a letter of reference and a small stipend. I will no longer be doing so."

"You cannot do that. You have no actual power here. I will tell the new master that you do not know what you speak of. Gentlemen like things to proceed in an orderly fashion. Without me, it would be chaos. He will not let me go."

"And you would be wrong to think so." Sebastian's voice had Lydia turning to see him standing in a doorway. He took the time to smile at Lydia before turning a glare on Mrs. Netter, stating, "What kind of man would I be if I did not stand with my wife in all things? I think you and everyone else will find that the management at Swarkstone is going to be very different from what it was under Mr. Blakesley."

Eyes narrowed, Mrs. Netter's glare flicked back and forth between Lydia and Sebastian. Then exclaimed, "You do not have the power to do anything, not yet. You have not been officially named that child's guardian."

Lydia moved to stand next to Sebastian, eager to appear united. Then, standing shoulder to shoulder with him, she said, "That is true, Mrs. Netter. We cannot do anything today, but know this, the day that we return, you had better be gone. If you are still here when we return, I will not think twice about suggesting to Mr. Burgess that you be charged with trespassing."

The odd puce color that she had been turning seemed only to intensify as Mrs. Netter stared at them both. Then turning with her head in the air, she stalked away. Lydia shook her head as she watched the woman leave.

Taking her by the shoulders, Sebastian ducked slightly to look into her eyes, asking, "Are you well, Lydia? Please tell me you did not let that woman's venom upset you."

Smiling fondly into his concerned countenance, Lydia was quick to respond. "She was so ridiculous I could not take her misconceptions seriously, though I will be glad when she is gone, and we can install someone who is actually capable of doing a good job."

Gesturing into the room with a warm smile, Sebastian said, "Would you care to come sit and talk with me and the steward, Mr. Burton, or did you have something else that needs your attention?"

Though Lydia would have liked to spend time with him, she knew that they were all working on a timetable. So, shaking her head no, she explained, "I still need to check in the nursery with my maid. If we are going to be bringing Clara back here, I want to make sure everything is ready for her. I would also like to speak with more servants before I have to change for dinner." Looking at Mr. Burton further in the room, she asked, "Mr. Burton, will you be joining us for dinner? I would love to get the chance to speak with you."

Glancing at Sebastian for a moment before he looked at her, he said, "If you are willing to have me, I will look forward to having dinner with you all."

"Then I will see you both then." She smiled at Sebastian before she turned to go. Lydia couldn't quite describe the mix of emotions she experienced in that moment. She did know that having Sebastian's immediate support felt comforting and reassuring to her. Taking to the stairs, Lydia could not keep the smile off her face on her way to the nursery.

Fanny watched the interchange with a smile on her face. Maybe her daughter would have a better marriage than she had originally thought. Mr. Burgess had not even hesitated to support Lydia. The man fully supported her against the horrible Mrs. Netter. If he kept this up, she would have to start liking the boy.

After Lydia had left to go look at the nursery, Fanny approached him, saying, "That was very well done, Mr. Burgess. It is always wise to stand united in front staff."

Mr. Burgess's eyes widened as he turned to face her. "Mrs. Hawkins, I did not see you there."

"That is understandable. You had your attention on the confrontation between my daughter and that horrible woman. It is my belief you will do much better without her at the reins." Gazing down the hallway in the direction that Mrs. Netter had slunk off, Fanny shook her head. Turning to her future son-in-law, she exclaimed, "That woman should not be trusted with anything more significant than a feral cat. At least a cat would have the ability to defend itself."

With his eyebrows raised into his hairline, Mr. Burgess gestured into the room he had been standing in the doorway of, inviting her to enter. "Mrs. Hawkins, would you have a moment to speak with me and Mr. Burton?"

"Of course." Walking quickly into the study, she smiled at the man sitting in one of the chairs in front of the desk. Taking a seat, she said, "Actually, I believe there are a few things that I found that you might need to be informed of."

Settling in behind the desk, Mr. Burgess asked, "What were you able to find, Mrs. Hawkins?"

"Lydia's inspection of the common rooms downstairs revealed most of them to be grimy and dusty. My inspection of the servants' quarters is what I believe was the deciding factor for Lydia when it came to dismissing Mrs. Netter."

"How so?"

"Apparently the lower servants, of which there are some ten odd people left, are housed in the most unacceptable conditions. I found leaking windows, drafts, and mold, not to mention inadequate bedding and furniture."

"We will have to make sure that we make repairs and bring in appropriate supplies for them all." Tilting his head, Mr. Burgess added, "I understand why that would upset Lydia, but I cannot see how that would have been Mrs. Netter's fault. Mr. Burton also has had problems getting permission to make repairs on the tenant farms."

Shaking her head, Fanny grit her teeth just thinking about what else she had found. Taking a deep breath, she explained, "Due to the number of staff that has left Swarkstone, there are actually many vacant servant rooms. Most of the vacant rooms are in much better condition, but Mrs. Netter forbid the lower staff to move into those rooms because they were *too good* for the lower staff. In fact, the staff is in all the worst rooms. All except for Mrs. Netter herself and the cook. Their rooms are practically opulent in comparison."

Mr. Burgess coloring darkened, and he ground out, "Mrs. Netter and the cook have been living in comfort while forcing the other staff to live in damp rooms with inadequate bedding?! No wonder Lydia insisted upon letting her go."

"I found it quite ironic that she found the dusty common rooms plenty adequate, but her own suite of rooms was spotless. I think she had the staff cleaning her rooms and the staff areas, not the rest of the house. There was more than a month's worth of grime in some of the rooms."

"Mr. Burton, do you know much about Mrs. Netter?"

Scrubbing his hand over his face, Mr. Burton said, "No, I do not live here. I have a small cottage of my own closer to the other side of the estate property. I have had minimal interaction with the staff here and no involvement in the management of the house. That has been under Mrs. Netter's foresight since the death of the former mistress."

Mr. Burgess nodded, looking away from them both, and Fanny wondered if he was thinking of his older sister who had died.

Eventually he said, "It seems that after five years without a mistress overseeing the household, she may have let matters get to her head. Regardless, she will no longer be an issue once Lydia and I have any say in the matter. I will add housekeeper to the list of staff we will be needing to acquire."

Fanny stood, saying, "I will go assist Lydia in exploring the nursery and determining what supplies may be required for Clara." Walking to the door, she stopped, her hand on the handle. "I wanted to make sure you know how thankful I am for the support you showed my daughter. If you continue to demonstrate your respect for her, I might find myself genuinely pleased with the match." Fanny only stayed long enough to see the bright smile creep across Mr. Burgess's face.

Shaking her head, Fanny made her way up to the nursery. She could see why her daughter might be inclined to agree to the match with the boy. His good looks were undeniable, and whenever he smiled, it was as if his charm multiplied.

STANDING IN THE ROOM that Clara had once occupied, Lydia couldn't help but feel a sense of unease wash over her. She knew that with a reduced staff and no child present, it would not make sense to clean it regularly, but it was more than the dust that was so off-putting.

Discolored and chipped paint covered the walls. While the color appeared to have once been a light blue shade, it had faded into an indeterminate gray in splotches. The entire atmosphere of the space was bleak and depressing in a way that no child's room should be. Shaking her head, Lydia began to catalog the furniture to see if there was anything worth salvaging.

Seeing her look of disgust, Oakley, her lady's maid, said, "I would never leave a child in this room. They would have nightmares for sure."

Inspecting the child's bed that was against the far wall, Lydia realized it was no better than anything she had seen in the servants' quarters. Frustrated, she gave it a kick only to have it teeter precariously. Getting down on the floor, she inspected the legs of the bed, only to realize that they were uneven. It appeared that a piece of wood had been wedged under one of the legs to keep it steady.

Lydia stood with a huff and stomped over to the old, worn toy chest against the other wall. Opening it, she found half a dozen broken toy soldiers and eight wooden blocks. The lone cloth doll that was missing an eye almost made her want to cry. Closing the lid, Lydia surveyed the surroundings, hoping to discover something that could have brought Clara happiness. There was no bookshelf, no soft blankets, and the windows were so caked with grime that they obscured any view of the garden below.

She felt like screaming. It was one thing to leave dust to pile up in a parlor or sitting room, but to have a child consigned to a nightmare inducing room with practically no toys was outrageous. Lydia looked at Oakley and said, "This is ridiculous. I will not allow Clara to stay here."

Stalking across the space, Lydia jerked open the door that presumably housed the nursemaid's room. The bed was in better condition than the one that Clara had been relegated to. There was a desk and an empty bookcase, but on the whole, the room was also depressing. It had the same chipped and faded paint, and its two windows were also so grime coated that they barely let any light in at all.

Lydia wanted to run her hand down her face in frustration but knew that she would just smear dirt all over herself. Going back out into the main room, she sighed, saying, "It will take much effort to remodel the space into something acceptable."

Oakley nodded and with a grimace said, "There is also an extension of the nursery through the door behind that chair that is in even worse condition that seems to have been closed up from the time of the first King George if what is left of the paper on the walls is any indication." Nose wrinkling, she added, "I wholeheartedly agree that Miss Clara cannot return to this room. But it will take time to correct. What will you do in the meantime?"

Lydia took a deep breath and blew it out through her pursed lips. Her first instinct was to keep Clara with her until she brought the nursery up to her standards. Surely Sebastian would not be offended by her care and consideration of his niece? It was not as if they had a love match like her sisters. They would not be sharing a room or a bed, at least not yet.

Scrunching up her face, she decided to go with her instinct. Facing Oakley, she smiled, happy to have come to a conclusion. "I will have her stay with me until it is done."

Eyes wide, Oakley asked, "Are you sure that is wise?"

"What is not wise?" asked mother as she walked into the nursery, frowning.

Facing her mother, Lydia explained, "I have decided that since Clara cannot possibly stay here in its current condition, she will stay with me in the mistress' suite until it can be remodeled."

Her mother looked around the room, her lips a hard line, before turning back to Lydia and saying, "While I agree, that she cannot stay here. I do believe that you should at least consult with Mr. Burgess about your thoughts on the sleeping arrangements."

Tilting her head, Lydia thought back to some of their previous conversations. While she suspected he would be fine with having Clara staying with her for a time, it would be rude to assume. Nodding her head, she said, "You are right. I should have that conversation with him. It is only fair." Lydia looked at her mother and Oakley and asked, "Do you think there might be any furniture we might use for the nursery in the attics?"

SEBASTIAN SUPPOSED THAT HE should not have been surprised that the dinner that night was not the best. He was not opposed to simple fare, but the meal had been so cold that the sauce had almost congealed. The question was, had it been the cook who was causing problems or Mrs. Netter?

Mrs. Netter was the one who had brought in the meal and served it. So it was possible that she had intentionally delayed serving them for that very purpose. After the way Mrs. Netter had acted, he half suspected that she would do something in retribution. Either way, he would be happy to not have to worry about her after they returned to Pemberley.

Looking down at the list he was compiling, he tried to distract himself from his grumbling stomach. There were so many things that they needed to see to and what they were able to do would be dictated by the funds that were made available by Mr. Coulson. Sadly, as he did not know what those funds were, he could not really make any plans to fix anything. He just had a list of things that needed to be accomplished.

He knew there would be some money at least, so he was trying to decide what order things needed to be done. A soft knock at the door allowed Sebastian to look away from his concern for a moment. Looking up, he said, "Enter." Lydia's smiling face came around the door, and Sebastian could not help but smile in return. He would spend time with her over ledgers any day.

Coming part way into the room, she asked, "Do you have a moment to discuss a few things?"

"Of course!" Gesturing to one of the chairs on the other side of the desk, he added, "Come sit. I have just been trying to make a few lists of what we need to take care of and decide in what order what order we will proceed. I know we will not have the funds to do everything all at once."

Leaving the door open as she came into the room, Lydia took a seat. Sebastian could see through the open door that her lady's maid sat in the hall, and he wondered if she was there for propriety's sake or to make sure that none of the staff were eavesdropping. Mentally shrugging, he determined it could very well be for both reasons. Lydia nodded as she made herself comfortable, saying, "I well remember that issue from my time back at Longbourn. We did not have the funds to see to all the problems, so it came down to determining what had to be handled first and sorting things out from there."

Smiling at Lydia across the desk, he asked, "Have I thanked you today for agreeing to be my wife? Having you at my side to help me muddle my way through the early days here is already proving invaluable." Sebastian loved the way Lydia's eyes sparkled at his comment.

"It brings me joy to be of use, and I genuinely hope we will be able to grow close as we work together. In fact, the first thing that I was hoping to work on with you was the issue we discovered with the nursery. Had you ever seen where your niece had been living?"

Casting his mind back to when he had arrived to get his niece not much more than a week ago. Sighing, he said, "I was not impressed with what I saw, but I did not spend much time there. I am curious to hear what your opinion of the nursery is."

A frown firmly settling on her face, Lydia's eyes grew hard. "What I found there is appalling. If I ever come across the person who thought that place was suitable for a child to spend their days, they will deeply regret their decision." Pausing, Lydia seemed to take several deep breaths before continuing, "There is no way that we could possibly have Clara stay in that room without extensive changes. At the very least, it will need a fresh coat of paint, a new bed, and thorough scrubbing. But with everything that needs to be done, I do not know when we can have her room ready for her to stay in."

"I completely understand not having her stay in there until we can fix it up for her. Clara deserves to have a bright and cheerful place to call her own. Though I am wondering where she will stay in the meantime."

"I am thinking we can create a play area for her somewhere and once we have a nursemaid for her, she should be fine, at least during the day. As for the nights, I was considering having her stay with me in my bed. Apparently, she has been having bad dreams and problems falling asleep and I wanted to be there for her as she adjusts. Only I wanted to discuss the idea with you before we put any plans in place."

Sebastian leaned back in his chair as he considered the implications of Lydia's statement. He loved that she was so concerned for Clara. It was her love for children and her care and concern for his niece that had promoted her to suggest that they marry. Her statement that she wanted to have his niece in with her at night, however, brought home the point that she was not in the marriage for him. Somehow, that made him feel a little lonely.

He was not the sort to demand husbandly rights, but he had hoped that they would grow closer, and things might naturally progress. His desire was for them to cultivate companionship and a sense of ease in each other's company, even if love should elude them. How would they begin the work of growing closer together with a five-year-old in their midst?

Was that Lydia's goal? To put off any unwanted advances on his part, at least for a time. Or was she truly just concerned with caring for his niece and thought nothing of the implications of her suggestion? Either way, Sebastian would not force the issue. Maybe it would be good and give them the time to work on their friendship. Reminding himself to smile, he said, "I am sure that your presence during the night will provide Clara with a sense of reassurance and comfort as she navigates this period of adjustment."

"That is what I am hoping for. If she feels more secure, she might start coming out of her shell."

Nodding, Sebastian picked up the list on his desk and handed it to Lydia. "While you are here, would you mind looking over the list of what needs to be done with me? I do not want to forget anything. I would also like your opinion on what we can put off and what we must take care of immediately." Though he might not have said it, Sebastian was already putting the remodeling in the nursery at the top of his list. He tried to convince himself that his only intention was to provide his niece with the environment she deserved. It was wholly unrelated to his desire to have his wife to himself.

Chapter Thirteen

The carriage ride back to Pemberley was not shorter or less arduous than the trip to Swarkstone Park, but at least it was less filled with uncertainty. Lydia knew what needed to be accomplished with the estate and she could begin planning. Facing her mother, she asked, "Do you think Kitty would mind if I stole the woman who has been training under her housekeeper at Matlock?"

Tilting her head, Fanny Hawkins considered the question briefly before saying, "No, I do not think your sister would be offended if you offered Mrs. Wilson the role of housekeeper at Swarkstone. I believe she was going to be wanting to take on a larger role soon, anyway, and Mrs. Belvedere will not be retiring anytime soon." Smiling broadly at her daughter, she said, "Besides, I foresee all of your sisters doing whatever they can to help establish you in your new home."

Glancing across the carriage at Sebastian, Lydia said, "I will write letters to Kitty and Mrs. Wilson as soon as we get back to Pemberley and we will at least have that one problem solved."

He responded, "I am relieved that you had a solution to our housekeeper problem. It will be reassuring to know we will have someone we know is reliable and hardworking. That is, if she accepts our offer."

"Oh, she is a dear, and very hardworking. Mrs. Wilson was widowed young when she lost her soldier husband on the continent not six months after they married. The then colonel knew her husband and arranged for her to find employment at his home estate. She has been working for the family for five years now and for all her losses, she is a very cheerful woman," exclaimed Lydia. Glancing at the list in Sebastian's hand, she asked, "What is next on the list?"

"The servants' quarters need repairs."

"That can certainly be put off. At least until we have more servants. There are rooms available for the servants that are in good condition. It was only the horrid Mrs. Netter who refused to allow them to stay in the nicer rooms as a way to make them know their place."

Grumbling under her breath, Fanny said, "It goes to show you that there are always big-headed people overly proud of their position in life in all spheres of society. Even considering the horrible condition of the house, I think the staff at Swarkstone will certainly do better under good management."

With a nod of agreement, Sebastian continued, "Additionally, two tenant cottages require repairs, and there's a possibility of the need to replace a barn due to a fire. I think those repairs should be prioritized over much of the other issues."

Fiddling with a ribbon that had come loose on her bonnet, Lydia wondered what the repairs would entail and how long they had needed fixing. Regardless of the issue, they would need to spend whatever necessary to care for their dependents. "Caring for the tenants' needs will certainly help toward gaining their trust. Surely they did not have an easy time of it under Mr. Blakesley. Trusting us will be hard for them all."

Lydia watched Sebastian's expression grow pensive, his eyebrows drawing together and his lips scrunching together for a moment before he said, "I can see how caring for Swarkstone Park might be good practice for one day taking over my family's estate."

Lydia worried for him for a reason that she could not quite put her finger on. She found herself wanting to reach out and clasp his hand. "Do you worry about the state of you family estate under your father's control?"

Rubbing at his eyebrow, Sebastian smiled weakly, saying, "My father understands tenants cannot do a good job of bringing in crops if they become sick from sleeping in a leaky cottage. Despite this, he maintains the stance that people he views as beneath him should only be given the most basic level of consideration. He does not believe trust is something he should have to earn or even consider. Respect and obedience are non-negotiable for him—he expects nothing less." Looking to Lydia, he shrugged, and continued saying, "My father has not made the lives of the tenants at Turnbridge any easier than he absolutely had to."

It took a moment for Lydia to take in what Sebastian had revealed about his father. Though the man did not seem as despicable as her own father, he did not, in fact, seem much better. It was no wonder Sebastian spent the majority of his time away from home. It was something that she had not expected for them to have in common. Casting about on her mind, Lydia attempted to find something to say to Sebastian. Something that might soothe his obvious distress. Finally, she said, "We shall start with Swarkstone. Tending to the needs of its people will give us valuable experience. This way, when we eventually assume control of Turnbridge, we will be fully equipped to care for its residents." Reaching across the narrow space between them, Lydia gripped Sebastian's hand. "Do not forget that we shall face it together and be stronger for it."

SEBASTIAN WAS GLAD THAT they had left Swarkstone Park as early as they had, otherwise it would have been much darker by the time that they had arrived at Pemberley. All in all, the journey to Swarkstone Park had been productive, if not slightly distressing. There was so much that would need to be corrected it was nearly overwhelming. However, with one sentence from Lydia, he had felt hope cement in his heart. She had said that they would do it together. That meant more to him than he had expected it would. Hopping down out of the carriage, he reached up to assist Mrs. Hawkins and Lydia down onto solid ground.

The late summer sun had provided them with ample time to travel. They made it before dusk had descended. There were several people on the steps coming towards them in greeting. Lydia wrapped her arm around his offered elbow and leaning into his shoulder as they walked. She sighed, saying, "I am that glad to be free of the swaying of the carriage."

"Yes, the swaying of the carriage gets to be a bit much after a long, hard ride. What do you think about breaking up the trip next time and staying overnight somewhere along the way?" asked Sebastian, as he fought a yawn.

Not bothering to hide her own yawn, Lydia responded, "At this moment, I want to put off another long ride for as long as may be. I would say stopping halfway might work, but I am uncertain of the inns along the way. We can always decide closer to the date we move in."

Sebastian's gaze shifted to Mrs. Hawkins, filled with concern. He couldn't help but think that if he and Lydia were fatigued, his future mother-in-law must be feeling even worse. However, his concern did not seem to be justified, as she seemed to be doing fine. The older woman was bustling across the gravel walkway in a hurry. In no time at all, she was embracing Mrs. Bingley. Glancing down at Lydia, he said, "It appears your mother has more fortitude than I do at this moment."

Chuckling, Lydia said, "When it comes to dispensing love on her children, my mother has all the energy in the world. I am uncertain if it is simply her, or a trait that comes with motherhood. I suppose I will find out once we begin building our own family."

Eyes widening at her causal mention of children, Sebastian was comforted to know that she wanted children as well. He had tried not to, but had begun worrying when she said that she wanted Clara to stay with her until they had the nursery done up. He wanted his niece to have only the best, so it was certainly at the top of his list to get that nursery ready for Clara. They also needed to find a nursemaid or a governess that they could trust. Sebastian swallowed thickly before saying, "Was your sister's visit planned or is this a result of our impending nuptials?"

Sebastian could feel the slight shake of her head from where it rested against his shoulder as they walked to the base of the Pemberley stairs. "Jane had always intended to come to see the new baby and visit with us. Though our wedding might have changed her timetable. Frankly, I am wondering about Kitty and Mary and Georgiana. I half suspect they will be showing up before the wedding. Though Kitty is probably great with child by now, I doubt Theodore will be able to keep her away. Mary and Georgiana are at

Longbourn, so if they are coming, it will take them longer to reach us."

Sebastian did not have much time to consider all of his future sisters-in-law descending on them before he was greeted by Darcy and Bingley, who had come over to shake his hand. Lydia left his side to go greet her sister, giving her a hug, and he was only slightly bereft at the loss of her warmth at his side.

Clapping him on the back, Darcy said, "Welcome back to Pemberley. I would ask you how things went at Swarkstone, but I can see you had a long, exhausting trip. We can discuss matters tomorrow if you wish."

"Though I would be glad to review several issues with you, I do not think I could keep any facts straight right now." Smiling ruefully, Sebastian admitted to his weariness.

Bingley, ever the cheerful chap, grinned and shook his hand, saying, "While I am not as versed in estate management as Darcy, I would be glad to be of use as well."

Fighting to keep a smile on his face, Sebastian asserted, "With what we found at Swarkstone, Lydia and I could use all the advice you are willing to provide." He knew his shoulders were drooping, and he did not much present the picture of confidence at that moment. He only hoped it did not make his future brothers-in-law doubt him.

"You shall have whatever advice and support you need," said Darcy, his voice encouraging if a little serious. Directing Sebastian to the steps with a steady hand on his back, he continued, "My first piece of advice is to get some rest. You are in the same room. There is water to wash up and a light meal will be sent up. Do not feel the need to socialize with us. Just get some sleep."

Grateful for the permission to rest his weary head, Sebastian nodded to the two gentlemen in thanks and moved to Lydia's side. Touching her elbow gently, he drew her attention from her two sisters and mother, saying, "It looks like you are in excellent hands. I am going to retire for the night, but I would love to meet with you in the morning. Perhaps we can make plans over breakfast?"

Eyes sparkling despite the weariness, he could see she responded, "As you say, I am in excellent hands. I am fairly certain my sisters and mother will have me tucked into bed in short order. I will look forward to seeing you in the morning."

LYDIA BLINKED SLOWLY AS she stared up at the canopy above her bed. Despite having slept soundly, she woke up feeling achy and longing for a few more hours of rest. Still, Lydia knew she could not laze about. There was much to do that day, starting with breakfast with Sebastian. So she lay there, willing her limbs to move to get ready for the day.

Finally, Lydia wearily sat up and, rubbing her face, swung her legs off the side of her bed. Pausing, she gathered her fortitude to get out of bed. A knock at her door had her swiveling her attention to Oakley as she came in with a tray. Perking up, Lydia was quick to say, "If you have brought me coffee, I will be eternally grateful."

"Yes miss, I knew you might be dragging this morning after the long distance you traveled yesterday, so I brought up some coffee with cream and sugar to drink while I help you get ready."

Accepting the cup, Lydia took a sip with a luxuriant sigh. After two more sips, she felt better, ready to face the day. Turning to Oakley, who was gathering her clothes for the day, she said, "Bless you, this was exactly what I needed to be able to confront the day. I have a number of letters to write today, as well as plans to draw up for Swarkstone."

"That estate is certainly in need of someone to take it in hand." Shaking her head, Oakley laid out the last of what they would need to get Lydia ready to go downstairs for breakfast with her fiancé. Turning back to her mistress, she smiled, saying, "I am quite sure you and your Mr. Burgess will do a marvelous job of it. Once you get that crabapple, Mrs. Netter, out of the housekeeper's position, I am sure everyone will be much better off."

"Oh, I cannot stand someone of such a sour disposition, and she was cruel besides. You are right, the whole place will do better without her attitude permeating everything in the house." Standing, Lydia gulped the last bit of her coffee down, feeling energized enough to attack the day. Putting her cup down on a side table, she continued, saying, "Right, let's get me dressed. I have too much to do today to laze about."

In no time at all, Lydia was dressed in a sprigged muslin creation that was both stylish and eminently comfortable and she was making her way down to partake of breakfast. Entering the room, Lydia was happy to see Sebastian standing at the sideboard, pouring himself a cup of coffee.

He looked up as she entered and, putting down his cup, came around the table to greet her, saying, "Good morning, Lydia. Did you sleep well?"

"Well enough, I suppose. I certainly slept soundly, though I always seem to need a day or two to feel like myself after a long carriage ride."

Nodding, Sebastian smiled, his white teeth flashing brightly as he replied, "I am much the same. May I get you something to drink? Tea or coffee, perhaps?"

"Coffee would be lovely, with cream and sugar, please." Going to get herself a plate of food, Lydia gathered her meal haltingly. She could not help but watch Sebastian as he prepared her coffee. She had often watched her brothers-in-law doing the same for her sisters. It felt incredibly special to experience such simple and sweet care. No wonder her sisters always relished it so.

Setting her plate on the table, she took a seat, only to have Sebastian approach her with the cup of coffee he had prepared. There was something interesting about knowing he was watching her drink the coffee he had prepared for her. While sipping the drink, she couldn't help but notice that it was exactly how she preferred it, which made her ponder whether he had merely guessed correctly or had been observing her closely. Realizing that Sebastian was waiting to make sure she approved, she reassured him, saying, "It is delicious. I will have to give you leave to prepare my morning coffee whenever I have you at my disposal."

Giving a little bow, he said, "It would be my pleasure to prepare your morning coffee." Moving over to the sideboard, he went about gathering his morning meal, only to return to her side and sit next to her.

For a while, they sat eating in companionable silence, until Sebastian said, "Have you had any ideas of how we can go about finding a good nursemaid for Clara?"

"I had thought perhaps of writing to Lady Derby and my aunt, Mrs. Gardiner, in London. Both of them have a number of children and even if they do not have someone whom we can take into service for us, they might know of an agency we can use."

Wiping his mouth, Sebastian replied, "That is a sound idea. I will hope that we can find someone adequate in the time frame that we have before us."

Tilting her head, Lydia pondered his statement for a moment while she chewed her latest bite of food. Then, swallowing, she asked, "What would you view as adequate? It is just now occurring to me that we might view what is adequate differently."

Sebastian paused with his fork on the way to his mouth, then putting it down, he looked at her, his brows drawn together. Opening his mouth, he hesitated before saying, "You are right, that is more complicated than I first thought. The first thing that comes to mind is someone who will make sure Clara is cared for and happy. I am sure that we will spend time with her ourselves. I like how involved your sisters are in their children's lives. I would hope for the same with Clara, but she will still need someone to care for her basic needs such as being dressed and fed. What do you think?"

Tapping her fingers on the table next to her plate, Lydia considered what she wanted in a nurse maid not only for Clara but also eventually for her own children. Looking at Sebastian, she said, "I would want someone kind but firm when necessary. I would not have Clara spoiled as so many children of the ton are. Someone literate is a must. I discovered a rocking chair tucked away in the attic, begging for a coat of fresh paint. It would be perfect for story time. The ideal person for me would be someone who has a deep affection for children and is fascinated by their charming idiosyncrasies, instead of being bothered by them."

Sebastian nodded and replied, "I think that finding someone like you describe may be difficult, but you are correct. I would want someone who enjoys Clara and not simply tolerates her."

"Good, I will put that in my letters this morning. Hopefully, we will get a good result back before the wedding." Satisfied with their decision, Lydia took another bite of food. With all the letter writing she had to work on that morning, she would need sustenance. Hopefully, she would have the chance to spend time in her garden later. She wanted to see about taking some specimens to propagate at Swarkstone Park. As it stood now, the garden at Swarkstone Park was sorely lacking order and care, though she could tell that someone had once loved it dearly. Despite its neglected state, Lydia envisioned the potential of Swarkstone Park and was determined to restore it.

KIERNAN KNEW HE WOULD find Lydia in the garden at this time of day and hurried to greet her before they both had to see to their various responsibilities of the evening. It did not take him long to spot her as she weeded one of the beds. He knew that the gardeners that Darcy employed would do the job, but that Lydia was fond of the task, similar to how Elizabeth was fond of her walks. They both seemed to need some form of outdoor activity to keep their spirits up.

Calling out so as not to startle her, Kiernan said, "I knew I would find you here."

Looking up from her task, Lydia swiped at her forehead with the back of her wrist, before saying, "Kiernan! I had hoped you would arrive in time for my wedding." She snagged the cloth that was next to her and wiped her hands as she got to her feet. Soon enough, they were hugging.

Leaning back from her, Kiernan realized that one day soon he would look down at her. He was constantly growing taller while she had stopped. Though she had ended up being the tallest of her sisters, despite being the youngest, it was evident that he would be taller. They were close to the same height, but at fifteen, he would certainly continue to grow.

Stepping back from her, he put his hands on his hips, exclaiming, "What is this I hear about you getting married all of a sudden? Not a word of a courtship and then news that you are marrying by the end of the month. I have a feeling that there is a story that I have not been told. I have not heard of any violence perpetrated by Darcy or any of your other brothers, so it cannot be too bad. Are you willing to tell your almost brother, or is it a secret?"

"You are right. There is a story, and I am more than willing to share, but let us sit first." Gesturing over to a nearby bench, Lydia moved to sit and Kiernan followed.

Settling himself at an angle so that he could watch her, Kiernan asked, "So what had been happening while I was away at school?"

Sighing, Lydia said, "You may recall meeting Sebastian and Selene Burgess at Kitty's wedding."

Nodding, Kiernan said, "Twins with black hair and blue eyes that befriended Kitty and the colonel." Kiernan still felt odd calling the man Fitzwilliam or Theodore and he certainly did not feel comfortable calling him the Earl of Matlock. When he had met him, he had called him the colonel, and it still felt right.

Not focusing on his response, Lydia continued, "Yes, well, not long ago, they showed up with their orphaned niece. It turns out that her father's will said that whoever gets custody of the girl must be married."

Kiernan instantly knew what happened. Lydia did not have to explain any further. Nodding his head, he said, "So you, seeing the need for him to get married, volunteered in order to protect the little girl. I assume there is some other family member that we are protecting her from, some sort of dissolute or shadowy figure that cannot be trusted with the care of a young girl. Who I am guessing is at least a moderately wealthy heiress, despite her tender age."

Smiling, Lydia affirmed, "You have it exactly."

Kiernan could easily understand why Lydia had jumped feet first into marrying Mr. Burgess. While she had Elizabeth's courage, she also was the youngest and used to getting her way most of the time. Beyond that, she absolutely loved children and the idea that someone was a threat to a child that she could protect would have moved her to act without hesitation. He had seen marriages based on less succeed. His parents had married for convenience and no matter how it began, they had found love in the relationship.

Trying to remember more of the man, Kiernan looked out into the garden but paid little heed to the blooms. After a moment, he said, "He seemed a good sort of man when last we met, so you have that in your favor. Then too, I am sure that Darcy and at least one other of your brothers have had a conversation about treating you well."

"Yes, Sebastian was in William's study for hours when I first suggested the solution to his problem. Elizabeth is not overly happy about my choice. She wanted me to find a man, fall in love and then get married. In her opinion, I am taking a risk of never having love in my life, but I do not see it that way. I am only doing things in a different order than she did. I know I have Sebastian's respect and support already. He is the sort of man I could love, and I hope he could love me. It will simply take time and effort on both of our parts, and that little girl is worth it all." Looking at Kiernan, her gaze full of anger, she said, "You should have seen where they had her, Kiernan."

Jumping up, she began to pace in front of him, growling as she spoke, "They had left Clara in a grim, dirty room without even a nurse to see to her and only a few toy soldiers and not enough blocks to build anything with. A child of five alone! She hardly speaks and is only begining to come out of her protective shell. I suspect that someone demanded she be silent at some point, and she took it to heart. Though Artie seems to do wonders with encouraging her to play, it will be some time before I think she will become the girl she is capable of being."

Facing Kiernan, hands clenched into fists, Lydia huffed, but he could not help but laugh. Lydia was the epitome of a mother tiger who had finally been gifted a cub. It may not have been hers, but she was ready to defend it with tooth and claw. Standing, he moved to walk with her, saying, "It seems as if the estate has been badly run. I am assuming that you will be moving there to take it in hand?"

"Yes, as part of the custody agreement, we must manage Clara's estate for her until she is of age. Half the staff abandoned their posts soon after they heard of Mr. Blakesley's death, which seems odd to me, but he had, for the most part, ignored the estate as much as he ignored the state of his daughter. We will need to hire a number of people both for the manor house and the grounds." Lydia moved down the path that would take her back to the house. It was probably time for her to clean up so she could attend breakfast with the family.

Considering how different this new estate would be, Kiernan frowned. Here at Pemberley and even when she lived back at Longbourn, she had been surrounded by staff that was very loyal to her and her family, but that would not be the case at this new location. It would take some time to weed out the disreputable and disloyal and to find good people to replace them. Glancing at her as they walked, he said, "I am not fond of the idea of having so many people there that you do not trust. Do you still remember what I taught you last summer when I came home from Eton?"

Grabbing Kiernan's arm and clutching him to her in a half hug, she said, "With as often as my sisters have found themselves in trouble, I would be foolish to forget how to protect myself and others if the need arose. Of all my brothers, I think you would have been the only one brave enough to teach me."

Chuckling, he replied, "The others have too many fancy manors to have thought of it. It's quite silly, actually, considering how often you girls get yourselves into scrapes."

Chapter Fourteen

Elizabeth looked around the room, happy to see all her family but frustrated as to why they had converged. The only sister who was absent from the sitting room was Lydia, who was spending the afternoon making plans with her future husband and William. She assumed a few other of the husbands were there helping as well. It was just as well because they were all gathered, for the most part, to discuss Lydia's choices.

"You seem to have recovered well from Gilbert's birth. How have you been adjusting?" This came from Mary, who was the most recently married. Elizabeth wondered how soon she would announce that her own little bundle of joy was on the way.

Smiling at Mary, Elizabeth replied, "The labor was no more difficult than my first one and I believe I am getting my strength back at a good rate. William tends to coddle me and would prefer to keep me cosseted and wrapped in lamb's wool, but I have been leaving my room and even took a short walk in the garden yesterday. I do not know where the silly notion that woman should stay in bed for a month complete after they have given birth came from, but it is stupid. Woman would do much better if they were to get fresh air and exercise."

Her mother laughed at her display of petulance, saying, "Not all ladies are as fond as you are of walking the trails and paths, so many of the high society ladies do not start off with the strength you have. You will have to forgive them if they prefer to be cosseted after such an ordeal."

Rubbing the large swelling of her abdomen, Kitty commented, "An ordeal that I am not quite looking forward to. Though I cannot wait to meet my little addition. Whoever they may be."

Reaching over, Jane grabbed her hand and gave it a squeeze. Smiling at her, Jane said, "I am sure you will do remarkably. You have proven yourself quite capable in the past of handling difficult situations with strength and grace. I am sure you will do no less in bringing your child into the world."

All the sisters nodded in agreement as their mother added, "If I can have five girls without a husband's support, I am sure that you can do no less with Theodore by your side."

Once everyone paused to take sips of tea and bites of the little delicacies that had been provided, Elizabeth took the opportunity to say, "Darling Clara aside, I cannot say I am thrilled that Lydia would chose to marry without love, but I have not attempted to stop her. What is everyone's opinion of Lydia's recent decisions?"

Setting her teacup down, Fanny said, "While I was ready to be disapproving and putting a stop to the marriage if I had to, my trip with them to Swarkstone Park was enlightening."

Mary took another sip of tea before asking, "How so?"

Tilting her head to the side, Fanny hesitated a beat before responding, "There was a very disrespectful servant who we soon realized would have to be let go if any true improvements could be made. As the housekeeper, her poor attitude was, of course, affecting most of the staff. Lydia confronted her and in the course of the conversation explained that since she refused to change or improve her attitude, she would have to be let go. The woman denied that Lydia could possibly have that power and insisted that Mr. Burgess would want her to stay. Her screeching, however, drew the attention of Mr. Burgess, who immediately supported Lydia's choice to dismiss her." Taking a sip of her tea, Elizabeth noticed her mother looked pensive before she continued, saying, "I believe he respects Lydia. Which is at least a firm foundation for a marriage, even if there is not love."

Kitty was quick to say, "I would not be quick to say that there will not be love in their marriage."

Turning to her younger sister, Elizabeth said, "You have spent a lot of time with Selene and Mr. Burgess, as they were frequently by your side while you were courting Theodore. Lydia also accompanied you on those walks. Did you see something that we have not?"

Repositioning her larger than typical bulk, Kitty sighed but then explained, "Though I will admit that I was, most of the time, otherwise occupied, I often noted how well the two got on. In fact, I distinctly remember thinking that they may one day form a match of it. Since the day they first crossed paths, they held each other in high regard and, if I may be so bold, were undeniably drawn to each other. I think this will end up far better than you suppose, Elizabeth."

Nodding in agreement, Georgianna said, "I believe Kitty is correct. While the order of things may be a bit jumbled, the fundamental components for a deeply loving marriage are all in place." Reaching out, she picked a little tea cake from the tea tray and took a bite.

Selecting her own miniature cake, Mary took a small nibble as if testing whether she would enjoy it. Elizabeth knew that her sister had not announced anything, but still she wondered. Taking a larger bit this time, Mary chewed contemplatively before saying, "I am happy to let Lydia make her own choices in the matter. We all know that she has her reasons for marrying Mr. Burgess and not one of us can say that she is wrong for wanting to protect that little girl. I believe her actions are noble. Think of the many women of the bible who took part in marriages of convenience or arranged marriages and were blessed for it. I think we should recognize Lydia for her courage and not doubt her for her choice to marry where is only the hope of love."

Mary's words resonated with Elizabeth, piercing straight into her heart. Lydia was being brave, and she should not be doubting her. Looking down at her teacup, Elizabeth watched the steam curl into the air. She would not like it if anyone doubted her convictions, even if it was one of her sisters. Sighing, she said, "I suppose you are right. Had I married William sooner, I would not love him any less today for having married before I was truly in love. Lydia's bravery is undeniable, and it feels almost unjust for me to question her."

As the days passed, the countdown to his wedding seemed to accelerate, leaving Sebastian feeling both excited and anxious. He would marry in two days' time and he had no idea where the time had gone. His days had been full of attempts to gain Clara's trust. Watching her play with the other children and smile more was heartening. In the moments he wasn't with Clara or Lydia, he busied himself with making plans and penning letters. He did not want Lydia to come to Swarkstone Park as a new bride and be confronted with inadequate and insolent staff, along with rooms that were in a state of disrepair. So he wrote to staffing agencies but found that most of the replies he received were not favorable.

He could not understand it. How were so many agencies experiencing a lack of applicants? If he did not know any better, he would have thought they were conspiring against him, but there was no reason to keep him from finding the staff that he needed. It made so little sense.

Then, too, there was the letter from his father. It was not even worth considering. His father's advice, which was usually questionable at best, was now completely devoid of any value. Sebastian would completely ignore the viscount's complaints and admonitions. He did not even deem them worthy of a response. It was fortunate that his letter to his father announcing his impending marriage would arrive too late for his father to intervene.

Deciding to take a break from reading frustrating correspondence, Sebastian went in search of Lydia. As they had worked together to plan for their future, their friendship had grown ever stronger. He found himself looking forward to the moments that they could spend together. She always had a smile for him and often was able to look at things in a better light than he did.

Lydia, Selene, and all the other females that had converged on Pemberley had been kept busy with their own arrangements, mostly for the wedding. Walking out into the sun dappled gardens, Sebastian was sure that he would come across Lydia and at least one of her sisters. Perhaps even his own sister. Lydia had been taking clippings and root stock from many of the plants so that she could add to the gardens at Swarkstone Park. He was sure that with her remarkable affinity for plants, Swarkstone's gardens would be a marvel in no time.

Sebastian found Lydia along with his sister and Miss Georgianna Darcy in amongst the roses. Miss Darcy was asking, "Are you sure you do not wish to take more than these two types of roses?"

"No, this is plenty for now. Besides, I do not know what the soil there is like, and these two varieties are the hardiest. I can expect them to thrive no matter where they are planted. I can obtain more once I know what I am dealing with," came Lydia's reply. Sebastian watched as she wrapped the root stock carefully with a burlap before tying it in place.

A gardener stepped up saying, "I will take it and put it with the others, and make sure they all arrive at your new home healthy and well."

She smiled kindly at the young man, saying, "Thank you, Mr. Roberts."

Feeling it was as good a time as any to make his presence known, Sebastian said, "I see you are hard at work preparing to make our future garden glorious."

Looking up at him from the ground, Lydia's smile widened dramatically and laughing, she said, "A lady needs to find a way to beautify her surroundings." Wiping her hands off on a nearby rag, she held one of her hands aloft and Sebastian was all too happy to help her to her feet.

Squeezing her hand, Sebastian replied, "Oh, but you take care of that merely by granting us your presence. Your beauty far outshines any flower." Sebastian did not know why he had been prompted to say such a flirtatious comment, but he definitely enjoyed watching the resulting blush creep across Lydia's cheeks. For a time, he only had eyes for Lydia, but realized his mistake when he heard the other women giggle.

Looking away from Lydia's flushed face, he smiled at Selene, who stood with her arm linked with Miss Darcy's. With all of Lydia's sisters showing up for the wedding, along with her mother, there was certainly a plethora of ladies present. He had never before spent so much time surrounded by feminine sensibilities.

He knew the look in his sister's eyes. She found his situation highly entertaining. Quirking an eyebrow, Selene said, "I see that you have left your papers and letters for a time, brother. Have you come to escort us to the house for tea?"

"I will admit that I had lost track of time, but enjoying tea with you all sounds quite pleasant after looking over letters for so long. Some people I am getting responses from have the worst penmanship," admitted Sebastian. Letting go of Lydia's hand, he offered her his arm, and the group began strolling to the house.

Miss Darcy and his sister seemed to walk faster than him and Lydia and quickly drew away from them. Sebastian suspected this was by design and could only be grateful for the opportunity to speak to Lydia alone. Lydia, however, spoke first. "Are the responses from the employment agencies not going well?"

Shaking his head, Sebastian resisted the urge to run his fingers through his hair. He wearily responded, "No, the employment agencies I have contacted do not have anyone to suggest or offer as workers. Something is not right about it."

Squeezing his arm as they walked, Lydia said, "I believe you may be right, but regardless, we can make do. Besides, Kitty has provided the two people we need the most."

Looking down at her, he said, "It was very kind of Lady Matlock to arrange for Mrs. Wilson and Nurse Harris to arrive with her. Having a housekeeper and nursemaid we can trust will go a long way towards making things go more smoothly."

Squeezing his arm, Lydia chided him, "You will have to stop calling my sister and her husband by their titles. Kitty and Theodore may have come up in the world with the death of his older brother, but they are still the same people." Resting her head against his arm in a way that he was growing rather fond of, she continued, "As for staffing issues, I am confident we will manage. I am not so dissimilar to my older sister, Mary. She took on our old home when it was completely in shambles and with only borrowed staff initially. Swarkstone is not nearly so dilapidated. Eventually, if we find that we really must get more staff, we can talk to my sisters and their husbands. With nine fully staffed estates, I am sure there must be some individuals looking for a promotion or a new location. If somehow there is no one interested in relocating to Swarkstone Park, we can always have Theodore contact the employment agencies. They cannot very well turn away the business of the earl of Matlock."

THE PARLOR WAS FULL of her family, and she was delighted to have everyone together for her wedding, even if she would have to by necessity say goodbye to them all. At the other end of the room, Selene was chatting happily with Georgianna, who had arrived with Mary and Gabriel the day before last. Her mother was sitting with her husband, Mr. Hawkins, and they were chatting with Elizabeth and William. Mary and Jane were seated together on a settee enjoying each other's company, their husbands close by discussing horses, she thought. What truly touched Lydia was that she noticed that her mother and two of her sisters appeared to be working on dresses for Clara as they socialized.

Even Kitty had made it with as far along as her pregnancy was. Lydia had been afraid Theodore might put his foot down and prevent her from traveling, but they had arrived that morning. Looking at Kitty and Theodore as they sat cuddled together on the settee next to her, Lydia said, "I am so very glad you both made it. With my wedding the day after next, I worried you would not be able to come."

"We took our time on the journey, making frequent stops to avoid overtaxing Kitty." Looking at his wife, Theodore kissed the back of her hand before putting a possessive hand on the swell of her stomach.

Kitty smiled fondly at him before turning back to Lydia and saying, "I could tell he thought about putting his foot down and saying no, but he knows me too well."

Laughing, Theodore said, "Yes, if I tried to put my foot down and stop her from making it to her baby sister's wedding, she would just stomp on it and find her own way here." This had the entire room laughing. Everyone knew how much Theodore doted on his wife and found it difficult to deny her anything.

"I want to thank you for bringing along Mrs. Wilson and Nurse Harris. Having them with us when we arrive at Swarkstone will be very helpful."

Kitty smiled brightly, saying, "It is not a trouble at all. In fact, I think that Mrs. Wilson is very excited to spread her wings, so to speak. As for Esther Harris, she is the daughter of one of our tenant families and was rather disappointed that I had already selected a nursemaid for our coming little one when she let us know she was looking for employment. She has plenty of experience with children and has the sweetest disposition."

Taking a sip of her tea, Lydia contemplated the young woman that she had met only briefly. She already seemed to be much better than whoever had been in charge of Clara's care previously. She certainly could not be any worse, not when the previous woman had let her live in that horrid room and then abandoned the child. Nodding her head, Lydia said, "Then I will look forward to getting to know her. I was hoping you would spend some time with Clara and myself before the wedding. You still have the best eye, and I would like your advice on decorating the nursery. I've organized fabric swatches, paper samples, and some color samples. I am hoping Clara will respond well to getting a say in picking her environment."

Her smile causing her cheeks to scrunch up, Kitty exclaimed with excitement, "I would be thrilled to! Was the nursery really so bad?"

Eyes going hard, Lydia frowned. "Worse." Taking another sip of her tea, Lydia intentionally worked at regaining her equanimity. This was a happy time. All her sisters were here, and she was about to get married. She was not about to dwell on what was in the past.

"How large is Swarkstone Park?" This question came from her newest brother, Gabriel.

Her mother spoke up, explaining, "Swarkstone Park's is not as large as Pemberley, but still quite large." Looking over at Lydia, she asked, "What do you think? Maybe twice the size of Longbourn?"

Biting her lip, Lydia tried to compare the two estates. That was a fair estimation, she supposed. "Yes, that seems about right, if not exactly correct. I did not see most of the spare rooms, but there is a whole additional wing. The building is a sort of U shape where Longbourn is an L and Pemberley is an E. Sadly, at the moment, I think the number of staff equals Longbourn, so it cannot present to the best of its ability."

Mary nodded, continuing the conversation with, "That is not ideal, but not completely impossible. If you shut up most of the unneeded rooms, you can get by in the manor house. What about the grounds?"

Lydia looked to Sebastian, as she was sure he knew more about the grounds and tenants. He said, "There is no one assigned to the grounds besides the two stable hands. One of them was a young stable boy. There are twelve tenant families, several in need of repairs to their homes. There was a fire that destroyed one of the family's barns recently. So that will need to be repaired."

This started a conversation around the room about similar issues that they had all faced and the best way that one might deal with a burned structure safely. Sebastian leaned over and whispered to Lydia, "I know that your family is not like most of the ton, but I still expected most of the conversation to revolve around our upcoming wedding. Yet there has not been one mention of lace, flowers, or fripperies."

Chuckling under her breath, she replied, "We have all the planning taken care of. I wanted to keep everything simple and there will be a few guests outside of the family. With eight ladies to help with the planning and arrangements, it was taken care of rather quickly. Actually, of all my sisters, I am the one who most enjoys fripperies, but for now I have more serious concerns to hold my attention."

"So once we have everything under good regulation at Swarkstone, can I expect you to shift your conversation from tenant concerns to fashion and lace?" Sebastian asked, his voice carrying his good humor.

Feeling playful in response to his comment, she whispered back, "Oh, do not worry too much. I am sure I will still talk to you about tenant and household concerns. My focus will be on important things like Clara's well-being and my garden. I promise to mention fashion and the design of my latest dress only every other week."

Selene followed her brother and Lydia as they walked out of the room. She had a few things that she wanted to say, and she was running out of time to say them. Before they could get too far away, she softly called out to them, "Sebastian, Lydia, do you have a moment to speak with me? With only the three of us?"

Turning back to face her, Lydia and Sebastian glanced at each other before looking back at her. Selene was left wondering at how good they were getting at communicating with one another without words. "Of course. Why don't we speak in here?" Lydia asked, gesturing to a small room that seemed to be a sort of study near the stairs.

With a nod of her head, Selene followed the pair into the room. Wiping her hands on the sides of her dress, she hoped the pair of them would not become offended or hurt by what she was about to suggest. Waiting until they were all settled, Selene cleared her throat and said, "I know you were expecting me to join you at Swarkstone, but I have been invited to stay at Pemberley and I have decided to take Elizabeth and Georgiana up on their offer. At least for now."

Leaning forward, her brother exclaimed, "Selene, you must know that you will always be welcome wherever I am. That does not change because I will marry Lydia."

Lydia was quick to follow with, "Sebastian is correct. You are family and we want you with us. Though I understand Pemberley's appeal, I would hate for you to feel as if you could not come with us. Clara is your niece, too."

Shaking her head, Selene tried to find the words to explain how she felt. "I know I am welcome. That is not in question." Reaching out to Lydia, she took her hand in her own. "Never once have you made me feel as if you are trying to supplant me in my brother's life. I know we will always be close, but you are getting married and taking over a poorly run estate. That is a big change, and I want to give you both a chance to adapt to that. Simply, eventually dealing with the poorly trained staff will be a trial. I do not want to complicate matters by giving them another person to look to for direction. It will be, for all intents and purposes, your estate until Clara is old enough to run it herself."

As she sat back in her chair, she attentively observed her brother and Lydia sharing a meaningful gaze, their connection palpable. That was the other part of why she wanted to stay away for a time. Most everyone was aware of their budding connection except the pair themselves. She wanted to give them the time alone to help it flourish.

Selene waited, knowing from her brother's expression that he wanted to say something but hadn't found the words yet.

Eyebrows drawn together and jaw hard, she could see his concern in the lines of her brother's face when he said, "Though I feel you would not be in the way as we take over the estate, I respect your desire to stay here at Pemberley. The Darcys are wonderful people, and I know they will make you feel welcome. I would hate it if you felt that you were unwelcome in my home. That is certainly not the case. I told Father years ago that you would always be welcome in my home wherever I was, and I will not go back on my word because of a change in circumstance."

Sighing, Selene replied, "Yes, I know. This is not because I feel unwelcome. It is more like my gift to you so you can start your marriage off on the right foot. I want you two to learn to depend on each other and to grow closer. I will not stay away forever. Only a month, maybe two." Hesitating, she decided the time to be ambiguous was past. "Remember, you are getting married and heading straight over to Swarkstone Park. You are not taking a wedding trip. You will both need time to adjust to all the changes in your life, and you deserve to do it without me hovering about the place."

Her brother took her meaning because he swiftly turned three shades pinker. Even though he stayed by Lydia's side, his body grew tense, his posture stiffening. He opened his mouth but only managed to say, "I... Well, uh..."

When he looked at Lydia, whose cheeks were similarly pink, obviously floundering with what to say, Lydia boldly said, "You need not worry about disturbing us, we are not...or rather... Clara will stay with me temporarily, until we can renovate the nursery and make it suitable for her."

If she wasn't so embarrassed as well, it would be comical to watch her brother and Lydia struggle. Clearing her throat, she said, "Regardless of your plans, I intend to give you time alone to adjust to everything."

After staring at one another for a time, her brother nodded finally, as if he knew he could not sway her. Or he had decided to forgo further embarrassment. Either way, he said, "Very well, but I expect you to come stay with us eventually."

LYDIA TOOK A SEAT on the floor of the nursery, glad that at least here she would not have to have such a horrifying discussion as she had just left. Selene was the sweetest to think that Lydia and Sebastian would need time to themselves after their wedding. However, theirs was not that sort of arrangement. They would not be constantly sneaking away the way that Elizabeth and William had. How all of her sisters had, really.

Hers was to be a different sort of marriage, and while she hoped that one day they would form some kind of love for one another, it certainly would not start out that way. She had rather hoped to fill her time alone with Selene's company, but she would have to be noble and allow Lydia time to bond with Sebastian. The question to Lydia was, did Sebastian wish to bond with her?

He had not protested when she said she would have Clara stay with her. It was only later that she had supposed that Clara could stay with her new nursemaid. Sebastian's lack of response made it evident that he had no plans to take advantage of his husbandly privilege, at least at that time. They had discussed their desire to have children eventually. So it would happen, whatever it was, just not anytime soon.

Shaking her head, Lydia moved her mind in a more profitable direction. She watched as Artie interacted with Mathew and Ellie. It was obvious that he was the leader of the group. Clara stood on the sidelines, uncertain. Talkative Artie approached her saying, "Here you can have this horse and play with us."

Eyes wide, she nodded and imitated the other children with helping her horse to prance around the area. Having been raised mostly alone and without the interaction of other children, it was a completely new experience for her, but Lydia was happy to see her adapting. Lydia watched them play for a time and eventually they even got Clara giggling with the rest. It was enough to make Lydia's eyes misty.

When there was a pause in the play as the children put away the horses in favor of a game with blocks, Lydia got their attention by saying, "Children, come over here for a moment. I have something I want to tell you." She waited as they came over and sat down around her, the youngest, her little brother Mathew, settling in her lap. She continued by asking, "Have you enjoyed getting to know Clara?"

Artie, ever the spokesman, said, "Yes, she is fun. I like having someone bigger to play with, even if she is a girl."

Mathew and Ellie both nodded in agreement with Artie's statement, though Ellie said, "I like Clara!" Leaning over, she gave the older girl an enormous hug.

Startled, Clara looked down at the younger blonde in surprise, but after a moment, she hugged her back and whispered, "I like you too."

"I am glad you like her because soon she will be family."

"Really?!" Artie exclaimed, jumping up off the ground.

"Yes, really." Lydia laughed.

Artie went over to the girls and, grabbing Clara's hands, asked, "Do you want to be my sister? I heard Mama say before that she wants a little girl, but she had baby Gill." Laughing, he hugged her and continued, "I bet she would be so happy if I could bring her you."

Lydia looked at Clara's confused expression and Artie's thrilled one, wondering how things had gotten so out of hand so quickly. She cried, "Wait, wait!" Getting all their attention, she explained, "Artie, she cannot be your sister because she is going to be your cousin. Of a sort, at least."

Leaning back, he looked over his shoulder at Lydia. His face scrunched up, he asked, "My cousin? Like Ellie?"

"Yes, like Ellie." Reaching out, Lydia smoothed her hand along Clara's pensive brow and explained, "Do you remember how you have an aunt and uncle named Selene and Sebastian?" The little girl nodded with wide eyes. Little Artie, possibly sensing her unease, sat next to her and pat her hand in comfort. Ellie looked on, her eyes uncertain, as she sat next to Clara.

Lydia continued, "Soon, Sebastian and I are going to get married, and that will mean that I will be your aunt, just like I am Artie and Ellie's aunt. What do you think of that?"

Clara did not look as if she knew what to say. Her eyes were still wide with upraised brows and her lips pressed together in a hard line. Leaning over, Artie hugged her, saying, "Auntie Lydia is the best aunt! She is so much fun. You will see."

Ellie nodded in agreement, but then asked, "Mr. 'bastian my un'cle now too?"

"Yes, Sebastian, or Mr. Burgess, will be your uncle, like Gabriel, William, and Theodore are your uncles."

"He builds forts?" asked Mathew from her lap.

While she was not going to point out that the much older gentleman was going to be his brother-in-law, she was happy to see his curiosity. Explaining the family tree more thoroughly was going to come later. Lydia grinned down at Mathew and said, "Yes, I am sure Sebastian can build forts with blocks, though if he does not, I suppose you can teach him."

With a nod, Mathew said, "Good."

Pausing in his enthusiasm, Artie asked, "Are you leaving like Mary and Kitty?"

Looking askance at Artie, the child really did understand more than he should at three. Sighing, she said, "Yes, Sebastian and Clara and I will be going somewhere nearby and making a home for ourselves. But we will visit and eventually you can come and visit us."

Artie nodded and said, "All right then." Then, studying both Lydia and Clara for a moment, he hugged Lydia. "Clara needs a good aunt. I can share you."

Shaking her head, Lydia once again wondered at her remarkable nephew and his precocious attitude about things. Setting Mathew up on his feet, Lydia said, "Why don't you go play a bit while I talk with Clara about her new room?" Smiling at the nursemaids who were chatting by the open window, she knew they would care for their charges. Getting to her feet, Lydia held her hand out to Clara, who promptly took it. She led the girl out of the nursery, and they made their way towards where Kitty was staying, asking, "What is your favorite color, Clara?"

The entire time she talked with Kitty and Clara about colors and flowers, Lydia's mind kept wondering back to the idea that she would be getting married. The prospect of the upcoming change in her life filled her with increasing excitement and anticipation. So much would change, and she could not wait to see what her future held.

Chapter Fifteen

Elizabeth sat in the pew with her husband and children, trying not to bawl. It seemed like the last day before Lydia's wedding had disappeared. In the midst of final dress fittings and last-minute arrangements, she realized that her time with her sister had vanished. Now it was time for Lydia to walk down the aisle and on to her new life.

She hoped with all that she had in her that Lydia would find love in the life that she had chosen by marrying Mr. Burgess. Kitty had told her that she suspected they were already halfway there, and she was certain they would find their own way to happiness. So she was going to hold on to that hope, but it was difficult to keep her worries at bay.

Lydia's infectious smile lit up her face, illuminating the room and overshadowing any negativity. Meanwhile, Elizabeth fought her anxiety. She knew from experience that even being married to someone you loved was difficult. Elizabeth worried how much harder it would be without that connection to unite you. All she could do at this point was to hope and pray that things would go as well as her sister hoped they would.

William wrapped her in his embrace, his arm around her shoulder, holding her to his side. He understood how hard this was for her. Absorbing his comfort, Elizabeth lay her head on his shoulder and watched the proceedings with slitted, tear-bleary eyes. She watched her sister walk down the aisle on their mother's arm. It was unusual, but quite fitting if you thought about it. Mama had done so much for them all, shielding them, teaching them and loving them with all she had. She deserved to walk her youngest daughter down the aisle. The pair of them were beautiful, Lydia a splendid reflection of their mother's grace and beauty.

For all that she fought her worry, it was easy for Elizabeth to admit that her baby sister was a beautiful bride. Even with a short time to throw everything together, everything that they had arranged turned out gorgeous. Lydia's periwinkle dress was beautiful, and the flowers and garlands were elegant. As she reached the altar, Lydia looked at her gentleman with such hope. If there was no love in her gaze, there was certainly respect and possibly more, possibly something on the way to love.

LYDIA MADE HER WAY down the aisle with her mother, the heady scent of the flowers in the air, making it seem like they could have easily been in a blooming meadow. There, at the end of her short journey, was her groom, the man she was entrusting all her hopes and dreams to. Despite the circumstances of their marriage, she could regret nothing.

Deep inside her, she knew that this was the right thing to do. It only took looking at the little girl who stood at the front. Clara was up there with Selene and Georgianna as her maids of honor. The little ring of flowers in her black curls was perfect in its simplicity. That little girl would be as good as her daughter, and she would see to her love and care. What better reason could there be to marry?

Looking up at Sebastian as she finally reached him, she admitted to herself that she was gaining a very handsome man in the bargain. Soon enough, her hand was in his while the vicar began to speak words of honor and duty, but she was paying more attention to the way her hand felt as it rested inside of Sebastian's larger one. His hand was warmer than her own and she could feel the calluses on his palm that came from some sort of hard work as it slid against her skin. She was marrying a good, hardworking man who loved his family and loved that little girl so much that he would do nearly anything to protect her. How did she get so lucky?

Then, out of what felt like the blue, it was time for her to repeat her vows, promising to have and to hold for better for worse, for richer or poorer, in sickness and in health, to love and to cherish.

Only death would part her and Sebastian, and she found she liked that part, maybe the most. She quite liked the idea of being bonded to someone so strongly. There was also the bit about pledging her troth, but she was not going to think of that later.

Soon enough, she was stepping back from the vicar, arm in arm with Sebastian as he said, "Mrs. Burgess," before kissing her on the cheek.

She could tell she was blushing by the heat she could feel in her cheeks, but that did not stop her from professing, "My, how lovely that sounds, husband."

He smiled back, his blue eyes twinkling, before replying in a hushed whisper, "And I find I like you calling me husband."

It was all the time they had alone together before all of her family descended them upon wishing them well. Of course, Selene was there, hugging Lydia, but she was far outnumbered by the many people who were connected to the Bennet ladies. Lydia found herself enveloped by hugs and kisses on her cheek, but she stopped when she felt a tug on her dress.

Looking down, she realized that Clara was becoming overwhelmed by the crowd. Her little fingers clutched at Lydia's dress in a white knuckled grip that was sure to have Oakley tsking at the wrinkles. Lydia quickly leaned down to comfort her. Wrapping an arm around her thin shoulders, she said, "My poor dear, this is quite a few cheerful people that you do not know, isn't it? But now that I have married your uncle, they are all your family and there is not a one of them who would not love and protect you."

Clara's eyes widened as she studied the crowd of people surrounding her. Lydia was just about to get Sebastian to pick her up, but then she saw Kiernan approach. Ever the gallant young man, Kiernan took notice of the girl's fears and crouched down in front of Clara. "Hello, Miss Clara. I am Kiernan, and I am a brother of sorts to your new aunt here. I know these people do not mean you any harm, but there are quite a few of them. I know that a large crowd of people can be scary." Nodding her head vigorously, Clara confirmed her fears and so Kiernan continued. "Would you prefer to be carried? That way, they won't be towering over you. I can carry you, if you wish."

Lydia watched as Clara bit her lip for a moment before nodding her head and whispering, "Yes, please, Mr. Kiernan."

Bowing with a flourish, Kiernan exclaimed, "Whatever my lady wishes." Then, scooping her up, he held her high in his arms so that she was able to look everyone in the eye.

As Lydia and Sebastian made their way out of the chapel through a sea of well-wishers, Kiernan followed closely with Clara in his arms. Lydia could hear him whispering to her about all the people they came across, letting her know who they were and how she was connected to them now. By the time they reached the carriages that would take them back to Pemberley for the wedding breakfast, he had her smiling and giggling.

Sebastian smiled at the pair, and asked, "Clara, do you want to ride in the carriage with your Aunt Lydia and I back to Pemberley or would you prefer to ride with some of the other children?"

She looked up at Kiernan with hopeful eyes and asked, "Can I ride with you?"

Laughing, he said, "You can, but I did not ride here in a carriage. I came on that mare over there. Her name is Epona, and I am sure she would love to have you ride her with me. But I understand if you do not want to ride a big horse with me. It is up to you."

Clara looked from him to the horse and back again. "I will ride Pony with you."

Kiernan looked at Lydia and Sebastian for approval before saying, "Wonderful. Have you ever ridden a horse before, Miss Clara?"

Watching them go, Lydia laughed. "And so the tradition continues."

Helping her up into the carriage, Sebastian asked, "What tradition?"

Lydia waited until Sebastian entered the carriage and the door was closed before explaining, "Darcy's horse was named Cadmus, but when Georgianna was little, she called him Crumpet instead, and Kiernan upheld the tradition. Then when Artie came along, he shortened Crumpet to Crumb. Now Epona, another fine and formal name, has been shortened to Pony. It is only fitting that Clara gets her turn at gifting a horse a nickname."

Kiernan smiled as the once quiet little girl before him continued to pet the mare's mane while talking to her. Clara, who had hardly spoken three words in all the time he had known her, seemed to be so fond of horses that she had found her voice.

"You are such a pretty horse, Pony. You have very soft hair. Does Mr. Kiernan brush your hair for you? It doesn't have no tangles. My hair always tangles." On and on she went. Of course, not a single word she said was to Kiernan. It was all to his horse, or rather, Darcy's horse.

Kiernan was helping to train Epona for Darcy. She was highly intelligent, and he found that like Crumpet, she seemed to like children. He was using methods that he had learned about from the former colonel, Theodore, the Earl of Matlock. He was hopeful that eventually they would have a horse that was gentle around his mistress but proved to be highly protective of Elizabeth. If it worked, they would use the methods for training other ladies' steeds. He and Darcy had even come up with the plan to breed Epona to Crumpet. Kiernan thought any horses to come from the union would be noble steeds indeed.

Deciding to try to speak to Clara now that she was a bit more open, Kiernan said, "You know Clara, I think Epona likes you."

Looking up at him with wide eyes and a grin, Clara asked, "Really?"

"Yes. Really." Kiernan laughed, happy to see her excitement. Curious if she would be more open with him now that her barriers seemed to be down, he prodded, "What do you think of moving back home with your uncle and your new aunt?"

Frowning, Clara wrapped her little hands in the horse's ebony mane. At first Kiernan thought he had pushed too hard, but after a moment Clara said, "I like my new Aunt Lydia, but I do not like my home."

Kiernan understood that the girl's home estate of Swarkstone Park was mismanaged and grim. It seemed from the conversations he had gleaned information from that Clara had been quite neglected before she was brought to Pemberley by Selene and Sebastian. Though they had no way of knowing for sure, the condition they had found her in was highly suspect. He could understand why she might not like it.

Ruffling her curls, he reassured her. "I like your Aunt Lydia too, and you know what?"

Looking back up at him, she parroted, "What?"

Grinning at the girl, Kiernan said, "Lydia has plans to make your old home much nicer."

"Nicer?" Clara asked, her eyebrows drawn together. From her tone of voice and expression, Kiernan wondered if she did not think it was possible to make her old home nice.

"Yes, she was talking about painting and fixing things and, of course, hiring more nice people. You remember Nurse Harris, don't you? She is coming with you, too."

Shaking her head Clara exclaimed, "But 'keeper said, I did not get a nurse anymore, I was big enough to 'fend myself.'"

Though he could not be certain what that conversation had gone like, it was obvious that the housekeeper Lydia and Sebastian were replacing had been cruel to the poor girl. It took Kiernan a moment to be sure that he could keep his voice civil before he said, "One of the things your new Aunt Lydia is doing is hiring a new housekeeper. I have met Mrs. Wilson, and I can promise that she will be very nice to you and all the workers there, like Nurse Harris."

Kiernan watched as Clara began running her fingers through Epona's mane again before she asked, "There will be no more 'keeper?"

"No, that woman will be gone from the place." Explained Kiernan.

Nodding her little head, Clara leaned over and hugged Epona's neck, hiding her face in the horse's mane. Still, he could hear her say, "That is very good."

Kiernan could not help but agree with her. Deciding to see if he could get her to laugh, he asked, "Clara, would you like to go faster?"

Jerking up right, she said, "We can go faster?"

Kiernan laughed. "Yes, Epona is only walking right now. She can go much faster if you do not think it will scare you."

He watched as Clara seemed to consider his offer. Tilting his head so that he could see her face from where she sat in front of him, he watched her lips as they scrunched up. Then, after a moment, she nodded her head and said, "Faster!"

They never went faster than a trot, but by the time they reached Pemberley, Kiernan had her giggling like the little girl that she was. He was happy to have discovered how well she did with horses. Maybe working with them would help her. He decided to suggest that Sebastian get her a suitable pony to ride.

Dismounting, he held her steady until he could swing her down, and she giggled all the way. She quieted somewhat by the time he had her delivered to the nursery where all the other children were to have their own celebration, but the moment she saw Artie she ran up to him and said, "Artie, I rode Pony, and we went fast!"

Being that the boy was just as horse mad, he grinned, and said, "Did you ride Crumb? I love Crumb!"

Shaking her head, she tried to explain. "No, I rode Pony."

Stepping in before it became an argument between the two, Kiernan said, "We rode Epona, but Clara has decided to call her Pony." Soon after, the two children were talking about the horses that they liked, and Kiernan was sneaking out of the room to join the wedding breakfast downstairs.

SEBASTIAN COULD NOT HELP but laugh at Lydia's story as they journeyed back to Pemberley. He was surprised that Clara had not been afraid of the large mare. She was normally so timid but had seemed to be quite eager to meet the horse. Then again, he and his sisters had all been quite horse mad when they were younger. Maybe it was something that she had inherited.

Looking across the carriage at his bride, Sebastian wondered at it all. Not even a month ago, he had just been learning that his former brother-in-law was dead, and he had begun his desperate rush to get to Clara. Now he was married to a remarkable beauty who had put his and Clara's needs before her own.

Watching her look out the window and smile at the passing scenery, he wondered if she was memorizing it. It would probably be some time before they visited Pemberley. There were so many challenges before them in handling such a badly run estate like Swarkstone Park. At that moment, Sebastian promised himself that he would always treat her well and even if she did not fall in love with him, he would do his best to love her. Lydia was remarkable, and she deserved to be loved. He would do everything in his power to ensure that she never had any reason to regret her decision.

Sebastian did not know if it was something in his expression or just happenstance, but Lydia looked back at him and asked, "What has you looking at me so?"

Feeling rather embarrassed to be caught staring, Sebastian struggled to come up with a suitable response. Fighting the desire to tug at his fancily tied cravat, he murmured, "I am finding it quite remarkable how much has changed in such a short time. There is going to be much to do at Swarkstone. It is going to be hard work, but I believe the rewards will be significant. In addition to securing Clara's happiness and future, we will work towards improving the circumstances of many families and at this moment, I cannot imagine undertaking this task with anyone else by my side. I find that I am eagerly looking forward to our future together."

The sight of Lydia's widening eyes and blushing cheeks made Sebastian's heart thud in his chest, and a silly grin spread across his face. He was certainly looking forward to spending time with his new wife. Maybe eventually they would develop the sort of relationship he had always envied. The kind her sisters all seemed to have with their husbands.

It was a few moments be before Lydia responded. "I have a feeling that our future together will be bright. I agree with you that it will be hard work, but it will be worth the effort." Then, with a little purse of her lips, she said, "I find I am looking forward to working side by side with you."

The carriage ride to Pemberley was not that long, but it was certainly convivial and full of hope. When Sebastian helped Lydia down out of the carriage and went into Pemberley, he saw her smile matched his own. Moving into the dining room where a grand wedding breakfast had been prepared for them, he was happy to see so much food. Sebastian had not eaten much before the wedding and was happy to enjoy a delightful meal with his bride.

The room was soon full of happy, laughing people also finding seats at the table. The children were led to a separate room, where they were treated to a lavish feast of their own. There was not a quiet moment to be had, even with everyone eating. Everyone was jolly and more than once he was welcomed to the family by one person or another. Even Mrs. Hawkins and Mrs. Darcy were being welcoming and kind. He did not doubt for a second that if he stepped one foot out of line, they would rain down their wrath upon him, but Sebastian liked that they were so protective of Lydia.

Sebastian, who had never had this kind of experience in his own small family, was thrilled to be so welcomed. Looking down the table, he spotted Selene laughing happily with Georgianna and Kitty, as he had been told to call them. He was glad that Selene had been accepted into the heart of the family as well.

"We are a merry bunch," commented Lydia from beside him.

Finishing chewing the bite of the pastry he had taken, Sebastian swallowed and said, "Yes, nothing like my past family experience, but I like it."

Spearing a piece of asparagus with her fork, she laughed. "I am glad. I have every intention of having large family gatherings as often as possible. It would be awkward if you did not enjoy them."

Shifting in his chair so he could look her more fully in the eyes, Sebastian said, "I have always wished I had a larger family. My father was always stern and imposing and with only my two sisters growing up, we did not have many happy family dinners and none like this."

"Well, your wish for a larger family has been granted. In fact, given time, our family dinners will grow even larger. We Bennet ladies seem to be quite happy to expand our numbers." Lydia was looking at her sister Kitty as she spoke.

Sebastian did not know how to respond to Lydia's comment, so he shoveled something from his plate into his mouth and chewed it mechanically. Was she implying that she would be happy to increase the numbers as well? Her returning blush might imply she did. He found himself wondering how long it was going to take until the nursery would be complete to Lydia's standards.

Chapter Sixteen

Sebastian gazed across the carriage at Clara and Lydia and frowned in concern. While the first day of travel had been short and passed with a certain amount of gaiety, this second day of travel was decidedly worse than the day before it. First thing in the morning, when he had gone down to settle his accounts with the innkeeper, the man had responded oddly. The innkeeper had seemed surprised by his thoughtfulness and had gone so far as to say that he should have known better than to trust the rumors. This had led to a discussion about the fact that there were rumors circulating about his and Lydia's reputation for being tight-fisted and hard to satisfy.

Even as he helped Lydia and Clara into the carriage, he worried about who would be spreading such rumors. He knew he had no way of discovering their source at that moment and tried, but failed, to think of more pleasant things. It did not help that he was beset by crying. For some reason he could not fathom, Clara had taken to fretfully crying and clinging to Lydia almost from the moment she had become fully awake.

It was not the day he had hoped for. He had hoped that he might be able to find a moment to talk more with Lydia. The time that they had spent together the night before had been quite enjoyable, and he was keen to repeat the experience. It seemed he was not about to have his wish, not with his new wife's attention so focused on Clara. Lydia had her arms full of the child at the moment, rubbing her back soothingly and humming to her. While she seemed happy enough to care for Clara, he saw lines of fatigue developing around her eyes.

He had tried to develop a relationship with Clara thus far, but she had almost seemed hesitant around him. Sebastian hoped that one day they would grow to be very close, and he knew it would take effort on his part to bridge the gap between them. Deciding to try again, he said, "Clara, would you like to come over her and sit with me? I can see a paddock with horses in it from this angle. Would you like to see?"

Clara picked her head up from where it had been cradled against Lydia's shoulder. She looked at him through puffy eyes, swollen from her long bout of tears. For a moment, she only gazed at him, as if weighing her options. Then she nodded and held her arms out for him to take her. Reaching out his long arms, he scooped her up from Lydia's lap and settled her in to his own. Sebastian did not miss the look of gratitude that crossed Lydia's face as she rubbed at the back of her neck.

Leaning so that Clara could see out the window, he pointed to the horses as they frolicked in the pasture. For the first time that day, Clara managed a small smile as she watched the horses play. It was not to last, however. They were traveling and eventually the horses passed beyond their sight. At least Clara did not demand to go back to Lydia or Nurse Harris. Though she slumped into him and hid her face in his waistcoat. Knowing that he was pressing his luck, Sebastian said, "I hate to see you so sad, Clara. Can you tell me why you are so sad?"

Clara peeked up at him through her lashes for a while before she whispered, "I do not want to go back to that place."

Happy to have stumbled onto the problem and that she had been willing to confide in him, he whispered back, "Do you mean Swarkstone Park? Or somewhere else?"

Lip trembling, Clara answered, "I do not want to go to that room again."

Sebastian was careful not to let his anger to leak out on to his face. Of course, he was not angry at his precious little niece, but at his former brother-in-law and the staff who had allowed her to whittle away her time in that horrid, dreary room. Wanting to reassure her, Sebastian said, "Can I tell you a secret?" Eyes widening in her pale face, Clara nodded. Happy that he had her attention, he continued, "I would not want to go to that room either. It is not at all like the nursery that Artie had, was it?"

Clara shook her head solemnly, adding, "Artie had toys and chairs and warm blankets. My room does not. It is sad, and I am scared and cold at night."

He had to look away from the pain in Clara's eyes for a moment, or else he knew that his fury would betray him and frighten her. It did not help that he met Lydia's enraged gaze from across the carriage. Letting a slow breath out through his nose, he managed to say, "I think that you deserve to have a better room, a room more like what Artie has. With warm blankets and pillows and rocking chairs and toys with walls full of pretty colors, and that is what you are going to get." They may have many things that they needed to see to on the estate and in the home, but he would make sure that his niece would have the sort of room she deserved.

From across the carriage, Lydia said, "Clara, do you remember when we talked about your favorite color?"

Clara nodded and said, "I like purple."

Lydia smiled at her and responded, "I know, and that is why before we left Pemberley, I arranged for people to bring paint and all sorts of things to Swarkstone Park so that we can paint your room and make it pretty. It will take time for it to be ready, but until it is beautiful and full of nice things like Artie's room, you will not have to be in that room." Clara beamed at Lydia's explanation and Lydia smiled back, then continuing, she said, "Even once your room is ready, you will never have to be in your room alone. You will have Nurse Harris with you, and she will stay the night in the little room next to yours. If you have need of her, she will be there for you."

For some reason, this seemed to upset Clara all over again and so Sebastian asked, "What is wrong, my dear? I thought you would be happy."

Looking up at Sebastian, she exclaimed, with more vigor than he had yet to see her demonstrate, "But that room is bad too." Looking across the carriage at Nurse Harris, she said, "Do not worry, Nurse Harris, you can stay with me if you want."

Startled, the kind woman's eyes widened slightly before she smiled and said, "That is very kind of you Miss Clara, but you do not have to worry. Your aunt has said that I can have my room fix too."

Clara nodded and then asked, "Do you get your favorite color, too?"

After that, the day improved. They were able to regain some cheerfulness despite the constant rocking of the carriage and ruts in the road. Clara fell asleep in his arms, and he realized just how much he enjoyed the feeling of holding a sleeping child.

THEY ARRIVED AT SWARKSTONE Park after dark and, like the time before, there was no one there to greet them. Sighing, Lydia waited with Clara sleeping in her arms as Davies, Sebastian's valet, tried the door. Knocking on the door yielded no response, leaving her feeling perturbed. Not that she expected anything else.

Once again, finding the door unlocked, their group made their way to the entryway. Lydia was tired and sore from the long day of travel and ready for a meal and bed, but doubted either would be forthcoming. Making her way into one of the dusty parlors with a moue of distaste, Lydia nevertheless sat down in an armchair with gratitude. Sebastian had tried to take Clara from her, to ease her burden, but the child had protested, and Lydia had said it was fine. While it was fine, her back and arms ached from the weight of holding her.

Shaking her head, Mrs. Wilson bustled over. Huffing in exasperation, she said, "And here I thought you must have been exaggerating. Pardon my saying so, ma'am, but the people here must be fools not to have prepared a welcome for you. If you will excuse me, I will find my way to the kitchens and see if I can scare up a meal for everyone."

Nodding, Lydia said, "Thank you, Mrs. Wilson. I must admit that I am becoming peckish."

Lydia had barely watched her go before Oakley said, "While she does that, I am going to investigate whether they bothered to make up your bed or Mr. Burgess' bed. After the day you have had, you deserve a good night's sleep." Lydia watched Oakley leave, her steps sharp.

No one was happy about the state of things at Swarkstone, but as tired as she was, Lydia felt there was no use complaining about it at the moment. She would whip things into shape tomorrow after she had a good night's sleep and possibly a good meal. Though she had doubts about the meal. She hoped that she would not need to get a new cook as well. There was so much to do.

Laying her head back against the back of the chair, Lydia watched through slitted eyes while Sebastian talked in hushed tones with his valet and several other servants that had accompanied them to Swarkstone. She wondered how he was directing them, but really could not find the energy to care. Closing her eyes, she rested, allowing the world around her to exist in a low hum she ignored in favor of lethargy. Lydia did not think that she had nodded off, but it was hard to know for certain because the next thing she noticed was Sebastian kneeling in front of her, his eyes full of concern. She smiled at him but found little energy to comfort him otherwise.

When Sebastian cupped her cheek and rubbed the arch of her cheekbone with his thumb, Lydia felt her lethargy being eaten away by the fire that seem to flood her veins. She had a hard time focusing on his words when he said, "Lydia, dear, I think that this day has done you in. Are you well?"

Sighing, she said, "I am perfectly fine, merely worn out. I will be back to my normal self after a good night's sleep and some food."

With Sebastian so close to her face, Lydia found herself focusing on his eyes. They were blue like her own, but now, looking closer, she realized that they were a different sort of blue. Her eyes had often been referred to as cornflower blue. Now that she was looking so closely, she realized that Sebastian's eyes were a deeper sort of blue, indigo to her cornflower. There was also a ring around his iris of dark navy. In her hazy state, she felt as if she could stare at his eyes indefinitely.

It took her a moment for her to realize that Sebastian had said something. Focusing with difficulty she caught, "… has left along with several other staff and possibly some artwork that is not hers, but frankly we are good to be rid of Mrs. Netter. I told Mrs. Wilson that we will be happy with something simple on a tray in our rooms." Standing, he held his arms out and leaned over. "If you hand me Clara, I will carry her upstairs."

Lydia released the automatic hold she had on the dead weight of sleeping Clara, hoping the child would not wake during the transfer. Gladly, the child stayed asleep. Holding Clara to his shoulder with one arm, he offered his other hand to Lydia to help her get to her feet. Lydia felt quite pampered as Sebastian guided her up the stairs with his arm around her shoulders.

She thought idly that they should have some conversation but could not come up with anything they might speak of. They progressed up the stairs and to the Mistress suite where she and Clara would stay at least for the night. Lydia only had a moment's hesitation at the thought of having a man in her bedroom. The thought of having a man in her bedroom would have once been scandalous, but now she simply shrugged it off. She was too tired to be concerned, and he was her husband, after all.

As he laid Clara on the bed, he turned to her and asked, "Can we leave her in her dress, or should we change her into something else?"

Smiling at such thoughtful consideration, Lydia said, "She will probably sleep better if we can get her in a night rail." Looking about the room, she spotted Clara's valise that Oakley must have brought up with her own. Opening it and pulling out what she was looking for, Lydia looked back at Sebastian and said, "I can change her and tuck her in."

Leaning over, he helped to sit Clara's pliant form up. "I can help."

It was simple work to get Clara out of her day clothes and into her night rail with Sebastian to help hold the child so she could work the buttons. Lydia knew she would marvel at how well they worked together to care for Clara at a later time, but for the moment, she was merely happy they had her settled with so little issue. After they settled Clara under the blankets, they stood together, looking down at her. Clara was what had brought them together, and if Lydia's intuition was correct, she was already drawing them closer.

Settling into a chair before the cold fireplace, Lydia sighed. It had been an exceptionally long day. Not only had she married Sebastian and had a wedding breakfast, but she had said goodbye to all of her family and traveled for eight hours on the way to her new home. She had woken a little after putting Clara to bed and now just wanted to take in some nourishment before she went to sleep herself.

When a soft knock came at the door to the sitting room they had reserved, Lydia sat up and called for whoever it was to enter. Sebastian peeked his head around the door and said, "I wanted to check in with you and make sure you were well for the night."

Smiling at his consideration, Lydia gestured him in. "Come and sit with me. They just delivered some tea and simple food. Would you like some?"

Coming to sit next to her, he said, "Yes, I would love a cup. It has been a long and eventful day."

Lydia was careful to pour him a cup and add just the right amount of cream and sugar. She had, after all, been paying attention to him so that she might find out such things about him. With a warm smile, she presented Sebastian with his tea, as well as a plate of buttered bread with a chunk of cheese. She said, "I am hoping that Clara will be so exhausted that she will sleep soundly throughout the night."

Though Lydia found herself eager to talk with her husband, she was more than aware of the unusual nature of their wedding night. There would be time enough to face that aspect of their marriage. For now, she was happy to adjust to all the changes going on and come to know Sebastian better.

Taking a sip of his tea, Sebastian smiled. "You got it just right."

Wrinkling her nose in pleasure, Lydia blushed at his approval. "I am your wife. After all, it would be bad if I could not even prepare a cup of tea according to your preference. How else will you know when I am angry with you, if you do not know that I know how to make you tea correctly? Now, if I serve it to you incorrectly, you will know there is a reason for it."

Her joke had been poorly timed because shortly before she spoke, he had taken another sip and nearly spit it out all over the sitting room. After a fit of coughing, he rasped, "I will be sure to remain on the lookout for your poorly crafted cup of tea, for I am sure to make many mistakes."

Handing him a serviette to wipe at his mouth, Lydia said, "Given that I am certain to commit my own fair share of mistakes, I kindly ask for the chance to extend forgiveness to one another."

With a grateful smile, Sebastian reached up to wipe his face clean. Then he turned to Lydia, and when their eyes met, something about it sent a shiver racing down her spine. Sebastian shared the connection with her for a moment before saying, "Then let us agree to forgive each other's mistakes, both honest and inevitable." Discovering the sudden need to take a sip of tea, Lydia could only nod her head in response to his lovely statement.

They sat for a moment, munching on the simple meal and sipping their tea in silence. All the while, Lydia wondered at how fast she was falling under his spell. He proved himself to be so considerate and respectful that Lydia found it hard not to be moved. Not that she wanted to resist it, only his potent gaze caught her off guard with its effect. In addition, there were countless moments when he graciously helped her in and out of the carriage, his touch at the small of her back or his arm extended for her to hold on to in a chivalrous manner. Was it only that they were married? Or did it mean more?

WAKING UP THAT MORNING had been difficult for Sebastian, but he had known that the lawyer, Mr. Coulson, would arrive sometime that morning. He arrived shortly after Sebastian and Lydia had enjoyed a pleasant breakfast together. Ever the professional, Mr. Coulson quickly had them settled in the study and going over matters.

"Everything looks in order," affirmed Mr. Coulson. Handing back the marriage papers to Lydia, he began to stack the papers that he had brought to be signed up. Looking up at Sebastian, he said, "I have set things so that you can have access to the funds I previously mentioned. I believe you will need the funds in order to make the needed improvements around the estate. In looking back over records of this estate, it appears that at one time it brought in nearly five thousand a year. Right now, it only brings in three thousand, but I am confident, Mr. Burgess, that you are the sort to turn things around."

Sebastian nodded his head in response to Mr. Coulson's comment. He would certainly work hard at it. An Estate the size of Swarkstone Park had no business bringing in so little profit. He was glad that they could finally make the needed repairs to the tenants' cottages with the money they now had access to. Shifting in his seat, Sebastian asked, "What happens to the profits from the estate every year?"

Putting his papers into a folder, Mr. Coulson said, "You keep the profits to use as you see fit. Though I would hope that you put at least some of it back into the property in improvements and such."

"But wouldn't the money go to Clara somehow?" Asked Lydia from where she sat beside him.

Smiling at Lydia, Mr. Coulson answered, "It is set up similar to how you would lease an estate. As you must know, someone who leases an estate gets whatever profits that come in after harvest. Though you are not paying rent, you will be caring for Miss Clara and providing for her by getting her a nursemaid and remodeling the nursery. You are also going to be putting forth a tremendous amount of effort to bring the estate back to what it should be. Having put in so much effort, you deserve to enjoy the fruits of your labor."

Nodding, Lydia said, "I suppose that makes a certain amount of sense. Do you need me for anything else?"

Shaking his head, Mr. Coulson responded, "No, we are done with everything."

Rising from her chair, Lydia nodded and said, "Then I will return to helping Mrs. Wilson oversee things. As you might have noticed, we are quite short of staff and those previously in charge let many things go far too long for my tastes. I am determined to have the house cleaned from top to bottom before we do anything else. Would you like to stay the night, Mr. Coulson? I am sure we could prepare a room for you."

Standing, Mr. Coulson said, "Thank you for offering, but I am eager to get back home. It is early enough for me to travel a good distance before I have to stop for the night."

Lydia dropped into a curtsy. "Then I will bid you goodbye, Mr. Coulson." Before she left the room, she smiled prettily at Sebastian.

Walking with Mr. Coulson towards the stables, Sebastian said, "Thank you for coming out here to help us get things in proper order. Having to make our way to London to meet with you would have made things much more complicated."

Waving him off, Mr. Coulson said, "I am used to a certain amount of travel with my role as solicitor." Pausing as they reached his horse and asked the stable hand to saddle him, Mr. Coulson said, "I must commend you on your choice of bride. Not only is Mrs. Burgess beautiful, but it is obvious that she already cares for Miss Clara. I could see how much affection she has for the girl when she brought her down to meet with me."

Glancing back in the direction they had come from, Sebastian smiled. Returning his gaze to Mr. Coulson, Sebastian said, "Mrs.

Burgess is always considerate of those she meets and already looks at Clara as her daughter. She has a deep understanding of how to run a home and an estate effectively. I couldn't be happier about this new chapter in my life."

Nodding, he smiled at Sebastian, responding, "Then I am glad for you. Though I cannot help but wonder at where you found such a paragon of virtues."

Leaning against a stall door, Sebastian thought about meeting Lydia. "Mrs. Burgess is the youngest sister of Mrs. Darcy and Lady Matlock. She was at Pemberley when we went there for aid. As soon as she knew I needed to marry in order to care for Clara, she volunteered."

Whistling, Mr. Coulson said, "Then you are now connected to two powerful families, but somehow I doubt that was something that influenced you."

Shaking his head, Sebastian said, "I never gave it a thought."

Taking the reins of his horse, Mr. Coulson led him out and swung himself up into the saddle, but before he left, he said, "Good for you. I will leave you with one further piece of advice. Do not get so lost in worry over the estate that you overlook enjoying time with your new bride."

Watching him go, Sebastian pondered his advice. Mr. Coulson was right. Even with a mountain of tasks ahead, he understood the importance of bonding with Lydia. However, he doubted it would be a problem with the way she drew him to her.

Chapter Seventeen

IT HAD BEEN A hard morning. While Mrs. Wilson was confronting the issues they had discovered in the kitchen, Lydia was training some of the maids on how she wanted them to clean a room. Some of them had worked too long under the old housekeeper and were resistant to having to take up a more thorough manner of cleaning, but Lydia would not accept *good enough* in her home.

"Mrs. Burgess, we will never get everything done if you expect us to clean this way," complained Suzanna, one of the older housemaids. Grumbling, she continued, "I knows you are a new bride wanting to impress people, but I still say the old way is good enough."

Lydia took a deep breath and counted to ten before releasing it through pursed lips. The youngest maid, May, looked at the older two maids with wide eyes. The woman who had spoken up, Suzanna and her friend Lilly, were giving each other knowing looks. As if they felt they need to train her on what to expect. It was very possible that she would have to let them go, but she wanted to give them the opportunity to learn to do better.

Poor Ann was the fourth of the group and seemed to be only slightly younger than herself. She had barely said a word the whole morning. It seemed as if she and May would be her hardest workers. Speaking only once she knew she could keep her frustration out of her voice, Lydia said, "I can assure you that once you clean a room properly, it is much easier to keep it looking nice. That starts with getting all the grime gone, and yes, even in the corners and behind the furniture."

It was easy to see the mulish looks on the older two maids' faces were not going away. It was equally easy to realize that the younger ones would not speak up and would hesitate to act due to the others' apparent seniority. So she said, "Is this room good enough for when my sister the countess comes to visit?"

Huffing, Lilly said, "Of course, should such an important figure come to visit, we would be sure to make everything presentable."

Hands on her hips, Lydia countered, "Why would my sister deserve better treatment than the people of this household?" If she wasn't so understaffed, she would have dismissed the two immediately for such insubordination, but she was trying to be understanding. The training they had received from Mrs. Netter was obvious in the way they spoke. She wanted to give them the opportunity to learn to do better.

Shaking her head, Suzanna spoke up this time, "Swarkstone is not Chatsworth or Pemberley. It is not grand, and Mrs. Netter always said that we should not pretend that it is more than it is."

Forcing herself to keep her arms regally at her sides and not crossed in frustration, she asked, "And what about being able to be proud of your work? What about wanting your home to be seen in the best light?"

Suzanna shook her head, a frown on her face. "This is not our home."

Lilly snorted and added, "It is not as if any of us will be enjoying these grand rooms."

Lydia watched the reactions of the other two girls and found that at least she had two supporters. Ann was frowning at the pair of rebellious maids, while May's reaction made her struggle not to laugh. With her mouth agape in shock, young May retreated from the other maid, as if anticipating a divine punishment.

Sighing, Lydia straightened her spine and stood tall, staring down at the two troublemakers. Deciding to stop mollycoddling them, she said, "By all means, speak freely. It is not as if I decide whether or not you will stay employed here." That had the two women looking at each other, eyes wide with concern. "As of this moment, you are both only here on a trial basis. If by the end of the month you have not improved both in attitude and ability to follow my or Mrs. Wilson's instruction, you will be let go. Perhaps you will be able to find an employer willing to accept *good enough*."

It was during that confrontation that the boy she had stationed at the front door in case of visitors came rushing in, out of breath. He cried, "Missus, there is an older gentleman here demanding to be seen. The toff is not at all happy. He gave me this card."

The card read Augustus Burgess, Viscount Trowbridge. Sebastian's father had come calling. Running her hand over her hair, she pulled the kerchief off her head and hoped that she looked at least remotely presentable. Shaking out her skirts, she looked at the maids and said, "Viscount Trowbridge is here to visit my husband. Ann and May, please go to the best guest room and prepare it for his lordship's stay. You know what I need you to do." Both girls gave little curtsies and scurried out of the room. Turning to Suzanna and Lilly, she said, "Go to the small dining room and work on it until it shines. If I spot one speck of dust or grime when we have dinner this evening, you will not last until the end of the month."

Lilly nodded and turned to go, but Suzanna got a mulish look on her face and said, "But you don't have enough maids as it is. You can lose two good works without the house falling down around you."

"I would not test my fortitude." Glaring at the woman she was already tired of working with, Lydia said, "Now go!" As the woman departed, Lydia's words were barely audible, a quiet murmur to herself. "While I go meet my father-in-law."

"I ASKED TO SEE my son, not the housekeeper," Augustus exclaimed angrily, looking down at the woman before him. She was younger than any housekeeper had a right to be with blonde hair and blue eyes. Had his son foolishly hired her for her looks? Her dress was mussed with grime, and he assumed that he had pulled her away from some onerous chore.

"Yes, My Lord, I know, but he is seeing to estate business. I have had him summoned." Huffing and rolling his eyes, Augustus was uncertain he could handle much more stupidity from his son. Sebastian was the son of a viscount. He did not need to be out in the field seeing to things himself. He was supposed to have people to see to things for him. Unaware of his line of thought, the woman kept speaking. "I am having a room prepared for you as we speak."

Shaking his head, he put his hands on his hips, ready to scold the obviously incompetent housekeeper. "Very shoddy, not having a room for guests ready. Do you know nothing of running a proper household?"

The woman blinked once before saying, "If I did not know how to run a household, I would not have had two maids go to our best room to prepare it for our unexpected guest. Who arrived, I may add, three days after we arrived ourselves? I may not know much, but I do know that it is common curtesy to allow a family time to settle into a new home before invading." Smiling boldly, she added, "If I did not know how to run a household, you would have been tuned away until I had the chance to confer with my husband."

Sneering at the woman before him, Augustus said, "And just who is your husband that you would talk to him regarding a guest as important as myself?" He had expected her to cower or simper at his scold, but she surprised him by maintaining her composure.

She stood tall, resolute in her bearing. Just who was this woman that she did not show him the proper deference? Her attitude, or lack thereof, did not match the expectations of a servant, especially one in a higher position. But what could he expect? His son had never taken his lessons to heart. He would have to explain to the boy that she had to be let go.

"It would be more productive to assist you in getting settled rather than talking about my husband." Gesturing for him to follow her, she walked to a nearby parlor and stood at the doorway. Driven by habit and the longing for respite after endless days on the road, he continued forward ungraciously, yearning to find a place to sit down without the movement of a carriage. As he entered the room, he heard her say, "I am sure you would like to sit down after your long journey. Make yourself comfortable. Dinner is to be served in two hours, but if you are hungry now, I can have a little something brought to you. Your room should be ready in short order. Once you make yourself comfortable here, I will check on it myself."

Collapsing on a nearby chair, Augustus allowed himself a moment to enjoy the comfort before turning and glaring at the impudent woman. "I only desire to see my son."

"I am sure he will come and find you as soon as he is able. I will send a maid to escort you to your room when it is ready." Her dress may have been dirty, and she may have been a mere servant, but her curtsy was executed with exquisite elegance. Who was this woman that she could not give him the respect that he deserved but knew exactly the type of curtsy to give a visiting viscount?

SEBASTIAN RUSHED TO THE house after helping fix the roof of the Clarke's cottage. He knew that his father might cause problems, but he had expected his wrath in the form of a sternly worded letter. He had never imagined that his father would travel all the way from Northumberland. Viscount Trowbridge hated traveling, and it had to have been at least a week's journey by carriage. His father would be in a very foul mood indeed.

Making it to the house, Sebastian considered changing before he went to speak with his father but decided that the added delay would only make him angrier. Walking through the house, he did not run into any staff who might know where his father was. With the state of the guest rooms, he knew that his father unexpectedly showing up meant he could not be shown to a room to change or rest. So he searched for his father in the nicer rooms near the front entrance.

He found him in the second room he checked, though on spotting him, he felt like turning around and leaving him there. Just from viewing his posture, it was obvious that he was furious. Straightening his shoulders, he walked into the room and said, "Hello, Father. What an unexpected visit."

This had his father vaulting from his chair and turning to confront him. Striding towards Sebastian, he chided, "Really, Sebastian, were you out working in the fields? I wrote to tell you to leave this place be. But no, the next thing I know, I get another letter saying you are following through with your foolish plan to marry some unknown girl in order to take up the care of your sister's child. I hurry to Pemberley, only to learn that the marriage has taken place, and you have come here of all places. This is utter madness!"

Sebastian watched as his father gasped for breath after his tirade. He had not seen him since he was twenty-one and they had had a great row over his father trying to force Selene to marry a titled cad. It appeared as if the intervening year had not been kind to his father. He seemed to have aged a decade instead of only a couple of years, and with the shade of red his father was turning, Sebastian was starting to fear for his father's health.

Regardless of his fears for his father, Sebastian knew that he could not in good conscience back down, not when there was so much resting on standing firm. Taking a breath, Sebastian tried to let go of his frustration before saying, "As I am now married and have become Clara's guardian, it is only fitting that I am here caring for her estate. I am sorry you went out of your way to try to stop it. You are more than welcome to stay here for a time to rest and recover from such an arduous journey."

This did not seem to appease his father at all. With his breath somewhat back, he shouted, "You do not need to be caring for an estate that is not yours. You will get Trowbridge when I pass as well as our satellite estates in Scotland. Besides, I am certain someone else could see to your sister's offspring. She is only a girl, after all, and will not even be a credit to our name. You know how much I disapprove of throwing good after the bad. This estate is obviously run-down, and the staff are apparently incapable of showing the appropriate deference."

Sebastian wondered who it was that had greeted his father. He would have to find out and apologize. His father was never capable of remaining civil after a long journey, not that it was any excuse for bad behavior. It did not help that it was obvious that his father had been looking to chastise him and would have been upset at the delay.

The maid walking into the room saved him from further argument. Turning to the girl, he struggled to remember her name for a moment before saying, "Yes, Ann?"

Ann smiled at him briefly and bobbed a curtsy. "Mrs. Burgess sent me to escort the viscount to his room now that it is ready."

"Thank you, Ann," said Sebastian. Turning back to his father, he said, "I am sorry for the delay, but now that your room is ready, why don't you take some time to relax and recover from your journey?

I can send someone to escort you to dinner. We can discuss matters afterwards."

Though his father's glare never wavered, his voice did remain civil as he said, "Very well. I will see you at dinner. I will meet the girl you married at that time." Turning with a disgruntled air, he followed the timid maid.

Sighing, Sebastian ran his hand through his hair. At least his father did not approve of airing family issues in front of staff, otherwise he would have continued on with his castigation. Looking down at his dirty clothes, Sebastian decided that a bath and a change of clothes were in order before he had to face his father again. Hopefully, there would not be an issue with getting hot water. With the state of the kitchen, he did not know.

Lydia watched in the mirror as Oakley worked to put her hair in some semblance of order and refinement. Her dress was not her best, but was much nicer than she would normally wear at a family dinner. Despite her poor beginning, she did want to impress her father-in-law. She had not intended to have their first meeting go so poorly and part of her wanted to make up for it. The other part of her wanted to rub her elegance and beauty in his face.

She knew she had not handled meeting her father-in-law for the first time the best, but the man's attitude had rubbed her the wrong way. She could forgive him for mistaking her for the housekeeper. After all, she was dirty from crawling around on floors and dusting mantelpieces. What she could not forgive, at least at the moment, was how condescending he was. Had she been the housekeeper and not the mistress of the house, his attitude would still be unacceptable.

Despite the prevailing belief that it was acceptable to treat others condescendingly, Lydia firmly rejected this viewpoint. Somehow, she would have to make the viscount see he could not behave in such a manner in her home. Of course, she did not want to upset Sebastian by angering his father, but there had to be a way to get her point across while being civil.

After she had put the last touches to his room, she had sent Ann down to collect him and check on the dining room. She only hoped he was civil to the maid. Mrs. Wilson was already informed about his arrival, and she was helping the cook to turn their simple dinner into something that would suit the viscount. She would have enough time to say hello to Clara before going down to dinner. Maybe spending some time with Clara would cool her ire.

The little playroom that Clara spent most of her time in now was in the same hall as the master and mistress suite. So as soon as Oakley was finished making her look presentable, Lydia walked a few doors down to check in on Clara. Peeking in the room, Lydia spotted the girl in her nursemaid's lap being rocked as she was read to. It was reassuring to see that Clara was becoming so comfortable with Nurse Harris.

Making her way into the room, she asked, "What story are you reading?"

Clara looked up from gazing at the pages that Lydia knew she could not read and smiled. She glanced at her nurse before refocusing on Lydia and whispered, "A tale about a girl in red and a wolf."

Lydia was so happy that she wanted to dance. It had been a struggle to get Clara to say much at all, but it was becoming easier with every day. Not wanting to startle Clara, Lydia only smiled and said, "That sounds very interesting. I would stay and listen myself, but I must go down and have dinner with your uncle. Would you mind doing me a favor, Clara?"

Eyes wide, Clara nodded, sending her curls bouncing. She whispered, "Yes."

Leaning down so that she was closer to Clara, she asked, "Will you pay careful attention so that you can tell me the story in the morning? I would love to hear what happens on an adventure that involves a wolf." Lydia met the nurse's eyes and was happy to see the way they crinkled.

Nodding her head again, Clara said, "I will pay attention and tell you in the morning."

"Wonderful. Now I have to go down to dinner. How do you think I look?" Turning in a circle, Lydia showed off her dress to the pair.

"Beautiful." Clara's comment was slightly more than a whisper this time.

Kissing Clara on the cheek, Lydia said, "Thank you for the compliment, my dear. Let's hope that your uncle agrees with you." Lydia mouthed thank you to nurse Harris before leaving the room and walking down to find her husband and father-in-law.

She was there in no time at all. Holding her head high, Lydia entered the parlor where she knew Sebastian and her father-in-law were waiting for dinner to be announced. As she walked in, she observed the pair for a moment before they realized she was in the room. The viscount was stalking about the room like a caged beast and though he did not speak, his glare said a lot about his displeasure. Turning her gaze to her husband, Lydia did not like the slump of Sebastian's shoulders. It seemed that his father had not been kind. That just would not do. Placing a practiced smile on her face, Lydia said, "I hope you have not been waiting for me."

Without hesitation, Sebastian hurried to her side and firmly held her hand in his own. She was unsure whether he did it out of concern for her needing support or out of his own need for it. Kissing her on the cheek, he said, "You are just in time."

The viscount, on the other hand, shouted, "You!"

Chapter Eighteen

Eyes narrowing, Sebastian glared at his father, shocked at his rudeness. "I would have you address my wife with respect, sir."

His father looked at him and then back at Lydia. His eyebrows raised and his color once again turning florid, his father thundered, "I thought she was the housekeeper! Just who is this woman? I will admit that she cleans up well, but did you know she was traipsing about with the look of a washerwoman?"

Sebastian immediately looked at Lydia, aghast at his father's horrible comments. Had Lydia been the one who had greeted his father? He had not known and now worried how very horrible he had been to her, especially if he thought her the housekeeper. Drawing her instinctively into his side, he hoped to shield her from some of his father's ire. Looking down at her, he pleaded, "I apologize for my father's inappropriate comments. I did not know that you were the one who greeted him. He is often put out after traveling, and not finding me available could not have helped."

Smiling up at him, she responded, "You are not your father, my dear. Only your father must answer for his behavior. How was he to know that his unexpected arrival interrupted my training the maids? He might have known who he was talking to had he stopped complaining long enough to allow me to introduce myself, but now he knows." Looking across the room at his father, she continued, "Would you prefer I address you as viscount? Or do you prefer something else? You do not strike me as the sort to be overly sentimental, so I will not call you father unless you ask me to."

Head tilted back and his body shifting away from Lydia, it delighted Sebastian to note that his father did not quite know what to make of his bold wife. It took his father a moment to compose himself enough to come up with a response. "Viscount, would be the most appropriate."

It seemed that his father was about to say more when Mrs. Wilson entered the room and announced, "Dinner is served."

They all moved into the small dining room together, Lydia on his arm, and Sebastian was happy to note that the place settings had been arranged informally. He had no desire to speak to his wife across the length of the table or be stuck only speaking with his father. His father, however, was not done complaining, "What sort of table setting is this?"

Lydia seated herself as Sebastian pulled out her chair for her. She was quick to respond to the viscount. "I had the staff set the table informally. We are, after all, family. There is no need to shout down the table to speak with one another when we can all be seated closer together."

Sebastian was delighted to realize that his father seemed to respond to Lydia's statement by sitting down. He frowned but said no more. Was it that he could not fault her logic? Taking his own seat, Sebastian observed the pair.

As they were being served, Lydia asked, "Is your room to your liking? Please let us know if there is anything lacking."

His father watched Lydia with narrowed eyes before nodding minutely. "The room is adequate, though I must admit that I appreciate the beauty of the flowers you have on display in my room."

Lydia smiled broadly, accepting the compliment with grace. "Thank you. I have a fondness for flower arranging."

"You have a deft hand with the art. It will reflect well on my son," acknowledged the Viscount.

Giving a dainty shrug, Lydia responded, "What can I say? It is as if they speak to me." Lydia looked at Sebastian as she spoke, her eyes twinkling with mirth and Sebastian nearly spit out the sip of claret that he had just taken. Heaven only knew what the flowers in his father's room said. Thank goodness his father was too stuffy to consider pursuing something like the language of flowers.

Sebastian went about consuming his meal, though he could not have said what they had if anyone had asked. He was too preoccupied with his father's presence and Lydia's reassuring smiles. She seemed to handle his father much better than Selene ever had, but he supposed that there was something different in dealing with your own parent versus someone wholly unconnected to you.

The table was quiet for a time, but eventually Lydia started a conversation by asking, "So, Viscount, how has the growing season been in Northumberland this year? I heard talk of heavy rains up north, causing flooding. Was that anywhere near your estate?"

Swallowing his most recent spoonful of soup carefully, he paused before saying, "Thankfully the heavy rains have not caused any flooding in my fields, though one or two neighboring estates have had issues."

Lydia took a delicate sip of her own soup before replying, "That is good. Too much rain early in the season is better than closer to harvest, but still it can harm the overall yield."

Eyebrows narrowing, his father said, "True."

Tuning to him, Lydia asked, "How did fixing the roof for the Clarke's cottage go?" In such a manner, Lydia kept the conversation at the table, going for the rest of the meal. As every course progressed. His father looked more and more confused.

When the meal had finally ended, Lydia stood from the table. "I am sure that you gentlemen need to talk with one another. I will be in my sitting room should you have need of me."

After she left, Sebastian looked at his father and waited for him to speak. He knew it was only a matter of time before he said something. The question was, what would it be? Somehow Sebastian thought that it was going to be what his father had originally come to say.

Augustus looked at his son as he sat at the head of the table realizing just how mature his son had grown. He had been ready to condemn him for his choice to marry a girl who was not born of the nobility; she was not even the daughter of a mere baron. Her father was a nobody, and yet... And yet she was not what he expected.

The woman knew about crop issues and could carry on conversation on a number of topics in a very refined manner. She was also of a strong character. Never once had she winced or cowered as he looked to find fault. That said, nothing of her beauty, which was notable. Somehow, she reminded him of his wife, despite her blonde hair. It was disconcerting.

He began, "I came here to tell you how disappointed I was in you." Watching his son's reaction, Augustus saw that Sebastian was not surprised that he had come to insult him. That, in fact, his son expected it. Deciding to go forward and not focus on the state of his relationship, he said, "However, choosing that woman to be your wife may not have been the worst decision."

"No, I already think that agreeing to marry her is about the best decision I have ever made."

"Wait, you agreed to marry her? Was she the one to ask you?"

Smiling, his son said, "She knew that I was determined to find a bride within the thirty-day allotment and saw how much of a struggle it would be. I think she was already half attached to Clara and wanted to be her mother figure. Lydia volunteered herself as my bride so that I could focus on bringing Swarkstone up to snuff."

Voice faint, Augustus said, "She reminds me of your mother." Gaze becoming unfocused, he remembered some of the early days of his arranged marriage. His young wife had not been at all what he expected. She had been energetic and constantly overseeing something. He had learned to enjoy her good-natured impertinence and good will to even the servants. His own father had been in charge at the time, and it had made for a few uncomfortable dinners, but when he had lost her at the birth of his heir, his life had shifted back to what it had been before she had brought so much light into his world. She had been a lovely aberration that could not last. Somehow, he had forgotten that light until recognizing it in his daughter-in-law.

"You never spoke of my mother. I have always wondered what she was like." Sebastian spoke up, his voice conveying shock.

"She was much like your wife, in equal turns, spirited and beautiful and hardworking. After she was gone from my life, it was easy to look back and view her almost as if she was a dream. Had I had her with me longer, I might have become a different man, but we were together less than five years, and I was still under my father's thumb for all that I was of age. I did not have your courage, your mother's courage really, and so I stayed in Northumberland." It felt odd to reveal so much of himself to his son. He had spent so much time being the *viscount*. Firm and unrelenting in the way he did things, he sought no council and gave nothing but commands.

"It is nice to think that I received more from my mother than just my black hair." Sebastian commented, his expression one that Augustus could not read.

Moving consciously away from reminiscing and moving to the problem at hand, he looked at his son with a hard stare, stating, "I still do not think that taking on this estate for the sake of your sister's daughter is a wise move. So much effort invested and for what? None' of it is going to be yours."

His son's visage likewise turned hard. Nearly growling, he said, "Can you not say her name? Clara is your daughter's only child. Would you see her left to the devices of an evil man who wants only to fill his coffers? I would die before I allowed my family, who I love, to be misused and neglected. It means more to me to love and care for my niece than to worry about putting my time and effort into my niece's inheritance. Besides, it gives me the opportunity to run an estate and gain experience. You would never allow me to help run any of your estates as I saw fit, and I would never let you arrange Selene's marriage as you wanted to." Sighing and rubbing at his eyebrow, Sebastian continued, "You have never even met your granddaughter."

It was an old argument. He did not agree with his son's new-fangled ideas and saw no point in letting him manage anything when he could still do so perfectly fine. He waited to take control until his own father passed and he saw no reason to change things for his son. As for Selene, that whole attempt to marry her to an earl had been a disaster. The moment Sebastian had gotten wind of it, he told his sister that he would support her decision to refuse the much older man. Sebastian insisted that Selene should have the freedom to choose her own husband and have the chance to fall in *love*, of all things. Even banning Sebastian from Trowbridge and his other estates for supporting his sister's choices had done nothing to sway him.

Suddenly, Augustus was very weary. The weight of years of arguments with his son seemed to be bearing down on him. Between that and his long journey to confront Sebastian, it was too much to take on. He needed to rest his weary bones. "I am too weary to argue with you anymore this evening. I am for bed. We will speak more on this in the morning." Getting up, Augustus walked wearily out of the room and made his way to his guest room. The visit to his son was not going at all as he had expected.

Lydia looked up from her sewing when Sebastian made his way into her sitting room. It was a habit that they had developed in the brief span of their marriage, meeting together in the evening to discuss matters of the day. Seeing the droop of his shoulders, Lydia put the dress she was making for Clara to the side. Sitting forward in her chair, she asked, "Did your conversation with your father go poorly?"

Sighing, he sat next to her on the settee in a slumping manner. When he did not speak right away, she scooted closer to him and ran a soothing hand along his arm. She did not push him to say anything, merely waited for him to find the words to express his pain.

Rubbing at his eyebrow, he said, "It was, oddly enough, the best conversation I have had with my father in years." Looking at her with a faint smile gracing his well-formed lips, he continued, "He told me you reminded him of my mother. I cannot recall a single instance where he had spoken about her before tonight. I think you impressed him. He actually almost said he approved of you as my wife, which is something I could have never expected."

Lydia was so used to fatherly disapproval that she had not even thought to care what his father thought of her. She supposed, though, that his approval might make things easier. It was heart-wrenching to realize that his father had kept him in the dark about his mother until that evening. She asked him, "How do you feel about what you learned of your mother?"

Drawing closer to Lydia, he rested his head on the back of the settee, nearly on her shoulder. Watching her with heavy-lidded eyes, he said, "Until this evening, the most I had truly known about her was that I get my black hair from her. When I asked the servants as I child, I mostly only heard that she was a true lady and was very caring. But tonight, father said that she was much like you, in equal turns, spirited and beautiful and hardworking. It is more than I have ever had, and it makes me happy to think I ended up with a woman so much like her."

It delighted Lydia to hear that she might be so like the woman who had birthed Sebastian. That she might be able to grant him a connection of sorts to the woman he never knew. Brushing a lock of hair out of his eyes, she said, "I am honored to know that you feel that way."

"Of course, things could not continue on such a positive note. He then felt he had to tell me how much he disapproves of my choice to take over Swarkstone. Father cannot see the good in it, in helping Clara." Lydia noticed the deep furrows of sorrow etched across her husband's brow, revealing a side of him she had never witnessed. Closing his eyes, Sebastian took a deep breath before seeking her with a pained gaze and saying, "He has never even met her."

She could see the pain in his eyes. She was familiar with that pain. The pain of not being accepted or loved the way you needed to be loved. Urged to comfort him, she soothed his brow with her fingertips as she would with Clara or even one of her sisters. Lydia quickly surmised that the action did not engender the same feelings of maternal solicitude. No, this was something else entirely, and she could not describe it. Determined to analyze her reaction at another time, she said, "Regardless of how your father feels about the situation, you know he cannot stop you from doing the right thing. We both adore your niece, and we will ensure that she receives the utmost love and care, which will undoubtedly make her feel cherished and protected."

Reaching out, he clasped the hand that had just left his brow and said, "How did I get so lucky? It hasn't even been a week since we married. It is a marriage of convenience and yet more and more I see that you are perfect. You are perfectly what I need to help manage things here in the house while I see to the estate, and you are exactly what Clara needs. You love her as much as I do, if not more."

It was not a declaration of love, but Lydia found herself happy with it, nonetheless. She was certainly very happy with the way her new marriage was progressing. She grinned at him and said, "Sometimes things just work out that way."

Chapter Nineteen

IT HAD BEEN A few weeks since his father had left Swarkstone Park, and he was glad of it. While his father's reaction to Lydia and their marriage wasn't as severe as he had feared, dealing with him regarding the estate and Clara had proven to be quite a struggle. His father did not understand why Sebastian would not give way to his suggestions, or rather, commands.

His father's argument was that he had more experience in running an estate and so he knew better. The viscount's way of doing things was inherited from his father and so on, while Sebastian was interested in attempting new methods of doing things. He was also interested in providing a better home environment for the tenants and their families as well as the staff.

When his father had learned that he and Lydia were arranging for a school to teach reading, writing and arithmetic two days a week, the viscount had gone on a tirade about educating the masses being the downfall of life as they knew it. Sebastian refused to argue about the matter and informed his father that he fully supported Lydia's idea for the school, and he would not be swayed otherwise. It was the next day that his father informed them that he would be leaving.

Neither he nor Lydia regretted his leaving much. If he regretted anything, it would have been the fact that though his father had finally met Clara, the man had no desire to spend any time with her or show her any love. It was sad the viscount did not want to have a relationship with his granddaughter. Sebastian promised himself that he would never allow himself to turn away from love and family the way his father did.

After the viscount's departure, Sebastian spoke with Lydia about the man that was his father. She had been very pragmatic about their relationship with the viscount moving forward, and that Clara would not be worse for not having the viscount's love and affection. With a comforting smile, she promised him that Clara would be surrounded by an abundance of love and support. It had been so reassuring to realize that Clara had love and attention that extended beyond the two of them. Lydia's family and Selene also held her dear.

Pulling himself out of his ruminations, Sebastian looked at the clock on the mantel, happy to see that it was nearly time for him to meet up with Lydia and Clara. They had developed the habit of taking a mid-morning stroll through the garden together. It was one of the highlights of his day. He enjoyed it almost as much as the quiet moments he shared alone with Lydia in the evenings.

Sitting and talking with her at the end of the day was both soothing and enjoyable. He looked forward to being able to engage in a conversation with her, sharing the details of their daily adventures. Sharing their concerns and victories strengthened their connection, and lately, it was as if their connection seemed to grow deeper. There was just something about sharing his dreams with her and hearing hers in return that made him feel captivated by her.

Pushing back from his desk, he left his office to make his way over to the stairway, where he was sure Lydia and Clara would soon be coming down to greet him. As he arrived at the base of the stairs, he heard Lydia's voice from above him saying, "Perfect timing." Looking down at Clara, who walked beside her, she said, "A charming gentleman has come to escort us on our walk, Clara. What do you think we should do?"

Smiling up at Lydia, Clara said, "We should thank him, Aunt Lydia."

Sebastian was happy to see how far Clara had come in the time they had her with them. She had gone from nearly silent to talking almost freely with them and almost joking. Lydia caught his eye and smiled, clearly as happy as he was at Cara's progress. Nodding to Clara, she said, "Then we shall thank him for his courtesy when we great him at the bottom of the stairs."

The words had barely left her mouth when something went wrong, and she seemed to lose her balance. Sebastian watched in suspended terror as she fell face first down the stairs. Things slowed down as he dove to catch her. If she had been a single step further up the stairs, he would have been helpless to save her. As it was, it was a near thing.

With his heart racing in his chest, he caught her in a one-armed embrace while desperately clutching the banister to steady themselves against her downward momentum. Gasping at the near disaster, he asked, "Lydia, are you all right?"

Her nod was barely perceptible, but he could feel the slight movement as she clung tightly to him, seeking solace. Had Clara not been there, he would have scooped her up in his arms and carried Lydia somewhere quiet so he could simply hold her until both of their shaking had stopped. It was not to be, however, because Clara was clinging to his leg, and looking up at him with tears in her eyes.

Swallowing hard, he looked down at her and said, "Your aunt is unharmed, sweetheart. She is simply a little startled. Why don't we go sit down for a moment? How does that sound?"

Clara nodded and then scampered off towards the parlor, giving Sebastian a moment to settle himself. Taking a breath, he slid his arm around Lydia's shoulders and, holding her into his side, supported her as they walked into the parlor. Escorting her to the closest settee, he sat down with her. Noticing how she still leaned into him, he asked, "Do you still think that you want to go for a walk outside in the garden or would you prefer to stay inside today?"

Sighing, Lydia said, "I am sure that I will recover after a moment." Smiling up at Sebastian, with a cute blush she added, "I am not so dainty that a fall down the stairs will keep me indoors for the day."

Finding he could not resist kissing her forehead, he then whispered, "Just let me know when you want to take our turn about the garden."

LYDIA SAT WITH OAKLEY and Mrs. Wilson as they went over lists of linens and the like. There were barely enough on hand to have sheets on even half the guest beds. Now that she had gotten the house thoroughly cleaned from attic to basement, Lydia wanted to see to everyone's comfort and the ability to have guests. It had been nearly a month since they had moved to Swarkstone Park, and Lydia assumed that Selene would be coming to stay with them. Despite knowing it would take time, Lydia remained committed to getting the house in order and would persist until she was satisfied.

"With the arrival of the trunk from my sister Jane, we should finally have enough bed lines for all the guest rooms. Jane is just the sort to send me something so practical and helpful. She even had my new initials sown into the corners. I'm also pleased to report that the fabric I ordered for the curtains has finally arrived." Lydia spoke while tapping at the desk with her finger. Looking up, she asked, "How are the maids with a needle?"

Mrs. Wilson said, "All of them are able to do simple work, though Ann is the best at finer work."

Nodding, Lydia wondered about having Ann work on producing the curtains for the front parlor. She was not about to drain their coffers to redecorate everything, but Lydia was determined that her home would not remain feeling so dismal. Now that they had cleaned all the rooms and properly had them closed off with the furniture covered and whatnot, they could keep the rest of the house looking more presentable. Lydia hoped to add one thing at a time to make her home beautiful. With the recent addition of another maid, they could afford to have Ann working on another project.

Lydia was so happy that Oakley had been willing to help with tasks that did not fall under the purview of lady's maid. Her stepping in to act almost as a second housekeeper had been a godsend. She was able to oversee some of the work and instruct May and Ann on some of the finer points of service while Mrs. Wilson focus on getting Suzanna and Lilly under better control as well as work with the kitchen staff. She also had to oversee the male staff, as they had yet to acquire a new butler. Though now that staff was starting to trickle in, Oakley could return to her more typical role.

When they had arrived at Swarkstone Park, Sebastian had asked the grooms which had come with them who normally handled his carriage if they would be willing to act as footmen. Both had been very obliging and, when not on duty near the front door, were seen helping move things about the house, helping to reorder things into a more pleasing and less ostentatious fashion.

Looking back at Mrs. Wilson, she said, "It would be nice to have Ann work on making the curtains. Once she has the basic stitching in, I will finish it off with some embroidery."

Oakley smiled. "I can help Ann. I think I know how to create the look you are going for, Mrs. Burgess. It's only a matter of time before your family makes an appearance and we will be sure to have your home is prepared to impress them." Looking at Mrs. Wilson with a nod, she added, "We won't let you down."

"Meals are already much better now that we have straightened out the cook," Mrs. Wilson smiled. "Once she learned she had a much better budget than before and with those recipes that you received from the Matlock and Pemberley's cooks, as well as from your good mother, things have improved tremendously. Mrs. Martin is not a bad cook; I think she was just under Mrs. Netter's thumb for too long. With her gone, Mrs. Martin has become a right cheery person."

Lydia had to admit that she had enjoyed the change of food being presented over the last week or so. Not that she had wanted to hurt the cook's feelings and tell her that her fare was not up to the standard she was used to. Yes, the food being presented would not embarrass her if her family visited. "I am glad she is able to enjoy her work now. I know when my mother visits she will be happy to see her favorite recipes in use."

"I believe your mother will have much to be happy with next time she visits." Oakley wore an unusual grin as she spoke that made Lydia wonder what she was about.

Tilting her head, Lydia questioned her, "While I know that Swarkstone has improved dramatically since the last time she saw it, I have the feeling that is not what you are alluding to."

Shaking her head at Lydia's comment, she replied, "Your mother was quite worried about your marriage to Mr. Burgess. Everyone could see it. I merely meant that she will be happy to see how much your husband adores you."

Lydia snapped her mouth shut or else risk it hanging open like a fool. That was not at all what she had expected Oakley to say. She was always the first to admit that she encouraged Oakley to be honest with her when she felt she needed it, but her comment blindsided her this time. It was hard to find the words that she wanted to use, but she managed to say, "While I hope that one day I will earn his love, it is far too soon to have hopes in that regard."

She was astounded when Mrs. Wilson and Oakley looked at each other and started laughing. It took them a few minutes to get themselves under control and by that time, Lydia was almost ready to become put out with them. Mrs. Wilson finally said, "Love does not follow a timeline, Mrs. Burgess. I know your marriage was not born of passion, but that does not mean it would not swiftly follow. You started your marriage on the sound foundation of goodwill and respect. This is merely an extension of that."

Rubbing her forehead, Lydia said, "I know that. I'm curious about the evidence you've seen that indicates my husband's feelings for me have grown beyond respect. Because I am certainly not seeing it."

Oakley looked at Lydia kindly, going so far as to reach out and pat her hand in a motherly fashion before saying, "Do you remember yesterday when you were going down the stairs and you tripped?"

"Of course, he prevented me from falling. He is a gentleman. It does not mean he is in love with me."

Shaking her head, Oakley's smile broadened as she said, "While I concede that he would have ensured the safety of anyone at risk, his extreme concern for your well-being can only stem from his deep feelings for you."

Adding her opinion to the mix, Mrs. Wilson added, "Maybe you are not seeing what we see because you are not looking for it. You are assuming that it cannot be love, so you are finding other ways to explain his actions and reactions."

Sitting back in her chair, Lydia tried to process all that she had been told. She had only recently admitted to herself that her feelings were delving into the realm of love, but she had never thought he would develop feelings for her so soon into the marriage. She had never even looked to see if he might be displaying any of the habits her brothers-in-law had demonstrated. Was it truly possible? And if it was, what could she do about it? She did not feel like declaring that she loved him over tea was the right thing to do at all. This was going to take some time to understand and figure out how to proceed.

THE COUNTRYSIDE AT SWARKSTONE Park was rather beautiful, though Sebastian wondered how it would change with the seasons. As Sebastian rode his horse to visit the tenants and view the improvements he had put in place, he relished the sights of the countryside passing by. Though, to be honest, he probably would prefer to spend his time with Lydia and Clara. However, his role in maintaining Swarkstone Park meant that he had to be attentive to the needs of the tenants, regardless of where his heart lay.

It seemed almost bizarre to him that the feelings that seemed to be so entrenched in him did not exist even two months ago. He was a man in love. Sebastian had gone into the marriage with the hope that one day he might develop a deep connection with Lydia. He could not have imagined that love would have come so soon.

Even his love for Clara had deepened. Oh, he had always loved Clara, but it was an ephemeral sort of love. He had never had the chance to get to know her before, but being here with her every day had changed things. He had seen her come out of her shell, talk more, and learn to play. Sebastian loved the walks they all took together in the morning in the garden. Clara had a way of scrunching her nose when she was thinking that was simply adorable. She had even started to call him Uncle S'batien. Was it any wonder that he would rather be back at home with the two ladies in his life?

Still, as he approached the Clarke's cottage, he slowed his horse and turned his mind to why he was visiting. Dismounting, he greeted Mr. Clarke. "Good day to you, sir. How are you and your family faring?"

Shaking Sebastian's hand, Mr. Clarke said, "We are all very well, Mr. Burgess, and especially grateful today after the rain we had last night."

Sebastian studied the house that he had come to look at. He could see nothing to be concerned about, so turning back to Mr. Clarke, he said, "That was one of the reasons that I had wanted to come by and check with you today. Did the roof hold up? Any leaks?"

Smiling, Mr. Clarke shook his head. "Nary a one. I cannot tell you how glad my Debera and I are that we do not have to worry about our children taking sick due to a leaky roof. Being able to keep our children warm and dry is a blessing."

"Everyone should be able to have a safe place to live. That includes a sound roof, Mr. Clarke. I may not have been managing Swarkstone for long, but I am determined that everyone on the estate has what they need to thrive." Sebastian waved at the children, who seemed to be gathering eggs as they moved about their tasks. He continued, "In fact, Mrs. Burgess is working on setting up a school for anyone wanting to learn reading, writing, and arithmetic. Once we have everything established, I will be sure to let your family know of the details." Sebastian was gladdened to see the smile that split Mr. Clarke's face. It was nice to be able to make people's lives better one little thing at a time.

Taking off his hat, Mr. Clarke clutched it in his hands. "I cannot tell you how happy that will make Debera. She has always wanted for our children to have some learning. She thinks that it will help them get farther in the world." Turning, he looked at his son and daughter at the chicken coop before he said, "There was talk when we first heard you were coming to take over things. Getting to know you and your missus as I have, I must confess that I am guilty of blindly believing what they said."

Waving off his concern, Sebastian said, "Do not worry about it, Mr. Clarke. There is always a certain amount of anxiety over the unknown. I won't trouble myself over talk that grows from that worry."

"You and you wife are good people. Did you know your wife heard of old Mrs. Walsh passing and she had a basket brought to her daughter and son-in-law? Talk is that she sent the prettiest little bouquet of flowers with a ham and various other things." Mr. Clarke smiled, putting his hat back on his head.

Sebastian did not know that Lydia had done it, but he was not surprised. He wondered what flowers she had sent, but suspected something that meant compassion. With a smile he said, "My wife is very fond of her flowers, and she loves making bouquets. I am not surprised that she would give one of them to someone who had lost a loved one."

Smiling, Mr. Clarke said, "I know you have not been married long, but I believe that you are well matched. Things always run better at an estate when the mister and missus care for each other as much as you both do."

It took a moment for Sebastian to realize just what Mr. Clarke was implying. People must be talking about his relationship with Lydia. Not only that, but they were under the impression that they cared for one another. Mr. Clarke could have simply meant that they did not argue, but he did not think that was what he meant. From the man's expression, Sebastian assumed the man spoke of their being in love and not just him in love, but Lydia in love as well. Could it be true?

Maybe reading his confusion, Mr. Clarke said, "No one means anything by it. It is just that people are happy to see how well you get on. My younger sister Ann works at the manor and says it is rather nice to see how in love you and your missus are."

Sebastian might have had more time to think about what Mr. Clarke had brought to light if he hadn't seen smoke rising in the distance. Realizing that there was another fire drew all his focus. Calling out, he said, "There is smoke rising in the distance."

Turning, Mr. Clarke cried, "My God, that is the Wright farm."

Chapter Twenty

Sebastian felt a headache coming on, and he knew that all the grinding of his teeth was not helping. Looking at Burton over the list of issues they had accumulated, he said, "I know I have no practical experience dealing with an estate, but two fires in such a short period seems unusual to me."

Running his hand through his already messy locks, Mr. Burton grumbled, "It is not just you that finds this odd. I have spoken with the Adams family and the Wrights. Both fires seem even more suspicious after talking with them. There was not a candle, or an oil lamp carelessly forgotten, and I trust them to be honest with me." Narrowing his eyes he continued, "What is worse is that one of the Wright boys said he saw a stranger near the house shortly before the fire broke out."

"I find that I am becoming more and more convinced that someone is out to hinder my management of Swarkstone Park."

Sebastian, having given voice to his suspicions, half expected Mr. Burton to reassure him that he was just imagining things. He did not.

Mr. Burton only sat there with his lips pursed and when he did not say anything Sebastian felt compelled to ask, "Do you have any other evidence that might prove that there is someone out there looking to bring harm to my family and or the Swarkstone estate?"

Mr. Burton grimaced before saying, "Cannot prove anything, sir, but I have noted some problematic rumors."

Eyes widening, Sebastian groaned, "What rumors?" It was hard enough trying to set things to rights, both in the tenant homes and his own. To hear that someone was disseminating negative information about him was disconcerting.

"There was talk when you first arrived about your cruel nature and your miserly tendencies. However, the talk has all but disappeared in the wake of tenant support. For one, the Gregson family has let it be known that you were quick to help them in their time of need. Going yourself to offer them aid. Then the tenants who had needed repairs to their homes let it be known that you spared no expense in making their homes more livable and indeed comfortable." Smiling, he added "Mrs. Burgess's visits to the tenants to check on their wellbeing and bringing remedies and handsewn items have also improved the neighborhood's view of you. Whoever started the talk cannot be happy because you have all but wiped out their efforts without even trying."

Tapping his fingers on his desk for a moment, Sebastian thought about the problem as a whole. He did not like the thought that someone might be harming his tenants because they were trying to hurt him. Laying his palm flat against the wood of the desk, Sebastian asked, "Is it possible that the fires have been an increase in the attacks against us, do you think?"

"Anything is possible. It would be advantageous to know more about the culprit. It is always better to understand one's opposition, if you want to defeat them." Mr. Burton answered with a shrug.

Standing, Sebastian went to the window. The first person he thought of in this situation was the former colonel, the Earl of Matlock. As a military man, his brother-in-law must know of some strategy that might be helpful. He would ask his opinion, but hated to bother him as his wife must be ready for her confinement and laying in. Maybe he should write him for advice, anyway? A letter could not hurt. It wasn't as if he was asking for a visit. He would ask Lydia's opinion when next he saw her. She would know if it would be a bad time to ask her brother-in-law for advice.

Sebastian found his gaze drawn in the direction of the gardens that Lydia enjoyed so much. It only took a few seconds for his shocked mind to process what he was seeing. Gripping the frame around the window with white-knuckled fingers, Sebastian had difficulty believing what he was seeing. There was smoke rising from the direction of the gardens. He wanted to believe that it was impossible, but no. There was yet another fire, and this time it was on the estate's grounds.

Running from the room, Sebastian shouted to Mr. Burton as he went, "There is a fire in the garden. I could see the smoke from the window. Go to the stables and get the men there to come and help. I am going now to investigate myself."

It was all a blur as Sebastian ran to the gardens, his outrage spurring him on. A third fire made it impossible to be just a series of accidents. This was intentional. Did they not care about who might be hurt? Beyond his worry of the injury to people of the estate, Sebastian worried what a fire in the gardens would do to Lydia. He knew how much Lydia loved her flowers and knowing that someone would strike against the woman he loved enraged him.

As Sebastian drew closer, he realized that it was none of the plants or little arbors that were on fire. It was the potting shed that held tools and supplies that Lydia used in her garden projects. As he ran, he began noticing the attention that the fire had gained. The littlest stable boy was there next to Mr. Roberts, the gardener. Calling out, he said, "Where is the nearest pump? We need to douse it with water!" The little boy quickly dashed off, and Sebastian hoped the boy was off on a quest for water.

Turning to him, his face a mask of horror, Mr. Roberts exclaimed, "The missus! She was gardening not five minutes ago, and now I cannot find her!"

He had never felt such all-encompassing fear than he had hearing those words. Sebastian wondered idly if it was possible to perish from fear. Rushing closer to the heat of the blaze, Sebastian fought the urge to cast up his breakfast. The flames were licking up the sides of the building as if the fire was a hungry beast eager to devour it whole and his wife very well could be inside. He collapsed to his knees, unable to stand, when he heard the first scream from within.

Lydia watched the smoke billow around her as the flames ate at the walls of the shed she was in. Trying to cover her mouth and nose with a handkerchief was not helping her breath any easier. She wished in vain for a large pitcher of water to soothe her throat or to dowse herself with and protect herself from the sparks and heat.

It was odd how her mind turned from horror at her situation to realizing that something was wrong with the fire. It was moving wrong. Besides the fact that there should have been nothing in her potting shed to spark a blaze, the burlap along the far wall seemed to be bursting into flames too rapidly to be natural. Someone had added something to feed the fire, some kind of oil, perhaps? She knew with utter clarity that someone had set this blaze. Had they known she was coming in to fetch supplies and seedlings? Was this more random damage or had their culprit stepped up their game and targeted her specifically?

She was now coughing continually, breathing far too much smoke. She knew she had to escape, but flames engulfed the door. Turning to the line of windows along the back of the shed, she wondered if she could climb on something to get out. She hoped she could force her way through, but they were too high off the ground to get through easily. Her cough had brought her to her knees, and she made a feeble attempt to let someone know she was inside the shed. Screaming hoarsely, she could not tell if anyone could hear her over the roar of the flames.

Lydia shoved a wooden box containing tools toward the back wall. It was too heavy to move easily, but she did not have time to empty it and make it lighter. She had not gotten very far when a covered figure kicked open the door behind her and dashed through the flames.

The blanket was thrown off by the figure as it smoldered, leaving Lydia curious about the intense heat it must have endured. It took only a moment in the hazy environment for her to realize that it was Sebastian. He rushed to her side, crouching below the smoke, only for part of the roof to come crashing down next to them. They looked at each other, knowing there was no time left. They had to get out of the collapsing fiery structure.

Lydia looked up into Sebastian's face and watched his expression grown determined. Leaning down, he claimed her lips and Lydia yearned to linger in the sensation of her first kiss, but his lips vanished all too swiftly. In a flash, he was wrapping her in the heat of the smoldering blanket and picking her up. Cocooned as she was, her senses were hampered, but she thought she heard him say, "Hold tight, Lydia, my love."

She only had enough time to realize what he was going to do before she felt him move and they were rushing through a heat so intense that she knew it could only mean that they were in fact, surrounded by fire. She wanted to scream at him to put her down, that they could come up with a better idea, but she knew it would do no good. Then she was falling, and Sebastian fell with her.

Flinging the charred blanket from around her, Lydia scrambled to check on Sebastian. Noting the flames on the sleeves of his coat, she was quick to smother them with the already smoldering blanket. Tears ran down her cheeks, creating grimy tracks in her soot blackened face. She cried, "You foolish man, you just had to risk yourself!" She would have said more if she had not broken off into another round of hacking coughs. Ignoring her desperate coughs and struggle to breathe unincumbered by smoke, Lydia hovered over Sebastian, afraid to hurt him by moving or touching him. As he lay on his side, his face appeared unharmed by the fire, but Lydia could discern his evident pain from the rigid lines of his mouth. She knew he had to have been burnt, but could not tell right off where he had been hurt.

"There was not enough time." He groaned, then said, "Could not risk you."

Halfheartedly glaring at the man she loved, she declared, "And you think I would want to risk you?"

Reaching out, Sebastian seemed to try to touch her face, but his hand dropped before reaching her. At first, Lydia was terrified that she had lost him, but she heard someone say, "He has just passed out."

Finally looking up, she realized that she and Sebastian were not alone. The clearing around the potting shed was alive with workers. There was even a team of people putting out the fire with buckets of water. Mr. Burton was there directing the movements of the people and Lydia wondered if he had become good at the process of putting out a fire. This was the third fire in as many weeks. Her gardener, Mr. Roberts, was next to her, ready to help. Lydia was confident enough in the workers to know they would care for the fire in the shed. Turning to face Mr. Roberts, she said, "We have to get Sebastian inside and see to his burns."

Nodding, Mr. Roberts said, "Right Missus, I will see about making a litter to bring 'im up to the house."

More and more people showed up, all taking things in hand and working together. On some level, Lydia was proud of how well everyone worked together. They had been working so hard to form a functioning team of staff and they had come together so smoothly in the time of crisis. Yet, in the recesses of her heart, the efficacy of their staff held no significance; her only concern was the well-being of her husband. Carefully observing him, she spotted the telltale marks of burns on the backs of his hands and arms. It was clear that he had received them while shielding her from the fire.

Her mind was a whirl of what she knew of burns and how to treat them. Which was next to nothing. Of course, they would summon the apothecary from the closest town, but she wished she had Jane and all of her knowledge with her. As soon as Mr. Roberts arrived with Mr. Davies in tow, they were moving Sebastian onto a makeshift litter and running him towards the house. Lydia followed as close behind as she could.

"LYDIA!"

Lydia looked up at Oakley in confusion. Oakley never just called her by her first name. She was always too proper for that. Was there something else that was going wrong? Concerned, she asked, "Is there something wrong?"

"Ma'am, I have been calling you, but you were not responding." Came Oakley's exasperated response.

Grimacing, Lydia said, "Oh, I am sorry. What do you need?" It was a struggle to keep her attention on Oakley as she spoke. Lydia wanted to turn back to Sebastian and continue to watch him breathe. She was so worried that something would happen to him if she took her eyes off him for a moment.

Oakley stepped forward and, placing a hand on Lydia's shoulder, she said, "Mrs. Burgess, you must take some time to see to yourself."

Lydia shook her head. "I am fine, Oakley. Besides, I cannot leave him." Lydia knew that she would have made a better point had she not burst into another round of coughing.

Oakley handed her a cup of tea liberally dosed with honey. Lydia took a grateful sip. Her throat had been so very sore since the fire, but nothing seemed to help for long. Oakley was of the opinion that honey cured most ills and so she had been plying Lydia with the stuff for the last few hours.

Looking back at Sebastian, she could not help but ache. Not only had he risked so much in saving her, but he did it not knowing how much she had come to love him. Despite everyone's assurances that he was sure to recover, she cursed herself for never having spoken the words he must have wanted to hear. Hadn't she been waiting for him to give some definitive sign before saying something? When he spoke to her amidst the fiery blaze, she had not had the time to fully process his words, but now all she could think about was how he had said 'Lydia, my love'. He loved her, and she hadn't known.

Clearing her throat, Oakley began again. "Your husband is in good hands with Mr. Davies. You need to see to your own needs. You can always return to him when you have refreshed yourself."

Shaking her head, Lydia was about to demur when Oakley continued, "What will your husband think when he wakes up and sees you like this? You will give him such a fright looking singed and overwhelmed." Hands on her hips, she added, "Besides, little Miss

Clara has been asking for you and I know you would not have *her* see you like this."

Looking down at herself Lydia, acknowledged that she presented a very poor image. Her clothes were soot stained and she could only imagine what her face and hair looked like if her hands were so grime covered. It was true that Clara would most likely be terrified by her current appearance. The poor child could probably see the residual smoke from her playroom's window.

Slumping in defeat, she looked back over to Sebastian, who was having his clothes carefully cut off of him by Davies. With burns like his, cleanliness would be vital, and here she was sitting, covered head to toe in soot and ash. It would not do. She had to step away and clean herself up. She would take the time to check on Clara and write to Jane, asking for her advice on caring for a burn victim. Nodding grudgingly, Lydia stood and, looking at Davies, said, "Have me summoned the moment he shows signs of waking or if his condition worsens."

Sighing, Lydia leaned over the bed and kissed Sebastian's cheek and whispered, "Be strong, my love. I will return as swiftly as I can."

Lydia was not surprised when she found her room already set up for her to take a bath. Oakley had always been quite efficient. In practically no time at all, she was clean, even though it had taken several rinses to get all the soot and grime out of her hair. Slipping into a simple dress that was more comfortable than stylish, Lydia noticed that May was hovering uncertainly as she came in to help empty out the tub.

Moving to sit by the fire to dry her hair, Lydia asked, "Is something troubling you, May?"

Putting her half full bucket down, May said, "I do not want to overstep, Mrs. Burgess, but my mother has always been right good with her remedies. She always seems to have a cure for everything, including burns. With Mr. Burgess getting burned, well...I thought you might like to know that she had a recipe for burns. I know you have summoned the apothecary but..." May shrugged as if she now questioned speaking up.

Sitting forward, Lydia exclaimed, "I would love to know how your mother has treated burns in the past. I am sorry to say it, but as I have never met this apothecary, I do not yet know if I trust him. Some are rather too fond of purging and bloodletting for my tastes."

Smiling, May picked up her bucket again before saying, "I believe my mother would be more than happy to come up to help. She and Pa are tenants here at Swarkstone, so I am sure she could be here in a trice."

Clasping her hands together, a glimmer of hope for Sebastian's treatment filled her heart. It would not stop her from writing to Jane, but it was wonderful to know where to begin. She reassured May by saying, "That would be marvelous. Could you please ask Mr. Burton if he could bring her?"

May nodded and started to leave with her bucket of water, but Lydia stopped her. "I am curious. Do you know what your mother uses to treat the burns?"

With a tilt of her head, May said, "She uses a salve made from beeswax, lanolin, and honey, and then she covers the wounds with boiled burdock leaves."

SEBASTIAN WOKE IN STAGES. The closer he was to awareness, the more pain he felt, but beyond the pain, he had the worst feeling that he had to check on something. That someone was in danger.

He was disconnected in a way that he recognized from a childhood injury when he had broken his arm falling out of a tree. They had given him laudanum; he did not like the hazy floaty feeling it gave him then and he did not like it now. It kept him from thinking properly. Who was it? Who needed him? He wondered as he tried to come to full awareness.

Lydia. Lydia was afraid and coughing. He had to help her. Jerking with awareness, he regretted the moment he tried to sit up. Fire erupted up his arms, and all at once, he remembered the fire in the potting shed. He had rescued Lydia from the potting shed, but was she alright?

He first looked down at his arms and was startled to see his arms covered with leaves. Was that some kind of treatment? He sure hoped so. Looking around, he realized he was in his room and in his bed. So he had made it back to the house somehow, and he was being treated, he hoped. Moving his arms hurt badly, but it seemed more of him than just his arms hurt as well. It was not the same kind of burning pain though, more aching, like he had fallen down hard.

The curtains were drawn, leaving the room in the dark. Trying to keep himself from moving too much, Sebastian peered about the room. Just then, the door opened, admitting Davies. Eager for answers about his missing time and how Lydia was, he tried to speak, but only managed an odd sounding croak.

It was enough to alert Davies, who rushed to his side. "Mr. Burgess! I am so glad you are coming around." Putting the tray he carried down on a table beside the bed, he grabbed the pitcher and poured a glass of water and brought it to Sebastian's lips, allowing him to drink.

Sebastian did not know how truly thirsty he was until the water touched his lips. Then he wanted to guzzle the whole glass down, only Davies pulled the glass away too soon. "Careful, sir, you do not want to make yourself sick."

Admitting grudgingly to himself that Davies was right, Sebastian cleared his throat, and this time managed to say, "How long?"

Putting the glass on the bedside table Davies, said, "Three days, sir. Part of that was due to the laudanum, but you also had a fever."

Sebastian nodded. Three days was not a lot, considering everything. Wishing he could sit up, he said, "What of Lydia?"

Smiling slightly, Davies said, "Apart from being extremely concerned about you, she is doing well. She has rarely left your side. Oakley has had to practically drag her away from your bedside so she could attend to her own needs." Nodding his head to the chair on the far side of the bed, Davies explained, "She only just drifted off before I went to gather supplies to change your dressing."

He couldn't help but look at her, feeling as though some external influence was guiding his gaze. She was peacefully asleep in the chair, her head and arms drooping onto the bed. He could not see her face, but her beautiful blonde hair was mussed and coming out of a simple knot at the back of her head. It was obvious that she had not been taking care of herself.

He wanted to be angry that he had been too unwell to enjoy her presence in his bedroom. How many nights had he lain awake wishing for her presence beside him? It was so unfair. She was finally spending time in his bedroom, and he had not been able to enjoy it. It was such a loss.

He was still watching her when she began coughing faintly in her sleep. Looking back at Davies, the man answered his unasked question. "She still has a cough from inhaling too much smoke."

More than ever, Sebastian wanted to be able to reach out and gather her close to him. He knew that he could not though, not in the condition that he was in. Sighing, he turned back to Davies and asked, "Am I covered with leaves?"

Smiling in a way that Sebastian could recognize as a suppressed laugh, Davies replied, "Yes sir. It seems that the way you were holding Mrs. Burgess protected your torso and face, but the backs of your hands and arms got the worst of the blaze. One of the female tenants suggested using the leaves as part of a remedy. Oddly enough, it seems to be working."

Sebastian tried to think back to when he was rescuing Lydia. He had tucked his face into the damp blanket as he ran through the blaze, but the heat on his arms had been excruciating. As he gazed at his arms, hidden beneath a blanket of leaves, he couldn't shake his curiosity about the state of his skin.

Seeing the direction of his gaze, Davies said, "Although the sleeves of your coat offered some protection, they briefly burst into flames before you fell to the ground. The backs of your hands are the worst off. I should change the leaves actually, unless you would like to wait until I can get you more laudanum?"

Shaking his head, Sebastian said, "No, no more laudanum."

The next interim of time was full of removing gooey leaves from his arms and, though he had expected his pain to increase, it did not, or at least not remarkably so. Once Sebastian was finally able to see his arms, he found that they were not nearly as bad as he had been imagining. While he knew there would be scarring, it would not be grotesque. The worst part was indeed the back of his hands. Looking at his arms, it was clear that they were inflamed, but his hands were even worse, covered in painful blisters and red twisted skin.

Realizing that he should not fixate on his wounds, Sebastian turned his gaze and focused on Lydia as she slept. He wanted to go over and settle her more comfortably on the bed. Despite the pain of his burns, he could not help but be happy that he was the one burned. He could withstand anything if it meant that he could protect her.

Chapter Twenty-One

"I am most severely displeased!" Baron Blackthorn's voice boomed across the room as he bellowed.

Chester watched the man prowl the room, hoping that if he held still enough, he would not draw the man's wrath. Of late, the baron had become more prone to violence and Chester was learning to fear for his safety. Not only that, but he was also starting to fear for his soul.

It had been one thing to bribe the workers to leave Swarkstone. It had not taken much really—a forged letter of reference to start over somewhere else and more than enough money to relocate. Bribing the employment agencies was even easier. Even encouraging the spread of rumors had been simple enough and had done little to actually hurt Mr. Burgess or his family. If he had been allowed to stop there, he could have dealt well enough with his conscience.

Though, of course, the baron found the results unsatisfactory. As a man who worked in the shadows and with many secrets, it had never occurred to him that someone else might not be easy to pull down into the muck. Mr. Burgess and his wife had proven too good and the people he had gone to help were all singing his praise. Everyone in the nearby estates and towns had quickly seen the truth. This had further enraged the baron, who was still determined to get his hands on the monies that had been granted to the child when his brother died.

"I will see that what is rightfully mine is returned to me!" The smashing of a vase near Chester's head accompanied the baron's continued rant. Chester tried his best to refrain from flinching, knowing it would draw the wrath of the baron. At this point in the baron's rambling, it was a relief that he did not expect Chester to say anything. Chester would have found little that he could have said in response to the baron's growing madness.

Though he had always found it distasteful, he had helped the baron with blackmail and rumor mongering. Now the baron was falling farther into depravity than Chester could follow. His stomach twisted in knots as he contemplated the consequences of the baron's recent foray into arson. He was certain that people would be hurt and what was worse, Chester had helped the baron find the arsonist who would do the job.

He was ever more certain that he must find a way out of his service to the despicable man. Thank goodness he had managed to see his mother and sister safely from England's shores. They were now on their way to Canada, looking to start over somewhere new. Now he only had to see to himself, and the baron could no longer threaten what remained of his family. Even with the threat of debtor's prison held over his head, like the sword of Damocles, he had to find a way out of the baron's clutches. Chester had begun silently planning his escape when something the baron said made his stomach drop.

"I am tired of trying to force Burgess's hand. Despite our efforts, he remains resolute in his commitment to care for the child and refuses to back out of the venture. And the current strategy to make the estate unprofitable is not proving to be sufficiently expedient. It's been quite a while, and the three strategies we got from that bribed clerk to have him lose custody of the girl are still not yielding results. At this rate, it could take years to get what I want." After kicking a chair and sending it skidding across the room, the baron suddenly grew still. When he smiled, Chester wanted to vomit, knowing the next words out of the man's mouth would be horrendous.

Moving calmly back to his desk, his face twisted in a cruel smile, Baron Blackthorn sat down and said, "I have gone about it all wrong. Why attempt to get custody of the child so that I can siphon off her fortune? I have it backwards. What I need to do is get my hands on what the man loves, what he needs, or what he wants, and I can simply demand all the funds I want."

Lydia woke slowly and was immediately aware of the kink in her neck because of sleeping oddly. Groaning, she lay there, trying to massage the pain away.

"You really should climb into bed with me instead of sleeping over there like that all huddled over." The slightly husky voice had Lydia jerking upright and gazing into the pained gaze of her darling Sebastian.

"You are awake!" Crawling over the bed in what she was certain was a very undignified fashion, Lydia drew as close to him as she dared. Goop and leaves still covered his arms, and she was terrified of hurting him, so she settled for hovering near him. Confused, she asked, "Why did no one wake me?"

Shaking his head, Sebastian replied, "It was obvious that you were completely exhausted. I was not going anywhere, and you needed the sleep."

It was just like him to try to protect her. Huffing, Lydia grumbled, "I was not the one who was burned trying to act the hero."

Sebastian laughed. "What else could I do? You must admit that you were in need of rescuing."

It irked Lydia that she had spent hours worrying about his unconscious wounded state, only for him to awaken in a jovial mood. Cranky, she complained, "Do you have no care for my poor nerves? Here I have been agonizing over you for four days. I have been in a constant state of guilt and fear, and you are joking?" Wiping angrily at the tears that were trailing down her cheeks, Lydia shook her head.

Then, gazing back up at him, she said, "It is a wonder that I love you so much because it has only brought me grief these last four days."

Covering her face with both her hands, Lydia allowed herself to cry in earnest. It was simply too much. Too much fear, too much joy now that he was awake. and too much relief to have finally said the words that had plagued her from almost the start of her marriage. She was astonished when she felt Sebastian pulling her hands away from her face. Mouth dropping open, she was about to admonish Sebastian for moving and possibly damaging himself when he hushed her with a look.

"I am well enough to move if I am careful. This salve that you have on me is doing wonders. Do not worry." Sebastian squeezed her hands before releasing them and laying his arms back down on the pillows that supported them. Offering her a reassuring smile, he continued, "You will forgive me if I do not want to speak of my love for you while looking at the backs of your hands while you cry."

Lydia knew that her mouth was hanging open, but she was incapable of doing a thing about it. He had once again spoken of his love, but this time there was no smoke or fire to distract her from his declaration. Now she was crying for more reasons than she had previously cataloged.

Shaking his head, Sebastian drawled, "It is painful to watch you cry or hear you declare your love and not be able to draw you into my arms with abandon. Sadly, I know if I attempted it, you would scold me soundly."

The impact of his statement was so significant that it nearly shocked her out of her teary state. Pouting, she said, "It is your own fault. I am sure we could have come up with a better plan had you taken the time to think."

"You will never sway me to your way of thinking because you see, I was successful. I got you out of there with little more than smoke damage. My own injures were inconsequential," he explained with a shrug of his shoulders, though it seemed to put a grimace on his face.

Despite her sympathy for his pain, Lydia became frustrated with his intransigence. No wonder Lizzie would get so frustrated with William. Were all men so hardheaded, or was it just the ones the Bennet sisters fell in love with?

With her weight shifted onto her heels, Lydia crossed her arms and stared at Sebastian, wondering if it was worth it to press the argument. It was not as if they could go back in time and change things. Nor could she have stopped him from saving her, even if they did.

She must have waited too long to speak, because Sebastian added, "From the time we met, I had always found you intriguing. You were energetic and bold, but also caring and compassionate, and I enjoyed spending time with you. The idea of biding my time, waiting for you to be ready for marriage, had crossed my mind. I wanted to get to know you better, and I half suspected that with time we would be good friends, or possibly more than that." He paused in his speech and Lydia watched his fingers twitch. She wondered if he wanted to run his fingers through his hair or rub at his eyebrow like he sometimes did.

After a moment he continued, "Then life intruded, and I was willing to settle for the sake of my niece, but you spoke up and upended my world. It was almost as if time had skipped a beat, and suddenly, I found myself immersed in the depths of love for you. I was no longer casually strolling by the seashore, but rather engulfed in a vast ocean of love for you."

She crept closer to Sebastian, but was careful not to disturb his healing burns. Lydia bit her lip, both eager to confess and terrified to do so. For a moment, Lydia found herself studying the man she loved. Besides the healing burns on his arms, Sebastian looked much different from how she had been used to seeing him. He was no longer clean shaven. In fact, he had more than a few days' scruff on his face. She admitted, if only to herself, that she much preferred him clean shaven. The sight of his strong jaw unobscured had always made her heart flutter. Regarding his shirtless state, she did not mind that at all, though it had taken a day or two to completely get over the shock of seeing his chest completely bare. Drawing her gaze back up to his eyes, she felt drawn into their depths. Somehow finding her courage there, she smiled at him, acknowledging that she knew he was watching her.

She was relieved to see that Sebastian was patient, giving her the time she needed to collect her thoughts. Tracing the outline on the pattern of the coverlet that she kneeled on, she finally admitted, "I had hopcd for love in our marriage, but I was willing to wait even years to develop it. Discovering my love for you was a shock so soon after our marriage. I probably was half in love with you when I proposed the idea of our union. Still, I was willing to wait and hope that you would develop feelings for me in return. I never thought I would feel this secure in your love for me so soon after our wedding."

WITH ALL THE LOVE he had for her stirred up and boiling to the surface, Sebastian did not want to resist the urge to hold Lydia. It felt as if there must be some divine consequence if he could not hold her in his arms. While his burns did hurt, what affected him more was this growing need of his that was becoming an ache. So he waited to gauge her reaction, hoping she would comply.

"Somehow, I cannot believe that we are finally both aware of our mutual affection and can do nothing about it. If I promise to try not to get leaves and salve in your hair, can I hold you?" he nearly begged.

The blush across her cheeks told him of her acceptance before she said, "Yes, as long as you are careful not to hurt yourself."

Holding his arms aloft, he encouraged her to crawl toward him and settle in on his chest. With gentle care, he placed his hands back down, cradling her securely against him as she rested her head at the crook of his neck. He sighed in contentment, simply happy to be so close in her company. Dreams of her embrace had been haunting him. Oh, there had been dreams of more, but just as precious to him were his dreams of simply lying with her in his arms. Sebastian was quick to note that reality was so much better than the misty impressions he had treasured.

Humming under his breath, Sebastian said, "I know that there must be a world of things that we must face and deal with. The consequences of the fire and the management of the estate, but I find that I do not want to move, nor do I want to think of anything of serious nature."

Tilting slightly, Lydia looked him in the eye from where she rested against his chest. In what he assumed was an attempt to be stern, she said, "While you are recovering, I expect you to while away your days in lazy pursuits. We can do without your diligent management for a time. You will find me capable of handling most things on my own." Laying her head back down on his chest, Lydia huffed. Sebastian found the action highly distracting, as the warmth of her breath curled along the bare skin of his neck and chest. He felt goosebumps shoot down his form and struggled not to shudder in pleasure as she continued speaking, "It would not surprise me if several members of my family were to show up in the near future. The minute they realize that we are being targeted, they will begin to close ranks."

Sebastian made a conscious effort to divert his mind from enticing thoughts, instead directing his attention towards the threats they faced. After all, it would be some time before he could act on any impulses his new closeness with Lydia might tempt him to, so he focused on maintaining self-control. Considering their problems, he said, "I should not have wondered if you would notice how we had been targeted."

Lydia seemed to ponder the question for a moment before saying, "If one fire is a horrible accident, and two fires is a questionable coincidence, then three fires in such a close period of time are evidence of a malicious attack. There have been too many odd experiences since we determined to take control of Swarkstone for there to not be some culprit hiding in the shadows."

Sebastian would have been better able to follow her well-reasoned logic if she had not started to trace some unknown pattern with her finger on the skin of his chest. For a moment, he found it very difficult to find the words with which to respond. After swallowing thickly, he managed, "Do you suppose they will show themselves eventually, or will we need to drag them into the light?"

"Well, if they do not come forward of their own volition, then we can always force the issue." Looking back up at him, Lydia said, "Though I think we both have our suspicions of who it is causing problems. There is only one man I know of who was angered by the results of Mr. Blakesley's will."

Eyebrows drawn, Sebastian surmised, "Yes, Mr. Herrington told me that Baron Blackthorn was not a man who appreciated being crossed. Not that we crossed him."

Huffing in a way that reminded Sebastian of a puppy, Lydia added, "No, it seems as if we simply stumbled into a family feud. Only the baron is the last man standing, and he is still not happy with the results."

Sebastian did not want their moment of bliss disrupted by such a man. He knew that he could not focus on the baron and retain the joy he felt just being with Lydia. So he said, "Is it wrong of me to want to ignore him? Not forever, only long enough to enjoy some time with you. I feel the need to just be with the woman I adore."

He could feel her nod against his chest, and, with a sigh, she said, "Our problems can wait. I only want to soak in the warmth of you and bask in the joy. We can face the realities of our situation soon enough."

Meeting with Mrs. Wilson had become an enjoyable part of Lydia's routine. They discussed the issues of running the house over tea and had developed a friendship of sorts. Taking a sip of her tea, Lydia listened as she spoke of the state of the employees.

"In fact, we have even expanded our staff by two yesterday, and I am hopeful that they will integrate well with our existing staff." Mrs. Wilson's smile grew wider as she spoke, her typically sunny disposition amplified by the addition of the much-needed assistance.

Lydia could easily see why even the addition of two people could encourage her so. To run efficiently, an estate the size of Swarkstone

Park should truly have a minimum of twenty indoor staff and ten outdoor staff. As it stood before the additions, they had eleven indoor staff and four outdoor staff. This meant that they were having to choose what could be worked on and what had to be ignored for a time. Both she and Mrs. Wilson shared a commitment to excellence in their work, never shying away from a challenge. It was irksome to know they were only handling the bare essentials. And that was before the additional issue of the fire and resulting problems.

Smiling, Lydia asked, "What can you tell me of the new workers?"

With a nod of her head, Mrs. Wilson said, "The first is a young woman in her twenties named Matilda Cole. She states that she was looking for a fresh start after some of her family members died in an accident. She has a wonderful reference from the housekeeper from her last position. I think with time she might become a good upstairs maid should she prove herself as hardworking as the reference suggests." After pausing to take a sip of her tea, she continued, "The second is a young man in his mid-teens who will work in the stables but is able to help elsewhere as the need arises. While I know that he can't have much experience at his age, he stuck me as energetic and hardworking."

For a moment, Lydia wondered how these workers managed to find their way to them. They certainly were not from the employment agencies that they had attempted to work with. She had a niggling suspicion that they may be receiving these workers through her family connections. It would be easy enough for them to spread the word that they were looking for good employees. Not one to look a gift horse in the mouth, she merely responded by saying, "I am glad to have them, as they shall certainly lighten our loads. On a different topic, have Suzanna and Lilly improved at all?"

With a frustrated purse of her lips, she let out a sigh and said, "I think Lilly is showing some improvement. The viscount visiting unexpectedly gave her enough of a fright make her realize why she should put in the effort to do a job well. I do not think she was ever trained to any standard that you or I would hold someone to, so I have been taking some time every day to show her how to do things better. With time, she will probably improve to be a middling worker. It helps that she is a follower and now that the other workers are showing their dedication, she is starting to follow along. On the other hand, if Suzanna does not show more improvement, she will eventually need to be let go. She only does the bare minimum and retains her petulant attitude."

"I suggest we try to keep her until the next hiring fair in September. Not only may we attempt to gain her replacement, but it will make it easier for her to find a new position." Taking a last sip of her tea, Lydia considered Suzanna. She hoped that the woman would improve, but suspected she would not. Setting down her now empty teacup, she changed the subject by asking, "I would like to reward those workers who are proving themselves to have good attitudes and are hardworking. Do you know of anything that they might use, or be appreciative to receive?" Lydia watched Mrs. Wilson as she looked off into the distance, thinking, glad that she was taking her question seriously. While Lydia had a few ideas herself, she knew that Mrs. Wilson was closer to the servants and might know something she didn't. Besides, it was always good to show your housekeeper how much you respected her judgment.

Turning her gaze back to Lydia, Mrs. Wilson said, "The first thing that comes to mind would be a cheerful blanket to keep them warm this winter, but that would take time to complete. More immediately, it might be better to offer something simpler like a small bag of chocolates or comfits."

Lydia knew it would not do to grin at her housekeeper, but she could not keep her eyes from dancing when she replied, "Both are lovely ideas. Next time I go to town, I will buy the supplies for both. I know you meet with the staff weekly. Would you mind distributing the gifts to those whom you consider deserving of the treats?" Lydia already had the thought of getting several lengths of ribbon to tie the bags with.

"Of course," came Mrs. Wilson's reply.

Looking at the clock that stood in the corner of the room, Lydia frowned, exclaiming, "I did not realize how late it was. I promised to take Clara on a walk through the garden and to visit the horses this morning."

Standing, Mrs. Wilson said, "Then I will leave you to do that and go check in on the maids." Then, giving a quick bob of a curtsy, she left the room, allowing Lydia to rush off in search of Clara.

CHESTER PATTED THE POCKET that had the letter he had finally received from his mother, reassuring himself by its presence. She and Gwen had arrived at their new home safely. It was finally time to make his escape. Once he had hoped he could work off his father's debt and start over in England. It had been hard to come to the realization that he could never return to the life that he once knew and had hoped to have. The baron would never willingly let him leave his service. As things stood, Chester was no better than a slave committed to doing his master's bidding.

With the baron unconscious after his excessive indulgence, Chester saw a glimmer of hope that he could make a swift and untraceable escape. Freedom was within his grasp. He just had to take the risk and grab it. He packed his bag and hid what little money he had been able to save over his years of servitude within its confines and fled.

Dashing down alleys in the dark of dawn, Chester knew that there was only one thing left to do. Using some of his precious funds, he had his letter sent by express. The baron's downward spiral was sure to hurt good people and Chester could not, in good conscience, leave good people in ignorance of the danger approaching them. He could only pray that the letter's recipient took his words seriously.

Chapter Twenty-Two

Kiernan brushed the horse before him with the skill that came with both experience and love for the animal. He had wondered if bringing Epona with him would prove to be a problem, but so far, it had not. When they had come up with the idea to have Kiernan pose as a worker at Swarkstone, Darcy told him to bring the mare. He had wanted him to have his own transportation in case Kiernan needed to get help for some reason. It was a sound argument, but Kiernan had worried that someone would question how a stable hand looking for work might have his own horse and especially one that was so obviously well bred.

It turned out that he needn't have worried. There were only three men working on the grounds. The youngest was a stable boy of about ten, who was excitable but willing to work hard. The only other person who worked in the stables was an older man named Jeb who did a good job but did not seem to give much thought beyond what was required of him. He was the de facto stable master, but only because all the more senior workers on the estate had abandoned their posts. When an extra horse had showed up in the stable, Jeb had merely shrugged. Not the best sort to be in charge of anything in Kiernan's opinion, but he would not point out his deficiencies when it was helping him.

The gardener, originally brought in to assist with transporting Lydia's plants, had ultimately chosen to remain on the estate as the third grounds worker. When he had run into Mr. Roberts, he had only winked at Kiernan as he introduced himself in front of the others, rightly assuming Lydia's family had sent him to check in on matters. Later, they met up in the gardens and discussed the state of the situation at Swarkstone. The situation impressed neither of them. The estate needed an infusion of good workers. And more than that, someone had been trying to cause harm to Lydia and her new family, and both of them were determined to do everything in their power to put an end to it.

Lost in thought, Kiernan was startled when he heard the young shout, "Pony!" Looking over at the source of the voice, he spied little Clara as she grinned exuberantly up at Epona from the front of the stall. Close behind her was Lydia, looking at him with a raised brow.

Grinning at being found out by Lydia, Kiernan quickly asserted, "Hello, my name is Kiernan, and I will be working in the stables and on the grounds."

He was glad Clara was too preoccupied by Epona snuffing about her face to catch him in his lie. It would not do for her to say anything about already knowing him. Lydia, on the other hand, was sure to understand the situation, so he was not worried about her reaction. His guess was confirmed when she said, "It is lovely to meet you and your fine horse."

Chuckling, he answered, "Oh this horse isn't mine, ma'am. I am only caring for it." Of course, Lydia would be the first person to point out the discrepancy. He offered his patently false explanation by saying, "I was dropped off by someone kind enough to bring me by cart on their way to another estate. I do not know where such a fine horse could have come from."

Wrinkling her nose, Lydia said, "Well, once Clara has her fill of our visit to the horses, I would appreciate it if you could help carry my basket and tools as we walk through the garden looking for blooms to arrange for or table." They both knew that Lydia did not need help to carry her basket, but it would give them a reasonable excuse to walk away from prying eyes together.

Turning his attention to Clara, he crouched down and asked, "Would you like to help me brush her?"

Nodding her head with vigor, she said, "Yes, please."

Handing her a currycomb, he said, "This is a currycomb, and we use it to get the dirt off her coat and skin." Then, picking her up around the waist, he held her so that she could stroke the horse with the comb. Continuing his instruction, he said, "Use gentle circular motions, like this." Holding his free hand over hers, he helped guide her efforts.

Looking on, Lydia said, "Oh look how pretty she is. You have done such a lovely job, Clara."

"Pony is a pretty horsey," exclaimed the little girl in happy agreement.

After a few minutes, Kiernan set her back on her feet. "Thank you for helping me groom Epona."

Handing back the comb, she said, "You're welcome." She then hugged the mare's front leg. "I love Pony!"

Kiernan inwardly cringed. With most horses, her abrupt movements could startle them, causing them to react by shying away from her or kicking out. Fortunately, Epona was steadier than most horses for all that she was young. Still, he felt Clara should learn how to act around horses if she was going to have such an affection for them. Kneeling, he said, "Clara, have you ever had someone startle you when you did not know they were there?" Eyes wide, she looked at him and nodded. Smiling softly, he continued, "I know you love *Pony,* but moving like you did can startle her. Some horses are more easily frightened than others, so it is important to move softly around them. It is important that you let horses know what you are doing so you don't scare them and they jump. Can you imagine what would happen if a scared horse jumped?"

Biting her lip, Clara looked back and forth between him and Epona. Then with a frown she said, "I am sorry if a scared you, Pony."

Then, walking slowly, she moved to where Epona could easily see her and said, "I would like to hug you now."

Lydia and Kiernan smiled at one another at Clara's cute antics, but the moment was disrupted when Jeb shouted, "Why are you allowing that child to be in there!"

Scared at the loud shout, Clara flinched in fear and clung tightly to Epona's leg. Epona remained still, her eyes locked on Jeb as he approached, emitting a furious snort in response to the older man's angry approach. As he continued to approach, his furious movements and expression caused the mare to snap at him.

Halting his approach, Jeb studied the mare with shock on his face. Epona leaned over and nuzzled at the top of Clara's head and softly nickered at her. Mouth dropping open, Jeb watched the scene with an expression of consternation. If Epona had looked at the older man and started to lecture in Latin, he might have been less thunderstruck by her behavior.

Speaking up, Lydia said, "Clara is rather fond of horses and Epona is rather fond of her. As long as Mr. Kiernan and I are here to supervise, it should not be a problem, Jeb."

Shaking his head, Jeb responded, "Whatever you say, Missus." Turning away, he walked to another stall muttering under his breath about crazy horses.

Lydia walked among the scant blooms of her garden at a sedate pace while Clara expended her energy running about. It was nice to see her looking more like a child and less like a somber little statue. She looked around, making sure that no one could overhear her before she spoke to Kiernan. "I suppose William sent you."

Rubbing at the back of his neck, Kiernan said, "It was a consensus of sorts. The letter you wrote about the fires and Mr. Burgess being burned in the most recent one did not sit well with anyone."

Lydia sighed. "I assumed someone would show up."

"Elizabeth wanted to rush over here, but Darcy put an end to that idea. Not without a struggle, mind you." This had them both laughing. Lydia could well picture that argument. Her older sister was ever the mother bear, always quick to run to the aid of those in need. Her recent delivery being only a few months past would not stop her, though William managed to. Kiernan managed to get his laughter under regulation before finishing, "If Kitty was not so close to her own confinement, I believe she and the colonel would both be here. I have a feeling that he will come to check on matters once their child arrives safely."

"But how did it come about that you were the one who came to my aid?"

Shrugging, Kiernan explained, "Servants are easy to overlook, and I will be able to act the servant easier than all of your brothers-in-law. I am hoping that I may overhear someone plotting evil or at the very least I may be present to help the next time something bad happens."

Sighing, Lydia moved to clip a bloom before saying, "I wish I could say that I do not think anything else bad will happen, but I can't. I can only hope that whatever transpires is not too bad." Placing the bloom in her basket with the others she had gathered, Lydia glanced back at Kiernan.

Examining her shears, he said, "Those are unlike the other shears I have seen you use."

Holding them for him to examine, she said, "They arrived shortly before I left Pemberley. They are quite useful. The cutting motion is smoother than typical and look at this." Holding the shears carefully, she undid a clasp, and the two halves of the shears came apart. Explaining, she said, "This makes them easier to clean and sharpen. They are my new favorites."

Lydia watched as a wicked grin spread across Kiernan's face. "I think it would be a good idea for you to keep these on hand when you are out here by yourself or only with Clara. I know Swarkstone is not like Pemberley. You do not have the staff on hand to accompany you as you work in the gardens. I would hate for you to be caught unawares."

Frowning, Lydia quickly scanned the area and spotted Clara happily playing not far off. She asked, "Do you really think that someone would be so bold as to attack me so close to home?"

Grimacing, Kiernan responded, "They caught the building you were in on fire and somehow got away without being noticed. It is better to be prepared than caught off guard and those shears could become valuable weapon should the need arise."

Remembering the suffocating heat and smoke, Lydia found her breath strangling in her throat. She had had more than one nightmare since the fire. In her dreams, she sometimes suffocated in the smoke when no one came to her aid. Other times, Sebastian perished from burns that were worse than reality.

Squaring her shoulders, Lydia chose not to dwell on her memories of the blaze or her nightmares and instead focused on how to protect herself and her loved ones. Her grim smile did not match Kiernan's fiendish one, but she did have the power to say, "I will keep them on hand."

With a nod, Kiernan changed the subject, asking, "How is Mr. Burgess recovering from his burns?"

Sighing, Lydia turned and inspected one of the rose bushes that she had brought with her from Pemberley. It was doing well for all that it was transplanted recently. Running her fingers along one of the stems, she said, "He has burns running from the backs of his hands and up his shoulders in patches. While he says he is well, and the apothecary said he is healing remarkably thanks to the treatment that was provided by one of our tenant wives, I still worry for him."

Kiernan spoke from behind her. "Of course you worry for him. The thought of someone you know needing help or being unwell weighs heavily on your mind. He is your husband, so it only makes things worse and unless I miss my guess, you have quickly grown to love him."

Lydia could feel her cheeks flame with embarrassment from being caught out so easily. She should have known that Kiernan would realize. He had been there for Elizabeth's romance and had encouraged William to propose. Kiernan had also been there when Mary finally confronted Gabriel, though a blizzard had also helped matters along. Finally, looking up at Kiernan, she managed to laugh, "I cannot deny it. Nor would I wish to. I have found myself thoroughly in love with the man, despite the way he goes charging into fires and scaring me to death."

THE WHOLE THING WAS ridiculous. He was too important to pay attention to his funds and spending. So, what if he should have waited for his estate's harvest to come in before buying that jewelry for his mistress? He knew he had to give her something to salvage their arrangement after his last drunken debacle. Growling, he punched at the nearby bush.

Who cared that they had record rain and a blight? Growing crops was so easy, even stupid peasants could do it, and yet somehow, they got it wrong. His tenants should have worked harder and had a better harvest. If they had done their job, he would have the money he expected and there would not be an issue of paying the jeweler or dealing with his very strong messengers. They were calling for better roofs and drainage for the fields. Baron Blackthorn chuckled quietly to himself, picturing how their complaints would turn to cries once he informed them he was raising their rents. He did not put up with loafers.

None of his previous plans had worked as he had counted upon and now, when he finally had something that would work, his minion had disappeared. He was Randell Blakesley, Baron of Blackthorn. He never actually did things himself unless it was threatening people, and that was only because he enjoyed it. Now he realized that he did not have people he could trust with something like this in his employ. Without his minion, he had no choice but to take matters into his own hands.

Grumbling as he went, the baron stalked among the bushes. His reports from his arsonist said that the little girl would be in the garden with a young blonde woman most mornings. Hoping for a swift getaway, he had tethered his horse in the small, untamed area just beyond the blooming flowers. Angry that he had been driven to something so beneath himself, he knelt in the dirt behind several large bushes with some sort of flowers that made him want to sneeze.

The sound of small footfalls sent a thrill through him. This would be the day that everything would come together. He could practically taste victory as he anticipated the moment when the little brat would be in his clutches. She was the key to all his money problems. By ransoming her, he could both pay off his debt to the jeweler and secure the funds needed to start horse breeding for races. He had heard it was becoming all the rage with the latest fast set he wanted to ingratiate him into. Once he had gained their trust and interest, he could throw a house party and get plenty of blackmail material to keep his ventures going.

Listening carefully, he heard the lower voice of the blonde intermingled with the higher annoyingly chirpy tones of the girl child. As he waited for them to come into view, he tried to remember if it was the nursemaid or the young wife that went with the child into the garden. It did not really matter she was just a girl and would not be able to stop him. No matter who she turned out to be, he would direct her to pass on his message to the Burgess fellow. Blackthorn needed Burgess to wait at Swarkstone Park to receive the ransom demand.

He had heard that Burgess' new wife had a significant dowry, so his plan had been to ask for it. His contacts had told him that she had been born from a lowly country squire, but several of her sisters had married exceedingly well and he supposed their husbands had increased her dowry so that they could get her off their hands. No man wanted to take care of a younger sister if he did not have to. Hopefully, there would be at least twenty-thousand pounds for the taking.

Just as the baron was about to rub his hands together in glee, the little girl came bouncing around the corner of the path, finally in sight. Knowing that he needed to be quick, he darted out from his hiding spot and grabbed the girl by the wrist, causing her to screech. Giving her a smallish shake, he told her, "You are going to come with me for a while, Laura."

The baron expected her to look up at him in fright, but she just looked confused for a moment before she started tugging to get her arm free. Looking up at him with blue eyes hooded by brows drawn together, she declared, "I am not Laura, I am Clara!"

Glaring at the child, the baron snapped, "I do not care who you are. You are coming with me." He would call her whatever he wanted, and she should be happy that he saw to her care while he had her.

The hard voice of a woman drew his attention when she thundered, "You will not be taking her anywhere!"

The baron studied her. It was obvious that she was the young bride. He could see that much from her method of dress. The baron observed her, noting that she was more than passingly pretty, although she was dressed far more respectably than he preferred. She was moving quickly towards him, obviously intent on stopping him, which almost made him laugh. Pulling the little girl out of her reach, he barked, "I am taking the child! Tell your husband that he will receive my ransom demand along with instruction on how to make the exchange by the end of the day."

The woman did not cry or act afraid, she merely said, "No." Then with a fierce look on her face she continued to approach him. Discomposed by her actions being the complete opposite of what he expected, he lashed out. "You are nothing but a female, foolish and powerless. What can you possibly do to stop me?" His laugh did not last long.

"You are nothing but a female, foolish and powerless. What can you possibly do to stop me?" questioned the baron.

Baron Blackthorn's chilling cackle quickly turned into a shriek of pain when Lydia thrust the flat of her palm into the bridge of his nose, breaking it. Grabbing Clara and moving back out of his reach when he brought both hands to his bleeding face, she taunted, "You know nothing of me, Baron. Engaging the enemy without proper intelligence was just the first of many mistakes you made. I may be female, but I long ago determined never to be foolish or powerless." Leaning over, she whispered something in Clara's ear before the child took off running.

"What the blazes? You struck me!" Giving up on stopping the bleeding, Baron Blackthorn dropped his hands into fists. "I will have you brought up on charges for striking a peer."

Knowing she had to keep the attention on herself, she continued to taunt the furious man, "Thinking that you have the power to have me brought up on charges is your second mistake. I am daughter-in-law to a viscount and sister-in-law to an earl. An earl who was once a colonel in the royal dragoons. Thinking that you can have me brought up on charges is laughable. You are the one who is trespassing."

"So you made me bleed. How brave you must think you are. How do you really think you are going to stop me? I am bigger than you." Stepping forward, he grabbed her arm and cajoled, "Why put up a fight? Your husband is abed recovering from his wounds. Let me take the girl and I will leave you alone. You do not want to get hurt, do you? Give up, you are just a lady."

Lydia grunted as he drew her close. He smelled of sweat and some sort of musk that made her want to gag. Had he said she was just a lady? The Baron began to drag her along down the garden path in the direction that Clara had run. Laughing, he said, "I will even let you have her back once your husband pays me enough."

"Threatening Clara was your third mistake. Haven't you ever heard not to threaten cubs when the mother is nearby?"

"How else would I get any money out of your husband? Besides, you are not her mother, she is nothing to you. Paying the servants to abandon the place didn't do anything. Spreading rumors backfired. Even setting the fires got me nowhere. That stupid lawyer would not find the pair of you unfit guardians. But I have discovered your weakness, and it's that brat. You will do anything for her. I will finally get what I deserve!" Lydia could feel his spittle slide down the side of her face as he ranted. While it was nice to have her suspicions confirmed, knowing that he had started the fire that had harmed Sebastian only made her angrier and more alert.

All the while he was dragging her around the garden, Lydia had been waiting for something very specific. Seeing what she was waiting for, Lydia knew it was time to act. When he put his foot down right alongside hers, she stomped hard with the heel of her boot on his instep.

She hadn't begun wearing her reinforced boots for nothing. She expected his scream and for him to loosen his grip around her neck, and she was ready. Shoving her elbow back into the middle of his chest exactly where Kiernan had shown her had the desired effect. He completely let her go and struggled to breathe. Facing him she snapped, "I am not just anything!" Driving home her point, Lydia grabbed him by the shoulders and brought her knee up and into his groin.

He might have wanted to scream or curse at her at that point, but he was incapable of either. The baron could only hold himself and look up at her in confusion. Glaring at him, she took a second to whistle shrilly. Then, reaching down into the gardening basket she had dropped on the ground earlier, Lydia pulled out her sheers. Undoing the catch that held the two pieces together, she was left with two incredibly sharp blades.

Eyes widening, the baron managed a strangled, "Who are you?"

"I am Lydia Bennet Burgess and I have faced worse men than you. My sisters have been attacked, survived blizzards, faced epidemics, been thrown off cliffs, and almost kidnapped, and every time we have come out on top. I have an adoptive little brother who saw the need to teach me to defend myself, and his methods have proved quite effective. The women in my family protect what is important, and we have learned to do what we must in order to protect who we love." Holding the blades at her sides, hoping that she would not have to use either of them, she declared, "I have claimed Clara Blakesley as my daughter, and you will never lay another finger on her."

"Do you think he is scared enough yet, Darcy?" said a familiar voice.

Lydia started for a moment when she heard the voice coming from behind her, but then relaxed when she realized reinforcements had arrived. Turning her head, Lydia spotted William, Kiernan, and Theodore standing there and glaring at Baron Blackthorn. She knew she could rely on them to take care of the matter. With a visible sense of relief, Lydia's energy seemed to drain from her body. Her shoulders sagged and her thudding heart no longer sounded in her ears.

Approaching her, William gave her a one-armed hug, while keeping his eyes on their adversary. Holding her to him in a supportive fashion, William said, "Why don't you go inside with Kiernan, while Theodore and I take care of this scum?"

With a nod, Lydia affixed her two blades back together into her gardening shears once again and then leaned down to gather her basket. With a faint smile directed at William and Theodore, she accepted Kiernan's outstretched arm and walked away, tuning out the unpleasant sounds of the disgruntled man's vociferous complaints.

Chapter Twenty-Three

Darcy looked down at the man before him with contempt. Baron Blackthorn was the sort of man who exemplified what was wrong with society: the desire to get what you want without working at it honestly.

Still huddled on the ground in pain from Lydia's last strike, the baron shouted, "Did you see what she did to me? I will have her charged with assault!"

"She did a good job of managing you. I will say it was almost a pleasure to watch her bring you down. It seems she takes after my Artemis in her ferocity." William could hear the fury in Theodore's voice, despite the laughter.

Glancing at Theodore briefly, William questioned, "I wonder, though, where she would learn such a skill."

Grinning, Theodore laughed, "I think we will have to blame that on Kiernan. I know he was learning to fight from some of his friends at Eton last year. Though if you think about it, it would be wise to at least teach something of defense to the women in our lives with as many muddles as they seem to get in."

Nodding his head in contemplation, Darcy wondered about the merits of Theodore's suggestion. He would like to think he could keep Elizabeth safe, but having her know how to better protect herself would be reassuring. Looking back down at the baron, Darcy could tell that the man was infuriated to be so ignored. Deciding to turn the knife, he said, "I do not think you will have to worry about Kitty. She is fairly handy with a knife and bow. Elizabeth would be happy to learn. Despite her desperate act of biting her attacker, she couldn't avoid hurtling off the cliff."

"She stopped you from being shot in the back, knowing she had no real way to defend herself. No one can deny that Elizabeth has courage, though a few additional skills wouldn't be amiss." Throughout their playful banter, William couldn't help but notice that Theodore's eyes never strayed from their adversary, a testament to his battle-hardened instincts.

As if he finally had too much, the baron struggled to his feet and growled, "Just who are you people to think you could ignore me?"

Offering a slight bow in irony, Darcy said, "Fitzwilliam Darcy of Pemberley at your service, and this is my cousin and brother-in-law, Theodore Fitzwilliam, retired colonel of the royal dragoons, and Earl of Matlock."

Beside him, Theodore placed his hand threateningly on the hilt of his saber. "It is a pleasure to finally meet you. I hear you have had some issue against our sister-in-law and her family, and we have come to handle matters." The expression on Theodore's face was one that had frightened battle-hardened soldiers. Against someone who had fancied himself intimidating, but had never faced anyone greater than himself, the result was utterly devastating.

The color leached out of the baron's face. Realization was finally sinking in for him—his failed attacks were about to come crashing back on him. Still, he blustered, "You cannot stop me from pressing charges, and two such individuals as yourself would hate to have your names so smeared."

William looked at Theodore and laughingly said, "Is the worm trying to threaten us, or blackmail us? I cannot tell."

Theodore laughed, the sound cold and devoid of all true humor. Smiling, he approached the baron and grabbed him by the scruff of his neck, and thundered, "Either way, he will soon learn the error of his ways. You are trespassing and have assaulted the sister of a nobleman. Everyone will applaud anything she did to protect herself and her family from you." Theodore dragged the baron over to the group of men that had surrounded them as they spoke. Muscled and armed, they were ex-soldiers who could handle any situation that came their way. Tossing the baron to one of his men, he said, "When I learned that you were coming to attack my sister in person, I gathered my best guards and came to Swarkstone. Frankly, I do not think a single one of them would blink an eye if I told them to kill you and bury you somewhere you would never be found, but I know my wife would be disappointed in me, so I will refrain."

William watched in satisfaction as the men put the baron in foot and leg irons. The baron's eyes bulged out of his face as he looked down at his hands, his expression filled with horror at the method of his confinement. "How did you know? How could you have known?" He whined in confusion.

Shaking his head Theodore, said, "I recently received an anonymous letter that warned me of an eminent attack by yourself. Though I already had you under investigation, either way, you would not have been free to persecute people beyond the month." Turning to the man who appeared to be in charge, he said, "They are expecting him at Old Bailey. I really don't care about his condition, but I would appreciate it if you made sure he arrives there alive."

William watched as they dragged him off towards the wagon that had been brought for just that purpose. In no time at all, he had been loaded with as much care as a sack of grain. The man shouting all the while, "You cannot do this to me! I am a baron! Don't you know who I am?"

One of his guards laughed as he secured him for the journey. "You be sure to say that to the folks at Old Bailey. I am sure they will be sure to show you the proper deference. Maybe they will give you a nicer cell."

As soon as she was out of sight of the baron, Lydia picked up her pace. Kiernan easily kept up with her, asking, "Where are we going in such a hurry?"

Slightly out of breath, she replied, "I told Clara to hide with Epona. I hoped that if Baron Blackthorn somehow got past me, the horse might be able to protect her until help came."

Nodding, Kiernan kept even with her as they rushed back to the stables. "That was a good plan, given the situation you found yourself in. I have been training Epona to protect her rider."

It did not take them long to enter into the dim space of the stables and Lydia was calling out, "Clara?" Looking into Epona's stall, Lydia at first panicked, but then she saw Clara pop up out of the straw near the back.

The mare looked at Lydia, while her ears flicked backed towards Clara. Lydia wondered if the mare would warn her away if she approached, but she needn't have worried because Clara was soon hurrying her way.

Crying out as Lydia scooped her up, Clara moaned, "He did not get you! I was so afraid."

Holding Clara close to her heart, Lydia crooned to her and ran her hand through her tangled black curls. "I am fine, darling," she reassured Clara. "You were so brave coming here to hide with Epona."

Looking back at the mare with a teary smile, Clara said, "Pony is nice. She would protect me because I love her."

Ruffling the girl's hair, Kiernan said, "I do believe you are right, Miss Clara."

Kissing Clara's brow and pulling a random piece of hay from her hair, Lydia added, "But I do believe it is time to head inside, Clara. I have had quite the morning, and I would like a warm cup of tea. What about you?"

Smile brightening up her face despite her tear-stained cheeks, Clara cried, "Can I have some biscuits?"

As they left the stable behind, Lydia assured Clara by saying, "Of course you can."

Looking over Lydia's shoulder, Clara waved goodbye. "Bye, Pony! Thank you for protecting me." Lydia knew that she should probably put Clara down. She was more than big enough to walk on her own, but she just could not. The recent attack was too fresh in her mind, and so she carried her into the house.

Clara noticed that Kiernan was following them into the house and asked, "Why are you coming too?"

Far from being offended by her comment, Kiernan merely laughed and said, "I want biscuits too!"

Clara's giggle was a balm to Lydia's anxious heart. Walking to the closest sitting room, Lydia placed Clara on a settee and then collapsed next to her. Kiernan pulled the bell cord before he sat down. Laying her head on the back of the settee, Lydia struggled not to cry.

Now that she was safe and Clara was safe, everything in her that she had used to fight was leaking out of her and it was leaving her weak and weepy. She resented feeling weak and weepy, and both in combination were even worse. When May came in response to the bellpull, she asked the girl for a tea service for four and plenty of biscuits. If William and Theodore wanted something more substantial than biscuits, they would let her know once they came in.

The sound of feet pounding down the stairs in a rush had Lydia jolting upright. Was there another problem at hand? The sight that came into view through the open doors was not something that she had expected. Sebastian, haphazardly dressed, was rushing down the hall. He had no cravat and was barefoot; it was obvious that he had left his room in a rush. She couldn't help herself—it was pure instinct that made her call out to him. "Sebastian, I thought you were asleep. What are you doing out of bed?"

Changing direction so fast that he nearly skidded into a wall, he rushed to her. Collapsing at her feet, he grabbed her hands in his and looked up into her eyes. "Davies said there was a rumor that the baron had attacked you."

Lydia shook her head, worried about the healing burns that were hidden beneath the sleeves of his loose-fitting shirt. "What about your arms?"

Shaking his head, Sebastian said, "I am healing and though they will probably hurt for some time, I have decided that I am well enough to leave my room. Right now, my focus is on you. Please tell me, are you all right?" As he had spoken, he drew her hands closer to him, holding them to his chest. Lydia could feel the pounding of his heart in the backs of her hands.

Blinking back a few errant tears, Lydia reassured him. "I am unharmed for the most part, though I may have a bruise or two. Baron Blackthorn tried to kidnap Clara with the thought that he could ransom her back to us. He was the one who had bribed our staff away before we got here and spread rumors and started fires. Or at least had all those things done."

Sebastian looked over to Clara and, freeing one of his hands, smoothed her wild hair away from her face. "Clara, are you all right?"

Nodding her head, she smiled at him and said, "Yes, I got to hide with Pony, and now I am getting biscuits."

Lydia wondered at the girl's resilience. When she had first met her, Clara had been nearly afraid of her own shadow, but now, here she was still talking and able to smile despite a kidnap attempt. Shaking her head, she said, "Clara was a very brave girl." Lydia heard her voice wobble and pressed her lips together to combat her ever-growing need to cry.

It was clear that Sebastian had heard it, as he swiftly lifted her up and settled her into his lap, cradling her against his chest in a firm, protective hold. He did not say anything, and simply held her. Lydia hid her face in the crook of his neck and gave way to tears. She hated the weakness of it but was unable to hold them at bay any longer.

Kiernan spoke up, saying, "Lydia was very brave too. She fought off Baron Blackthorn so that Clara could get away. She was amazing."

Sebastian clutched Lydia tightly, feeling her tears soak through his shirt, a silent testament to the intensity of her struggle to protect Clara. Despite her claims of being physically fine, it was clear that emotionally she had been profoundly affected. He could only imagine how terrified she must have been having to fight the baron to protect Clara.

He was both relieved that she was safe and furious that the man had dared to attack his family. Sebastian wanted to go after the baron with revenge in mind. He wanted to hurt him for hurting Lydia, but he knew she needed him, and she would always be his priority. So he stayed, holding her to his chest and absorbing her pain as her tears soaked into his skin.

The sound of boots approaching had him clutching her tighter and his head coming up and looking for danger. He relaxed when he saw Darcy and Theodore come into the room, though why they were in his home, he could only guess. Actually, after a moment, he realized he could guess quite easily. Somehow, thcy had learned of the danger his family faced.

Taking a seat across from him, Theodore said, "The scum is on his way to face justice at the Old Bailey, accompanied by four of my old military friends who serve as guards for me. They were more than happy to help when they learned that my wife's younger sister was being threatened by an entitled fool."

Smoothing Lydia's hair as he spoke, Sebastian said, "I am grateful for your assistance, though I do wonder why, or rather how, you are here to offer that assistance."

Darcy and Theodore looked at one another for a moment before Darcy said, "When we received news of the fire, Kiernan came to help keep an eye on things, and Theodore and I set our people investigating matters. It is not that we did not want to come to help, but we knew Kiernan would go unnoticed more so than we would."

Picking up where Darcy left off, Theodore said, "I wanted to help but did not want to leave Kitty."

This had Lydia jerking away from Sebastian and looking at Theodore, saying, "Is Kitty all right? Why did you leave her? She should be having her baby any day now."

Laughing, Theodore said, "I came at her command. She is my general, after all. You will be happy to know, however, that she and baby Cedric are doing well back at Matlock."

Collapsing back against Sebastian with a smile, she said, "I am so glad she and the baby are well."

Sebastian was pleased that Lydia had stopped crying. Though there was no shame in her tears, he was always happier to see her smiles. Her smile changed into a blush when the maid entered the room with the tea tray. It seemed that Lydia had overlooked the fact that she was in his lap until the maid's shocked expression reminded her. When Lydia got up to serve tea, she did so with a bright blush that amused him.

Lydia quickly asked the maid for an additional cup for Sebastian and to ask for Nurse Harris to come and gather Clara. Her relaxed demeanor and the way she idly swung her legs indicated she had overcome her fright and was now getting restless after devouring her biscuits. In quick order, the maid provided an extra cup and Nurse Harris took Clara away.

As Lydia sat back down with her tea, she positioned herself next to him, and the group delved back into their discussion. Theodore began by saying, "Shortly after Cedric's birth, I received an anonymous letter stating that the baron was most likely going to strike soon. So Kitty sent me here to make sure you were safe. I sent a note round to Darcy, and it seems we arrived just in time."

Darcy took up the tale there, saying, "We had just started to talk with Kiernan when we heard the whistle and rushed to Lydia's aid."

Looking back and forth between Lydia and his guests, he asked, "Whistle?"

Rolling her eyes, Lydia said, "When Kiernan arrived, he told me to whistle loudly if I needed help, assuring me that he would come running." Then, shrugging, she added, "It seemed to work well."

Setting his empty teacup down in its saucer, Theodore laughingly said, "By the time we got there, Baron Blackthorn was already on the ground writhing in pain. So it was simple work to have him shackled and taken away."

"Regardless of how easy it was, I want to thank you all for coming to help us in our time of need."

Waving him off, Darcy said, "You are family. I would like to think that you would do something similar to help me and mine should the need arise." Sebastian was quick to nod. Should the need arise, he would not hesitate to lend his aid. It was just who he was.

He looked down at where Lydia sat beside him. Watching her, Sebastian felt his heart turn over. Gratefulness washed over him as he realized that she had made it through the morning's danger without any harm. Things could have gone much worse.

Finishing her tea, Lydia set her cup down and said, "If you gentlemen will excuse me, I am going to see about having rooms prepared for William and Theodore."

After she left the room, Kiernan found his voice, saying, "I am glad you figured out how much you love her. The woman you married is remarkable though I would be careful about making her angry. She really took the lessons I showed her to heart."

Chapter Twenty-Four

Lydia had woken up early, which was surprising, considering the drama she endured the day before. She had gone to bed feeling like she would sleep for years. Yet she woke early, unable to stop thinking of all that had happened. Glancing over at Clara, Lydia was happy that she had slept well through the night. Lydia had been afraid the little girl would have nightmares, but she had slept better than Lydia herself.

Carefully sliding out of bed so as to not disturb Clara, Lydia grabbed her wrapper and put it on. Walking across the room, her bare feet cool on the wooden floor, Lydia sat before her mirror and brushed her hair. A faint light seeped through the windows, creating a muted gray hue that hinted at the approaching dawn. She did not really need to see herself in the mirror; it was only out of habit that she sat there as she methodically brushed her hair.

Lydia had always thought there was something soothing in the rhythmic motion of brushing her hair. She allowed her mind to wonder, thinking of the attack by Baron Blackthorn, which thankfully had failed. She also thought about how grateful she was to have the skills that Kiernan had taught her, without which she would not have been able to protect Clara nearly as easily. Lydia was confident that she would have stopped the man somehow.

With her hair free of tangles and once again a golden waterfall down her back, Lydia put her brush down and began a simple braid. Once complete, Lydia wound the braid around the back of her head to create a simple knot that would be adequate for a simple morning at home. Placing a few pins to hold it in place, Lydia was done with her hair for the morning.

Walking across the room, Lydia went into her sitting room, being sure to leave her bedroom door ajar so that she could hear Clara if she cried out. Taking up a seat at her desk, Lydia lit a candle and took out a sheet of paper. With Theodore and William both heading back to their homes, Lydia felt she should send letters with them to her sisters. Only as she gazed down at the empty page before her, she could not think of what to say. Oh, she could congratulate Kitty for her new baby boy, but what did she put after that?

Lydia found she did not really want to put her experience with the baron to paper, and when it came to the developments in her relationship with Sebastian, well, she could not find the words to express it adequately. Thinking about Sebastian and their relationship moved her to put her quill down all together. For a moment, her mind wandered back to the feeling of Sebastian's comforting embrace as tears streamed down her face. Without uttering a word, he gave her the space to let go, without any demands or expectations. He hadn't even really needed her to tell him that she was falling apart; he had seemed to just know. Through it all, she had felt so safe, so loved. How could she put that down on paper and catch the magnitude of it? Which was why her page remained blank.

She did not know how long she had been staring at that page when she heard tapping coming from the door that led to Sebastian's sitting room. Moving to stand, Lyda saw Sebastian peek his head around the door. Greeting her with a smile, he said, "I saw your light on, and I wanted to check in with you and make sure you were all right after the day you had yesterday."

In that moment, Lydia realized what had felt off that morning. She was missing Sebastian. Since they married, she had been grateful for his companionship, but now she was realizing just how much she missed him when he wasn't by her side. She was even starting to crave his presence. Gesturing for him to enter the room and join her, she said, "I am well. I just could not sleep so I thought I would try to write my sisters, but I have been just staring at a blank page, unable to come up with what to write."

Moving to a comfortable settee, she patted the space next to her, hoping he would sit with her. As he walked towards her, she noticed that he was wearing his banyan. She had to tell herself not to be shocked. She had certainly seen him in less when she was helping to care for him after the fire. As he sat down next to her, he casually draped his arm along the back of the seat, creating a comforting cocoon around Lydia.

Thinking of his recent injury moved her to ask, "How are your arms? Only yesterday, it seemed like you were staying in bed and now you are up and about and dressed."

"My burns were not so terrible. The apothecary admitted to me that he had seen much worse and that I could move about as soon as I felt capable, and I was careful. I am still putting on the cream, but I have left off the leaves." As if to demonstrate, Sebastian pulled up his sleeve and showed her his scarred hand and wrist. The skin looked to be healing well with no open wounds, so she supposed he was well enough.

Swallowing, she said, "That is good. I have always known you to be a busy person. I am sure you will prefer to be out of bed and handling things."

Curling her into his side, Sebastian admitted, "I think I will be happy to just be up and about with you. It terrified me yesterday to hear about the fact that you had been in danger, and I had not been there to help you. I do not think I want you to go very far from my side again."

She was only too happy to snuggle into him and soak up the love and comfort that he offered. She was too caught up in enjoying the warmth of him to say anything at first, but after a moment said, "I was terrified too, but only afterwards. At first, I was furious that the baron had thought it would be so easy to just kidnap Clara. Not only would he have re-traumatized her, but he called me a powerless female. I was livid. At least until it was all over. Then I was weak."

Sebastian gently brushed a strand of hair from her forehead, his lips pressing against her temple, igniting a surge of electricity that traveled down her body, tingling all the way to her toes. Trailing a series of kisses from her temple to behind her ear, he whispered, "I would never describe you as powerless. You are magnificent. You protected Clara and yourself. I want you to know that just because you were afraid after the fact and you cried, it doesn't detract from the fact that you were strong when you had to be." Turning so he could look her in the eye he continued, "I marvel at your strength, and I am happy to watch it as you take on the world, but I am also ready to be a soft place to land when it becomes too much for you. You mean everything to me and with each passing day, my adoration for you grows stronger. Tell me what you need."

Sebastian watched Lydia's eyes fill up with tears, hoping they were good tears and that he had not just said something wrong. He did not have to worry long because Lydia swiftly blinked away her tears and said, "You know just how to say what I need to hear. I feel unequipped to express how you make me feel, and sometimes I wonder how I can ever compare to your eloquence."

Offering an encouraging smile, Sebastian revealed, "I do not need eloquence. I only need you and your love. The words are immaterial. I will view any words of love you give me as a gift, and I have a feeling that any description of your feelings will be more potent than you may comprehend. Will you tell me how you feel?"

It had always been easy to admire Lydia's beauty, but there was something special about the way she blushed as they spoke. It heartened him and let him know that even if she struggled for something to say, she was not unaffected by him. Though she moved closer to him, settling her forehead into the crook of his neck and robbing him of the sight of her, he was not disappointed in her show of affection.

"Your idea of being a safe haven resonates with me; I want that for both of us. I crave the idea of being there for you when you need me. My love for you is not so fragile that it cannot handle the weight that will come with life. While I love that you are committed to sheltering me, please do not forget that I want the same thing for you." Lydia's voice as she spoke grew stronger. Sebastian could feel the strength of it in the vibrations on the skin of his neck. He almost did not want her to stop talking, and was very happy when she continued, "I need you to promise me that you will not be someone who hides his problems. I want to be someone you can gain comfort from when you need it."

In response to her declaration, he pulled her closer, wrapping his arms tightly around her. Kissing her forehead again, he said, "Then I shall do all in my power to share my troubles as well as my triumphs with you. I will warn you though, it may not come easily."

Pulling back from him slightly, Lydia looked him in the eye and said, "I will not be the type of person who just takes and doesn't give in this relationship." She paused and then with a slight look of hesitation and a deep blush continued, "Though I have had an idea of how to remind you that you should be sharing your burden with me."

Raising his eyebrows in puzzlement, Sebastian asked, "What did you have in mind?"

He was astounded when she swiftly moved in and pressed her lips to his own. The interaction started off innocently enough, but as soon as she offered her gift, he wasted no time in returning the favor. As his hand glided through her hair, he found himself caught in the elaborate knot at the base of her neck. Nothing could dampen his enjoyment of the exquisite taste of her on his lips and the mesmerizing sound of her sighs in his ears. The intensity of their kiss was palpable as his heart thudded in his chest.

Locked in the moment of their first true taste of expressing their love, only the need for air moved him to pull his lips from hers and find other places on her face to settle his kiss. Though he did not stray from her lips for long. He had been nurturing his love for her for so long that he couldn't help but thoroughly enjoy such a precious moment. He could see a few problems with her idea if she meant to use a kiss to get him to share his problems with her, though to be fair, it would have the very good advantage of entirely distracting him from whatever might be bothering him at any given moment. They might have continued their glorious exploration had they not heard something that reached them through the haze of passion.

"Auntie?" Clara's plaintive voice had them freezing in place before slowly untangling. Calling out, Lydia said, "I am coming, darling. One moment." Standing up, Lydia smoothed out the wrinkles in her dressing gown and moved the door to her bedroom. As she reached the door, Lydia looked back over her shoulder and smiled at him.

Sebastian knew he would have to settle for that smile for the moment. Their day was starting, and they were not likely to have many moments alone together with their newly realized love. He sprawled back against the settee, slightly overwhelmed that he had been so taken over by a simple series of kisses. Sebastian wondered idly just how soon the nursery would be done.

"Since it is such a rainy, gloomy day, I thought instead of going for our normal garden walk, I might treat you both to a surprise. What do you think?" asked Lydia. It was two days after her brothers-in-law had left and Lydia had been working feverishly to prepare the gift for them both.

Clara, clearly happy for a surprise, beamed at Lydia. Running up to her, Clara grabbed her around the legs and asked, "What is the surprise? I would love a surprise!"

Leaning down, Lydia kissed Clara's forehead and clasped her in a hug. As she straightened up, she stole a quick glance at Sebastian, finding joy in the fact that he appeared to be genuinely interested, if not as excited as Clara.

Sebastian took one of Clara's hands and asked, "Where is the surprise hiding?"

Taking Clara's other hand, Lydia said, "It is upstairs. Though when we get closer, I will want you to close your eyes. That way, it will be a much bigger surprise. Can you do that for me?"

Nodding, Clara jumped slightly on her toes in excitement, exclaiming. "Yes, Auntie, I can close my eyes if you hold my hand and don't let me fall."

Sebastian smiled down at Clara, squeezing her tiny hand in his, and said, "Of course we won't let you fall. Now why don't we go upstairs so we can get our surprise?"

Tugging both of them with her, Clara rushed to the stairs. Once they got to the top of the second flight of stairs, Clara asked, "When do I close my eyes?"

Scooping Clara up, Sebastian said, "You can close them now. I will carry you."

Lydia smiled as Clara cuddled into Sebastian's hold, her eyes squeezed shut. Leading them both to the nursery, Lydia opened the door and followed them in. She was giddy to see Clara's reaction to the newly finished nursery. Lydia waited until Sebastian was in the middle of the room before saying, "You can open your eyes now."

Clara opened her eyes and gasped. Sebastian, on the other hand, said, "Oh my, Lydia, this is splendid." Once Sebastian put Clara down, she wasted no time exploring every nook and cranny of the room, her giggles filling the air. On one side of the room, there were two beds, each with their own charming canopy, adding a touch of elegance to the space. A short table adorned with several miniature chairs sat proudly in the center of the room. By the windows, two rocking chairs sat invitingly, ready to be occupied. There was also a toy chest filled to the brim and a small bookcase with books.

From start to finish, Lydia had incorporated a soothing lavender and sage theme into every detail. A tranquil ambiance filled the room, with its walls painted in a gentle sage hue interspersed with lavender stripes, while the lavender pillows and bedclothes added a hint of femininity. In Lydia's opinion, the green and purple color scheme struck the perfect balance, making it a suitable choice for both boys and girls who might come to live there.

Coming over to Lydia, Sebastian embraced her, saying, "It is beautiful. I love the painting on that wall."

Looking at the painting, Lydia leaned into Sebastian. It was a lovely painting of several children playing on a grassy hill dotted with purple flowers. Lydia said, "The painting was a gift from Kitty. She knew the color scheme of the room, so she was able to make it fit in perfectly."

Holding Lydia in front of him, Sebastian put his chin on her shoulder, saying, "Your sister is an amazing artist."

Nodding, Lydia said, "I have always thought so."

From the center of the room at the child-size table, Clara said, "There is a tea set for me!"

Grinning, Lydia said, "Yes, honey. I asked them to bring up some biscuits so that we may have a treat in your new room."

Clasping her hands together, Clara asked, "Is this is my very own new room?"

"Yes, darling, the room is yours. Nurse Harris will be in that little room through that door." Pointing at the door that was painted cream, Lydia continued, "So you will not be alone, and you can pick whichever bed you want to be yours. There is an extra bed so that you can have your cousins visit and spend the night in here with you. There are more little beds coming that will be in the next room for when everyone is here."

Clara ran towards Lydia and Sebastian, throwing her arms around their legs in a tight embrace. "I love my room, Auntie. It has purple and toys! I love you, Auntie Lydia, and you too, Uncle S'Bastien."

With a warm smile directed at Clara, Lydia cooed, "I love you too, my sweet little love."

Settling in at the child-sized table, Lydia helped Clara serve pretend tea to go with the biscuits. Sebastian was too large to sit on the tiny child-size chairs, so he sat on the floor without a fuss. When Clara left the table to get her new doll so she could have more guests at her tea party, Lydia leaned over and whispered to Sebastian, "Thank you for putting up with this silliness. I know it means a lot to Clara."

Whispering back, he said, "She deserves to be happy. I can manage a tea party or two. Besides, you said that this was my surprise as well. You did a wonderful job getting this room ready for Clara."

"Thank you."

Coming back with a doll, Clara set it on one of the small chairs and placed a teacup in front of her. Suddenly looking worried, Clara looked at Lydia and said, "If I am sleeping here with Nurse Harris, will you be lonely all by yourself, Auntie Lydia?"

Lydia glanced at Sebastian, her face heating in a blush. She said, "It is so sweet that you are worried about me. Your uncle said I can sleep in his room so we can keep each other company."

Nodding, Clara said, "That is good." Then, looking at Sebastian, she added, "You take good care of Auntie Lydia, Uncle S'bastien. I love her."

Reaching out, Sebastian ruffled Clara's hair and said, "Of course, I will take good care of Auntie Lydia. I love her too."

As they made their way out of the room and left Clara to play with Nurse Harris, Sebastian walked to the stairs with Lydia on his arm. Ever since she had terrified him by tripping that one time, he preferred to have her on his arm. He knew it was foolish, but he could not help but worry about her safety. He loved her so intensely that the mere thought of her becoming injured pained him. Now that he knew she returned his feelings, he was determined that they would have no less than fifty years together.

Arriving at the hall near their rooms, Lydia hugged his arm to her and said, "You know, now that the nursery is finished, I think my next project will be the mistress suite."

Looking down at Lydia, Sebastian asked, "What exactly are you wanting to do?" He knew it was the done thing for married couples to sleep apart, but he had not expected her to want to make improvements to her room. He had hoped they would be spending more time together, not less.

Smiling up at him, Lydia said, "You may not know this, but none of the women in my family sleep in their own room. Some have even converted part of their rooms into a mini nursery for when their babies are small or if one of them is sick and needs to be kept from infecting the others. I hoped that we might start work on it right away. Do you know where I might sleep while my room is being redone?"

Sebastian could not have kept the tremendous grin off his face if he tried. Turning to face Lydia, he blurted, "Let me get this straight. You want to move into my room? Permanently?"

Smiling up at him with a rosy blush spreading across her cheeks, she replied, "Only if you want me to."

With a swift motion, Sebastian reached out and captured Lydia by the waist, and effortlessly swung her around in a joyful arc. He only stopped so that he could capture her lips with his own. Once he pulled back, gasping for air, Sebastian declared, "I am not a stupid man, my love, only a stupid man would not want to spend his every night with his beautiful wife."

Giggling, Lydia pressed her fingers to her swollen lips before saying, "I suppose I can take that as a yes?"

Going in for another kiss, Sebastian said, "That is so much more than a yes!" Their passionate kiss was abruptly interrupted by Sebastian's realization of their conspicuousness in the hallway, where any of their staff might see them. Scooping up Lydia, Sebastian couldn't help but smile when he heard her startled squeak, but the joy in her eyes reassured him. He loved her so much and promised himself that he would make sure she knew it every day of her life.

Epilogue

"YOU GOT ME ANOTHER set of twins! Now I have more babies than everyone else!" Clara knew better than to squeal around new babies, but that did not stop her from bouncing on her toes as she looked down at the two little bundles. Looking at Lydia where she lay in bed, she asked, "What are we naming them?"

Lydia smiled at Clara, despite her exhaustion. Giving birth to twins was definitely no easier this time than it had been the first time around. Never having had a single birth, she wondered if that would be any easier. Lydia leaned into Sebastian, her head resting gently on his shoulder, before saying, "Well, I was thinking that since we have an A and B with Adelaide and Benedict, and we have a C in our family with you, that we could name them Diana and Elizabeth."

Clara looked back at Lydia. "So I get to be C?"

Sebastian nodded and said, "Yes, I was hoping that you would like to be the C. It was your idea to do the alphabet after all."

Whispering to Sebastian, Lydia said, "Though I can promise you right now, we are not having twenty-six children."

Lydia could feel the vibrations of Sebastian's soft chuckle in her back and smiled, glad that he saw humor in her statement. They had fallen with child shortly after Clara had moved to the nursery and had their first two children close to their first anniversary. Their second set of twins came almost eighteen months later. Lydia felt entirely outnumbered. Though that would probably fade as she recovered.

Elizabeth came into the room with a maid carrying a tea tray. Lydia tried not to roll her eyes at Elizabeth's insistence on keeping her drinking fluids. Clara immediately went to Elizabeth and asked, "Aunt Elizabeth, have you seen my new twins?"

"Yes, my dear girl, I have seen them." Elizabeth smiled at Clara and then Lydia as she spoke. As she had been there at their birth, she had indeed seen them, though Lydia supposed they looked much better all clean and swaddled.

"When will Artie, Gill, and baby Thea get to see my new twins?" Swirling around, Clara faced Lydia and Sebastian and asked, "Have Adie and Ben seen their new sisters?"

Happy to see Clara's excitement over their two little bundles of joy, Lydia said, "You are the first to have seen them, my dear. We will bring Adie and Ben in to see their new sisters after their nap."

Kneeling down next to Clara, Elizabeth said, "It is time for your Aunt Lydia and your new cousins to take a nap. I am sure the boys would love to have you tell them about their two new little cousins."

After smiling at Elizabeth, Clara turned back to Sebastian and Lydia and said, "I am going to tell Artie and Gill about my new twins. Have a good nap, Auntie." She gave Lydia a kiss on the cheek and then with a bouncing step she was on her way to the nursery, her governess trailing behind.

Elizabeth, meanwhile, poured a cup of tea for Lydia, preparing it as she liked and handed it to her younger sister, saying, "Now you drink this and get some sleep. You have expended a lot of effort to bring those two darlings into the world."

Taking the tea, Lydia said, "Thank you for being here, Elizabeth, and being so attentive."

Reaching out, she brushed a strand of damp hair back from her sister's forehead, saying, "How could I not? You are my baby sister. Besides, you know how much Artie and Gill love spending time with their oldest cousin. Now I'm going to leave you to rest. Don't forget to drink your tea."

Lydia sighed as her sister left, slumping even further into Sebastian's comforting side. She felt as if someone had torn her apart, but knew from experience that it would not last. Besides, it was not as if she was going to blame darling little Diana and Elizabeth. It was not their fault that twins ran in his family.

"Drink your tea, my love." Sebastian whispered and kissing her brow before continuing, "You know you will just fall asleep if you do not drink it soon and it probably has willow bark in it to help you feel better."

Lydia wanted to grumble about being so directed, but she knew Sebastian was right. So she took a sip of her tea, enjoying the way it made her sore throat feel. Gazing over at the two little ones in the bassinet next to her bed, Lydia made sure they were well. Both girls were sleeping. They were small, but Lydia figured that if they had been any larger, she would have burst. Taking another sip of her tea, Lydia sighed in contentment.

Once she was done with her tea, Sebastian placed her cup on his bed-side table and helped Lydia get comfortable laying down. Instead of leaving her to her rest, he climbed in bed with her. Chuckling, Lydia said, "What do you think you are doing, Sebastian? I am supposed to be napping."

Pulling Lydia into his powerful frame, Sebastian said, "I didn't get any rest last night either. I need a nap too."

"Oh, you poor baby, you didn't get any sleep. Why couldn't my big, strong husband get any sleep?" Lydia yawned drowsily.

Kissing her brow, Sebastian murmured, "The woman who holds my heart above all else was tirelessly bringing our beautiful daughters into existence, and I couldn't find peace until I knew you were all out of harm's way."

Smirking, Lydia grumbled, "The one you are so in love with better be me."

Hugging her tight, Sebastian grumbled, "You know it is."

"Yes, I know," she replied.

Lydia was just about to nod off when Sebastian murmured, "Have I told you yet today how glad I am that you said you would marry me?"

"Not that I can remember," Lydia yawned, adding, "Though I was rather otherwise occupied today."

"Well, I do." Sebastian kissed the spot behind her ear, continuing, "I cannot imagine my life without you and our children in it."

Lydia murmured, "Get some rest, my love. You know Elizabeth will not be able to hold off the hoard of children for long, and our newest little loves will be hungry soon enough." Sighing, Lydia fell swiftly towards sleep with a last mumbled, "Love you."

Epilogue: Part Two

Twelve and a half years later

Lydia shook her head, tears in her eyes as she exclaimed, "I am not ready for this. She is too young."

Sebastian rubbed his hands up and down her arms and leaned down to kiss her forehead. "Clara is twenty, my love. She is two years older than you were when we married."

Lydia sighed and rested her forehead against her husband's chest. It was hard to admit that Sebastian was right. She loved Clara like a mother, and it was time for her to say goodbye to her little girl. Lydia just did not know how she would be able to do it. Looking up at Sebastian, Lydia asked, "I know, I know, it is just do you realize that she will be the beginning of me losing them all?"

Chuckling, Sebastian smoothed a lock of hair out of Lydia's face. "My dear, Adelaide and Benedict are fourteen, nowhere near being old enough to leave the nest." Reaching down, he rested his hand on the swell of her stomach and asked, "Do you think your condition might influence your emotions?"

Lydia rolled her eyes and intertwined her fingers with Sebastian's on her swollen abdomen. It was very possible that her fifth pregnancy was making her teary. "I suppose you may be correct. It seems that I handle pregnancy with ease except for how it affects my sensibilities. You know, I believe I am having another set of twins."

"If you are, I doubt any of your sisters will be able to match our brood," he added with a smirk. Sebastian smiled at Lydia and gently encouraged her, "Take a deep breath and savor the joy of the day, rather than dwelling on what you are losing." Turning Lydia, he pointed out Clara and continued, "Look at how happy Clara is standing next to her new husband. Look at how much she loves him."

She gazed across the room at her little girl, who stood holding on to her new husband's arm, gazing up at him adoringly. It was easy to see how much Clara loved Lord Granville. Lydia realized that she could not hamper so much joy and happiness. She would have to be done with tears for the day. She could always indulge in them later. Just then, Clara caught Lydia's gaze from across the room, their eyes locking in a moment of silent acknowledgment. Clara smiled at Lydia for a moment before turning back to the conversation she was holding with her group of friends.

Lyda's voice caught in her throat as she swallowed, and she managed to say, "I am so proud of her, Sebastian. We married in order to take care of a fearful and vulnerable girl, and she has blossomed into a strong and resilient woman."

Sebastian held Lydia to his side as they watched Clara. Leaning down, he kissed her temple. "Our girl has grown up to be a remarkable woman. Somehow, we must have done something right along the way. I am so grateful that you told me to marry you all those years ago."

Lying her head against Sebastian's shoulder, Lydia replied, "I know what you mean. I could almost say it was the best day of my life, but it was only the beginning of a beautiful journey, full of remarkably amazing days."

AFTER SEBASTIAN HAD SPENT time reminiscing with Lydia and buoying her sentimental tears, he moved off to chat with his brothers-in-law. He was very touched that every one of them had made the effort to be at Clara's wedding. Turning to his one unofficial brother-in-law, he asked, "How is your horse breeding program going, Kiernan?"

Grinning, the younger man said, "It is doing very well. The line of horses out of Crumpet and Epona is proving remarkable. By the way, I am still grateful for your gift of their colt, Darcy. He has grown into an amazing stud."

Shrugging, Darcy responded, "Think nothing of it. I knew he was destined for more than just work as a farm horse or another one of my mounts for riding around Pemberley."

Looking at Sebastian, Theodore asked, "How has it been adjusting to the role of viscount?

Grimacing, Sebastian took a sip of champagne while he pondered how attaining his title had come about. It was two years earlier when he had been contacted by his father's steward, who informed him of the master's poor condition. It took a week and a half for them to arrive at Trowbridge Hall, with two carriages needed to accommodate all the children and servants.

Traveling that far with six children between the ages of twelve and two had been quite the event. The fact that Clara, at the age of eighteen, was able to exhibit patience and helpfulness towards her younger cousins was a crucial factor in maintaining their sanity amidst the chaos. Arriving at Trowbridge Hall after so many years had been quite a shock. Learning that his father had been bedridden after suffering an apoplexy had been even more of a shock.

His father was paralyzed on one side of his body and found speaking and doing things for himself nearly impossible. It had not been easy for his father to adjust to the change and though he had somewhat recovered, he could never walk or oversee his estates again. Unfortunately, he experienced another apoplexy within the year, and this time it proved fatal. Lydia's steady presence by his side was like a comforting anchor, helping him navigate his father's impotent rage and the overwhelming task of overseeing multiple estates.

Knowing that Theodore understood the difficulties he had faced, Sebastian felt able to say, "It was hard to see my father so angry that last year, but I think we managed a reconciliation of sorts before he died. At Trowbridge Hall, we are far removed from the constraints of high society. There, the burden of our title is diminished. Thanks to Lydia's efforts, the Hall has transformed into a cozy home rather than a symbol of the past. As a result, things have greatly improved."

Sebastian knew that the other gentleman had also experienced the same hardships he did when he unexpectedly became an earl. Theodore's understanding nod confirmed this shared struggle. For a moment, they were all quiet, enjoying their various drinks and the view of all the happy socializing taking place.

Artie was laughing with Clara and Lord Granville across the room. Lord Granville's younger brother, Stewart, was one of Artie's closest friends from Cambridge. It had been through Artie that the loving couple had met at a dinner party in London. Only Artie, Ellie and Mathew were present at the wedding breakfast. The younger children were all outside playing on the lawn, carefully watched by their various nursemaids and governesses. It was a wonderful day for the family.

Reaching out to clutch Darcy's shoulder, Sebastian said, "I am immensely thankful that you agreed to host Clara's wedding at Pemberley; I know you are not overly fond of crowds. Trowbridge

Hall is too far out of the way and Swarkstone Park is not big enough to hold everyone. This way we were able to host our expansive family as well as Granville's."

Darcy smiled sheepishly, saying, "You know that Elizabeth would accept nothing less than having the wedding here. Her oldest niece was getting married, and she wanted everyone there for the celebration."

The gentlemen's attention shifted, drawn to the sisters who were engaged in lively conversation on the opposite side of the room. Elizabeth and Lydia were laughing at something someone said. The former Mrs. Bennet had her arm linked with Jane and was shaking her head fondly at her girls. Mary and Kitty were wearing broad smiles as they watched the interaction between Lydia and Elizabeth.

Turning back to face Darcy, Bingley said, "I am just grateful that you were able to help liberate our ladies all those years ago. Without Jane, I would not have my darling Ellie or Edward. Without Jane in my life, I would only be half a man."

Gabriel added, "I must second that, Darcy. I most certainly would not have been able to marry the love of my life, my sweet Mary. Nor would we have had our three boys. You paved the way for me to become a Bennet and the master of Longbourn."

Rubbing at the back of his neck, Darcy said, "You are making too much of it. I only did what I did because of my love for Elizabeth."

"And yet, if it weren't for your actions, Darcy, I doubt any of us would have found the women we were all meant to be with. Nor would all our children be here," asserted Theodore.

Seeing Darcy's discomfort with the attention, Sebastian said, "Regardless of Darcy's action, I believe each of our wives worked hard to become the amazing women they are today, and moreover, none of us would be anyone without their love."

A round of agreement followed his comment, but if any other conversation took place after that, Sebastian missed it. He was far too interested in watching his glowing bride of many years. Eventually, she noticed his gaze fixed on her, and she responded with a radiant smile from where she stood. Lydia was the woman who held his heart, and he couldn't help but adore her with every fiber of his being. He could not wait to see what his life with her still had to offer.

Acknowledgements

Before you go, I'd like to express my gratitude to all those who assisted me in bringing the Bennet sisters' stories to the world. I'd like to start by acknowledging and thanking the people closest to me. It was thanks to my sister Megan's encouragement that I began writing. Then there is my mother, who serves as my alpha reader and sounding board for fresh ideas. My sister Chelsea's support is invaluable, just like the inspiration I find in my nieces and nephew for my younger characters. If you haven't had the pleasure of debating with a one-year-old who can articulate their thoughts in complete sentences, you're missing out. It is an absolute delight!

Additionally, I would like to extend my appreciation to my Beta readers and the people who show support through my newsletter. Doris, Debra, Carol, and Frankie, working with you to bring my stories to the world has been an honor. The encouragement and feedback I get from you helps me more than you know.

Lastly, it has been an utter pleasure working with my editor, Tayler. Your feedback not only helps me ensure that my story flows and my characters shine, but I also thoroughly enjoy reading your comments. I always love seeing your emojis in the comments, especially the ones with heart eyes!

Most importantly, I would like to thank you. It's been a joy to create this work of love, but without readers, it would be an exercise in futility. The fact that you chose my book to read is an honor. Thank you for taking the time to finish my book, I hope the characters and their stories resonated with you.

If you enjoyed reading this book, please consider leaving an honest review on your favorite site. It does not have to be very long, but I would really appreciate the feedback.

About the Author

My journey with words started out as a painful one. The letters on the page seemed to taunt me, and I spent countless hours with my mother trying to decipher their meaning. Our reading journey started with Little House on the Prairie and continued with other books, mostly in the historical fiction genre. Slowly but surely, I started reading independently, advancing from historical fiction to fantasy and science fiction.

The stories I found in the books I read held me captive, and I often lost track of time. The realization of the true power of the written word inspired me to pursue writing. Unfortunately, I had to put it on the back burner in order to deal with pesky things like paying for food and housing. Then a dare from my sister brought back memories of my passion for writing in high school. It was a passion that I was determined to rekindle.

When I got back into writing, I turned to my latest reading addiction for inspiration, Pride and Prejudice Variations. My mind was fixated on the regency era and the romance of Elizabeth and Darcy, making it hard to write anything else. So I went with it and here we are.

Visit jaimemariewrites.com to delve into my world of words, or find me on Instagram @jaimemariewrites for a glimpse into my creative process.

Books by Jaime Marie Lang

The Bennet Ladies Liberation Series

Darcy's Gallant Gambit

Kitty Catches Kismet

Mary's Daring Demand

Jane's Fragile Façade

Lydia Acquires Adoration

Elizabeth & Darcy True Love Multiverse

Murdered on a Wednesday: A Pride and Prejudice Mystery

Darcy, Knight Errant

Access my linktree account by scanning this QR code and discover the different places where you can find my books.